# THE TRIAL

## FRANZ KAFKA

Translation and Introduction by
DAVID PETAULT

Copyright © 2024 by David Petault

All rights reserved.

This book has been translated from the original German text, which is in the public domain. No part of this book may be reproduced in any form or by any electronic or mechanical means, including information storage and retrieval systems, without written permission from the author, except for the use of brief quotations in a book review.

ISBN: 9798345977767

# CONTENTS

| | |
|---|---|
| Introduction | v |
| 1. ARREST · CONVERSATION WITH MRS. GRUBACH · THEN MISS BÜRSTNER | 1 |
| 2. FIRST INVESTIGATION | 27 |
| 3. IN THE EMPTY COURTROOM · THE STUDENT · THE OFFICES | 41 |
| 4. THE FRIEND OF MISS BÜRSTNER | 61 |
| 5. THE BULLY | 69 |
| 6. THE UNCLE · LENI | 75 |
| 7. LAWYER · MANUFACTURER · PAINTER | 93 |
| 8. MERCHANT BLOCK · DISMISSAL OF THE LAWYER | 135 |
| 9. IN THE CATHEDRAL | 159 |
| 10. END | 179 |
| AFTERWORD | 185 |

# INTRODUCTION

Franz Kafka's *The Trial* is a haunting exploration of bureaucracy, guilt, and the struggle for justice in a world devoid of reason. Written in 1914 and published posthumously in 1925, this novel is one of Kafka's most profound works, delving into the surreal nightmare of Josef K., a man who finds himself arrested and prosecuted by a mysterious, faceless court for an unspecified crime.

This new translation seeks to capture Kafka's unique narrative style while making the text accessible to modern readers. Unlike previous versions that can be bogged down by archaic language or dense prose, this translation emphasizes clarity and readability without sacrificing the tension and absurdity of Kafka's vision. By maintaining the eerie simplicity of Kafka's language, it allows readers to experience the chilling detachment and relentless anxiety that defines *The Trial*.

Kafka masterfully blends the absurd with the ordinary, creating a sense of unease that lingers throughout the novel. The story's relentless bureaucratic nightmare, where logic is suspended and guilt is assumed, serves as a powerful metaphor for the individual's struggle against oppressive systems. Themes of power, alienation, and the loss of iden-

INTRODUCTION

tity resonate with modern readers, making *The Trial* as relevant today as it was nearly a century ago.

This translation of *The Trial* brings Kafka's world to life for a contemporary audience, ensuring that the novel's dark humor, existential dread, and profound philosophical insights remain as impactful as ever. Whether you are reading Kafka for the first time or returning to his work, this edition provides a fresh, immersive experience that captures the timeless essence of Kafka's genius.

# I
## ARREST · CONVERSATION WITH MRS. GRUBACH · THEN MISS BÜRSTNER

Someone must have slandered Josef K., for without having done anything wrong, he was arrested one morning. The cook of Mrs. Grubach, his landlady, who brought him breakfast every day around eight in the morning, did not come this time. That had never happened before. K. waited a little while, watching the old woman who lived across from him with an unusual curiosity, and then, feeling both confused and hungry, he rang the bell. Immediately there was a knock, and a man he had never seen in this apartment entered. He was slender yet well-built, wearing a tight black outfit that resembled travel suits, complete with various folds, pockets, buckles, buttons, and a belt, which made it appear particularly practical, though it was unclear what it was meant for. "Who are you?" K. asked, sitting up halfway in bed. The man, however, ignored the question as if his presence had to be accepted, and simply said, "You rang?"

"Anna should bring me breakfast," K. replied, initially trying to quietly assess who the man was through observation and thought. But the man did not remain exposed to K.'s scrutiny for long; he turned to the door, which he opened slightly, to tell someone apparently standing just behind it, "He wants Anna to bring him breakfast." A small laugh followed from the next room; from the sound, it was uncertain whether several people were involved. Despite the fact that the stranger could not have learned anything from this that he did not already know, he now told K. in a reporting tone, "It is impossible."

"That would be news," K. said, jumping out of bed and quickly putting on his trousers. "I want to see what kind of people are in the next room and how Mrs. Grubach will justify this disturbance to me." He immediately realized that he should not have said that out loud and that it somehow acknowledged the stranger's right to oversee him, but it did not seem important to him at that moment. Nevertheless, the stranger interpreted it that way, saying, "Wouldn't you rather stay here?"

"I neither want to stay here nor be addressed by you until you introduce yourself."

"It was meant well," the stranger replied, and now voluntarily opened the door. In the next room, which K. entered more slowly than he intended, it looked almost exactly as it had the night before. It was Mrs. Grubach's living room, and perhaps today there was a little more space than usual in this room filled with furniture, blankets, porcelain, and photographs, though it was not immediately recognizable, especially since the main change was the presence of a man sitting by the open window with a book, whom he now looked up at.

"You should have stayed in your room! Didn't Franz tell you?"

"Yes, what do you want?" K. said, glancing from the new acquaintance to the man named Franz, who had remained standing in the doorway, and then back again. Through the open window, he spotted the old woman who had stepped to the now opposite window with truly elderly curiosity to continue watching everything.

"I want to see Mrs. Grubach—" K. said, making a motion as if he were breaking free from the two men, who were standing far from him, and wanted to keep going.

"No," said the man at the window, throwing the book onto a small table and standing up. "You may not leave; you are under arrest."

"It looks that way," K. replied. "And why is that?"

"We are not appointed to tell you that. Go back to your room and wait. The proceedings have been initiated, and you will learn everything in due time. I am overstepping my duties by speaking to you so amicably. But I hope no one else hears this except Franz, who is being unusually friendly to you against all regulations. If you continue to have as much luck as you have had with the determination of your guards, then you can be confident."

K. wanted to sit down, but now he saw that there was no seating available in the entire room except for the armchair by the window.

"You will come to realize how true all of this is," Franz said, moving toward him simultaneously with the other man. The latter, in particular, towered over K. significantly and patted him on the shoulder several times. Both examined K.'s nightshirt and said that he would now have to put on a much worse shirt, but that they would keep this shirt as well as his other laundry and, if things turned out favorably, return them to him.

"It is better for you to give the things to us than to the depot," they said, "because things often go missing in the depot, and moreover, all items are sold there after a certain time regardless of whether the relevant proceedings are concluded or not. And how long such processes can last, especially lately. In the end, you would indeed receive the proceeds from the depot, but that amount is already small in itself, since the sale is determined not by the amount offered but by the amount of bribery, and such proceeds tend to decrease further as they change hands and years go by."

K. hardly paid attention to this talk; he did not think highly of the rights he might still have over his belongings; it was much more important to him to gain clarity about his situation. However, in the presence of these people, he could not even think properly; the belly of the second guard—who could only be a guard—kept bumping against him in a seemingly friendly manner, and when he looked up, he saw a dry, bony face, completely unsuitable for the stout body, with a strong, sideways-turned nose, communicating with the other guard over him.

What kind of people were they? What were they talking about? To which authority did they belong? K. lived in a state governed by law; everywhere there was peace, all laws were upheld, who dared to invade him in his own home? He always tended to take everything lightly, believing the worst only when the worst actually occurred, making no provisions for the future even when everything threatened to go wrong. Yet here it did not seem right to him; he could certainly see the whole thing as a joke, a crude joke that his colleagues at the bank had played on him for unknown reasons, perhaps because today was his thirtieth birthday. It was certainly possible; perhaps he just needed to laugh in the faces of the guards in some way, and they would laugh along with him. Perhaps they were men from the street corner; they did not look too different from them—yet since the very first glimpse of the guard Franz, he had been determined not to give up even the smallest advantage he might have over these people.

K. saw very little danger in later saying that he did not understand the joke, but he did remember—without it being his habit to learn from experience—some seemingly insignificant instances in which, unlike his friends, he had behaved recklessly and consciously, without the slightest feeling for the possible consequences, and had been punished by the outcome. It should not happen again, at least not this time; if it was a comedy, then he wanted to play along.

He was still free. "Excuse me," he said, hurrying between the guards and into his room. "He seems reasonable," he heard someone say behind him. In his room, he immediately pulled open the drawers of the desk; everything was neatly organized, but in his agitation, he couldn't find the identification papers he was looking for. Finally, he found his cycling permit and was about to go to the guards with it, but then it seemed too trivial to him, so he continued searching until he found his birth certificate. When he returned to the adjoining room, the door opposite him opened, and Mrs. Grubach was about to enter. They only saw her for a moment; as soon as she recognized K., she appeared embarrassed, apologized, disappeared, and carefully closed the door. "Please, come in," K. had just managed to say. Now, however, he stood in the middle of the room with his papers, still looking at the door, which did not open again, and was only startled by a call from the guards, who were sitting at the little table by the open window and, as K. now realized, were eating his breakfast. "Why didn't she come in?" he asked. "She's not allowed to," said the tall guard. "You are under arrest." "How can I be under arrest? And in this manner?" "Well, here we go again," said the guard, dipping a piece of bread into the jar of honey. "We don't answer such questions." "You will have to answer them," K. said. "Here are my identification papers; now show me yours, especially the arrest warrant." "Good heavens!" said the guard, "that you can't accept your situation and that you seem intent on provoking us, who are probably closer to you than anyone else at this moment, is pointless." "It's true, believe me," said Franz, not bringing the coffee cup he held to his mouth but instead looking at K. with a long, likely significant but incomprehensible glance. K. found himself, without intending to, engaged in a silent exchange of glances with Franz but then struck the papers down and said, "Here are my identification papers." "What do we care about those?" the tall guard shouted now. "You're behaving worse than a child. What do you want? Do you think you can hasten your damned trial by discussing identification and arrest warrants with us, the guards? We are lowly employees who hardly understand identification papers and have nothing to do with your case except to keep watch over you for ten hours a day and get paid for it. That's all we are, yet we are able to realize that the higher authorities, whom we serve, make sure to thoroughly inform themselves about the reasons for the arrest and the person being arrested before they issue such an order. There's no mistake in that. Our authority, as far as I know it—and I only know the lowest levels—does not seek the fault in the population but is, as the law states, drawn to the fault and must send us guards. That's the law. Where would there be a mistake in that?" "I don't know that law," K. said. "The worse for you," the guard replied. "It probably exists only in your minds," K. said, trying to worm his way into the guards' thoughts, to turn them to his advantage or to establish himself among them. But the guard merely said dismissively, "You'll find out." Franz interjected, saying, "Look, Willem, he admits he doesn't know the law and simultaneously claims to be innocent." "You're right, but you can't make him understand anything," said the other. K. did not respond anymore; he thought, should I allow myself to be further confused by the chatter of these lowest of officials—they even admit to being such? They are talking about things they don't understand at all. Their security is only possible because of their ignorance. A few words I exchange with a person of equal standing will clarify everything incomparably better than the longest speeches with these. He walked back and forth a few times in the open space of the room; over there, he saw an old woman who had pulled a much older man to the window, holding him close. K. had to put an end to this display: "Take me to your superior," he said.

"Not until he wishes it; not before," said the guard, who had been called Willem. "And now I advise you," he added, "to go back to your room, behave calmly, and wait for what will be decided about you. We advise you not to distract yourself with useless thoughts but to collect yourself, as great demands will be placed upon you. You have not treated us as our courtesy deserved; you have forgotten that we, whatever we may be, are at least free men in relation to you at this moment, which is no small advantage. Nevertheless, we are willing, if you have money, to bring you a small breakfast from the café over there."

Without responding to this offer, K. stood still for a while. Perhaps the two would not even dare to stop him if he opened the door to the next room or even the door to the anteroom; maybe it would be the simplest solution to push things to the limit. But perhaps they would seize him, and once he was brought down, he would lose all the superiority that he still maintained over them in a certain sense. Therefore, he preferred the security of a solution as it must naturally unfold, and he returned to his room without a word from either himself or the guards.

He threw himself onto his bed and took a beautiful apple from the washstand, which he had prepared for breakfast the night before. Now it was his only breakfast and, as he assured himself with the first big bite, much better than what he could have gotten from the dirty café, thanks to the grace of the guards. He felt comfortable and confident; although he missed his duty at the bank that morning, it could easily be excused given the relatively high position he held there. Should he provide the real excuse? He intended to do so. If they didn't believe him, which was understandable in this case, he could call Mrs. Grubach as a witness, or even the two old people from across the way, who were probably now on their way to the opposite window. K. was surprised, at least from the guards' line of thinking, that they had driven him into the room and left him alone here, where he had multiple opportunities to take his own life. At the same time, he wondered, from his own thought process, what reason he would have to do so. Was it because the two next door were sitting and had intercepted his breakfast? It would have been so pointless to commit suicide that he, even if he had wanted to, would have been unable to do it due to that pointlessness. Had the mental limitations of the guards not been so striking, one might have assumed that they, too, saw no danger in leaving him alone for the same reason. They could now, if they wished, watch as he went to a wall cabinet where he kept a good schnapps, how he first emptied a glass as a substitute for breakfast, and how he prepared a second glass to give him courage, the latter only out of caution for the unlikely event that it might be necessary.

The shout from the next room startled him so much that he hit his teeth against the glass. "The supervisor is calling you," it said. It was only the shouting that frightened him, that short, clipped military yell that he would never have expected from the guard Franz. The command itself was quite welcome to him; "finally," he called back, locked the wardrobe, and hurried into the next room. There stood the two guards and, as if it were the most natural thing, they pushed him back into his room. "What do you think you're doing?" they shouted. "You want to go before the supervisor in your shirt? He'll have you beaten and us too." "Leave me alone, to hell with you," K. shouted, already being pushed back to his wardrobe. "If someone attacks me in bed, you can't expect me to be dressed for a formal occasion." "It won't help," said the guards, who always became very calm, almost sad, whenever K. yelled, confusing him or bringing him to a sort of realization. "Ridiculous ceremonies!" he grumbled, but already lifted a coat off the chair and held it for a moment with both hands, as if presenting it for the guards' judgment. They shook their heads. "It must be a black coat," they said. K. then threw the coat to the ground and said—he didn't even know in what sense he said it—"It's not the main hearing yet." The guards smiled but stuck to their point: "It must be a black coat." "If this speeds things up, so be it," K. said, opened the wardrobe himself, searched for a long time among the many clothes, selected his best black outfit, a jacket dress that had caused quite a stir among acquaintances because of its fit, then pulled out another shirt and began to dress carefully. Secretly, he believed he had achieved a speeding up of the whole process by the fact that the guards had forgotten to force him to take a bath. He watched them to see if they might remember, but of course, that didn't occur to them; however,

Willem did not forget to send Franz with the message that K. was getting dressed to the supervisor.

Once he was fully dressed, he had to walk just past Willem through the empty adjoining room into the next one, whose door was already wide open. This room, as K. knew very well, had recently been occupied by a Miss Bürstner, a typist, who used to leave for work very early, came home late, and had exchanged little more than greetings with K. Now, the bedside table from her bed had been moved to the center of the room to serve as a negotiation table, and the supervisor sat behind it. He had crossed his legs and rested one arm on the back of the chair.

In one corner of the room stood three young people, looking at the photographs of Miss Bürstner, which were framed and hanging on the wall. A white blouse was hanging on the handle of the open window. In the opposite window lay the two old people again, but their company had grown, for behind them, towering over them, stood a man with an open shirt on his chest, who was pressing and twisting his reddish pointed beard with his fingers.

"Josef K.?" asked the supervisor, perhaps just to draw K.'s distracted gaze to himself. K. nodded. "You must be very surprised by the events of this morning," said the supervisor, adjusting with both hands the few items on the nightstand—a candle, some matches, a book, and a pincushion—as if they were items he needed for the proceedings.

"Certainly," K. said, and he felt a sense of relief at finally standing in front of a reasonable person with whom he could discuss his situation, "certainly, I am surprised, but I am by no means very surprised."

"Not very surprised?" asked the supervisor, now placing the candle in the center of the small table while arranging the other items around it.

. . .

"You might be misunderstanding me," K. hurried to note. "What I mean is—" Here K. paused and looked around for a chair. "Can I sit down?" he asked.

"It's not customary," replied the supervisor.

"What I mean," K. continued without further pause, "is that I am indeed very surprised, but when you have been in the world for 30 years and have had to fend for yourself, as I have, you become hardened against surprises and don't take them too heavily. Especially not today's."

"Why especially today's?"

"I don't want to say that I see the whole thing as a joke; the events that have occurred seem too extensive for that. All the members of the boarding house would have to be involved, and even all of you, which would go beyond the limits of a joke. So I don't want to say it's a joke."

"Quite right," said the supervisor, looking to see how many matches were in the matchbox.

"On the other hand," K. continued, addressing everyone and even wanting to turn to the three by the photographs, "on the other hand, this matter cannot be of much importance. I conclude this from the fact that I am accused but can find not the slightest fault for which I could be accused. But that is also secondary; the main question is, who is accusing me? Which authority is conducting the proceedings? Are you officials? No one is wearing a uniform, unless you want to call your outfit—" he directed this at Franz, "a uniform, but it's more like travel attire. In these matters, I demand clarity, and I am convinced that after this clarification, we can take our leave of each other in the warmest way."

The supervisor slammed the matchbox down on the table. "You are greatly mistaken," he said. "These gentlemen here and I are completely irrelevant to your matter; in fact, we know almost nothing about it. We could be wearing the most proper uniforms, and your situation would not be any worse off. I cannot even tell you that you are accused, or rather, I don't know if you are. You are arrested, that is correct; beyond that, I know nothing. Perhaps the guards have said something else, but it was just talk. However, even though I cannot answer your questions, I can advise you to think less about us and what will happen to you, and think more about yourself. And don't make such a fuss about your feeling of innocence; it disrupts the otherwise not bad impression you make. You should also generally be more restrained in your speech; almost everything you said earlier could have been inferred from your behavior if you had just said a few words, and besides, it was not particularly favorable for you."

K. stared at the guard. He was receiving school-like teachings from perhaps a younger person? For his openness, he was punished with a reprimand? And he learned nothing about the reason for his arrest or who had ordered it?

He became somewhat agitated, pacing back and forth, which no one stopped him from doing, rolled up his cuffs, felt his chest, smoothed his hair, passed by the three gentlemen, and said, "It's pointless," prompting them to turn to him and look at him seriously yet kindly. He finally stopped again in front of the supervisor's desk. "Prosecutor Hasterer is my good friend," he said. "Can I call him?" "Of course," said the supervisor, "but I don't see what sense that would make, unless you have some private matter to discuss with him." "What sense?" K. exclaimed, more disturbed than annoyed. "Who are you? You want a sense and yet you are doing the most senseless thing there is. Isn't it maddening? The gentlemen ambushed me first, and now they are just sitting or standing around, letting me perform for you all. What sense would it make to call a prosecutor if I'm supposedly under arrest? Fine, I won't call." "But you should," said the supervisor, extending his hand toward the anteroom where the telephone was. "Please do call." "No, I don't want to anymore," K. said, walking to the window. Over there, the group by the window seemed only now to be disturbed in their quiet observation by K.'s approach. The older men wanted to get up, but the man behind them calmed them. "There are also such spectators over there," K. called loudly to the supervisor, pointing with his finger outside. "Get away from there," he then shouted across. The three immediately stepped back a few paces, the two older men even retreating behind the man, who shielded them with his broad body and, judging by his lip movements, was saying something unintelligible from a distance. However, they did not completely disappear, but seemed to be waiting for a moment to approach the window again unnoticed. "Intrusive, thoughtless people!" K. said as he turned back into the room. The supervisor possibly agreed, as K. believed he could tell from a sidelong glance. But it was equally possible that he hadn't listened at all, for he pressed one hand firmly on the table and seemed to be comparing the length of his fingers. The two guards sat on a trunk covered with a decorative cloth, rubbing their knees. The three young men had their hands on their hips, looking around aimlessly. It was as quiet as in some forgotten office. "Well, gentlemen," K. called, feeling for a moment as if he were carrying all of them on his shoulders, "judging by your appearance, my matter should be resolved. I think it would be best not to think any further about the legitimacy or illegitimacy of your proceedings and to conclude the matter amicably with a handshake. If you agree with me, then please" — and he stepped up to the supervisor's desk and offered his hand. The supervisor raised his eyes, gnawed at his lips, and looked at K.'s outstretched hand; K. still believed the supervisor would shake it. However, the supervisor stood up, took a hard round hat that was lying on Miss Bürstner's bed, and carefully placed it on his head with both hands, just as one would do when trying on new hats. "How simple everything seems to you!" he said to K. "You think we should conclude the matter amicably, do you? No, no, that really won't do. Which I certainly do not mean to

# THE TRIAL

imply that you should despair. No, why should you? You are simply under arrest, nothing more. I had to inform you of that, and I have done so and have also seen how you took it. That is enough for today, and we can say goodbye, albeit only temporarily. You probably want to go to the bank now?" "To the bank?" K. asked. "I thought I was under arrest." K. asked with a certain defiance, for even though his handshake had not been accepted, he felt increasingly independent of all these people, especially since the supervisor had stood up. He toyed with them. He planned that if they were to leave, he would run after them to the front door and offer them his arrest. That is why he repeated, "How can I go to the bank if I am under arrest?" "Oh," said the supervisor, who was already at the door, "you misunderstood me. You are under arrest, of course, but that should not hinder you from fulfilling your profession. You should not be impeded in your usual way of life either." "Then being under arrest isn't very bad," K. said, stepping closer to the supervisor. "I never meant otherwise," the supervisor replied. "But then it doesn't even seem very necessary to have communicated the arrest," K. said, moving even closer. The others had also stepped closer. They were all now gathered in a tight space by the door. "It was my duty," said the supervisor. "A foolish duty," K. said stubbornly. "Perhaps," replied the supervisor, "but we don't want to waste our time on such talk. I had assumed you wanted to go to the bank. Since you are paying attention to every word, I will add: I am not forcing you to go to the bank; I merely assumed that you wanted to. And to make it easier for you, and to ensure your arrival at the bank is as inconspicuous as possible, I have kept these three gentlemen, your colleagues, here at your disposal." "What?" K. exclaimed, staring at the three. These so uncharacteristic, pale young men, whom he still only remembered as a group from photographs, were indeed officials from his bank, not colleagues — that was too much to say and already a gap in the supervisor's omniscience — but they were certainly subordinate officials from the bank. How had K. overlooked that? How had he managed to accept being shielded by the supervisor and the guards to the point of not recognizing these three? The stiff, hand-swinging Rabensteiner, the blonde Kullich with the deep-set eyes, and Kaminer with his unbearable smile, caused by a chronic muscle strain. "Good morning!" K. said after a while, extending his hand to the gentlemen, who bowed correctly. "I didn't recognize you at all. Now we can get to work, can't we?" The gentlemen nodded, laughing and eagerly, as if they had been waiting for this the whole time. Only when K. noticed his hat was missing, left behind in his room, did they all hurriedly go fetch it one after another, which still indicated a certain embarrassment. K. stood still and watched them through the two open doors; the last one, of course, was the indifferent Rabensteiner, who merely had a stylish gait. Kaminer handed over the hat, and K. had to explicitly tell him, as was often necessary at the bank, that Kaminer's smile was not intentional, indeed that he could not smile intentionally at all. In the anteroom, Frau Grubach, who didn't look very guilty, opened the apartment door for the whole group, and K. looked down at her apron string, which cut unnecessarily deep into her ample body. Below, K. resolved, looking at his watch, to take a car to avoid unnecessarily increasing the already half-hour delay. Kaminer ran to the corner to fetch the vehicle, while the other two evidently tried to distract K. when suddenly Kullich pointed to the opposite front door, where the tall man with the blond pointed beard appeared, stepping back against the wall for a moment, a little awkward about showing himself in his full height. The older men were probably still on the stairs. K. was annoyed with Kullich for drawing attention to the man he had already seen before, even expected. "Don't look," he hissed, without realizing how conspicuous such speech was toward independent men. However, no explanation was needed, as the car had just arrived, they got in, and drove off. Then K. remembered that he had not even noticed the departure of the supervisor and the guards; the supervisor had concealed the three officials from him, and now the officials had concealed the supervisor. That didn't show much presence of mind, and K. resolved to observe himself more closely in that regard. Yet he involuntarily turned around and leaned over the back of the car to possibly see the supervisor and the guards again. But he quickly turned back and leaned comfortably into the corner of the vehicle without even attempting to look for anyone. Although it did not seem so, he could have used some support just then, but now the gentlemen seemed tired; Rabensteiner was looking out the right side of the car,

Kullich out the left, and only Kaminer stood there with his grin, over which it was regrettable to make a joke, as humanity forbade it.

*

This spring, K. spent his evenings in such a way that after work, when it was still possible—he usually stayed at the office until 9 PM—he would take a short walk alone or with colleagues and then go to a beer hall, where he would usually sit at a regular table with mostly older gentlemen until around 11 PM. However, there were exceptions to this routine, such as when K. was invited by the bank director, who highly valued his work ethic and trustworthiness, for a drive or for dinner at his villa. Additionally, K. visited a girl named Elsa once a week, who worked as a waitress in a wine bar during the night and only received visitors from her bed during the day.

On this particular evening, however—the day had passed quickly under intense work and many respectful and friendly birthday wishes—K. wanted to go home immediately. In every small break during the day's work, he had thought about it; without exactly knowing why, it seemed to him that the events of the morning had caused a great disorder in Mrs. Grubach's apartment and that he was needed to restore order. Once that order was established, every trace of those incidents would be erased, and everything would return to its old routine. In particular, there was nothing to fear from the three officials; they had again become immersed in the vast bureaucracy of the bank, and no change could be noticed in them. K. had often called them individually and together to his office, not for any other purpose than to observe them; he had always been able to send them away satisfied.

When he arrived at the house where he lived at 9:30 PM, he encountered a young man standing in the doorway with his legs spread apart, smoking a pipe. "Who are you?" K. asked immediately, bringing his face close to the young man, as not much could be seen in the dim light of the hallway. "I am the son of the caretaker, sir," the young man replied, taking the pipe out of his mouth and stepping aside. "The son of the caretaker?" K. asked, tapping the ground impatiently with his cane. "Does the sir require anything? Should I fetch my father?" "No, no," K. said, his voice carrying a hint of forgiveness, as if the young man had done something wrong, and he was choosing to forgive him. "That's fine," he then said and continued on, but before he climbed the stairs, he turned around once more.

He could have gone straight to his room, but since he wanted to speak with Mrs. Grubach, he knocked on her door. She was sitting at the table with a knitting project, and there was still a pile of old stockings on it. K. distractedly apologized for coming so late, but Mrs. Grubach was very friendly and didn't want to hear any excuses; she was always available to talk to him, and he knew very well that he was her best and favorite tenant. K. looked around the room; it was completely back to its old state, the breakfast dishes that had been on the small table by the window had already been cleared away. Women's hands can accomplish a lot quietly, he thought; he might have broken the dishes on the spot, but certainly couldn't have carried them out. He glanced at Mrs. Grubach with a certain gratitude. "Why are you still working so late?" he asked. They were both sitting at the table now, and K. occasionally buried his hand in the stockings. "There's a lot of work," she said. "During the day, I belong to the tenants; if I want to get my things in order, I only have the evenings left." "I certainly gave you some unusual work today." "How so?" she asked, becoming a bit more eager, her work resting in her lap. "I mean the men who were here this morning." "Oh, that," she said, returning to her calm demeanor, "it didn't cause me any special trouble." K. silently watched as she resumed her knitting. She seems surprised that I'm talking about this, he thought; she doesn't seem to think it's right for me to bring it up. All the more important that I do. Only with an old woman can I speak of this. "But it certainly did cause some work," he then said, "but it won't happen again." "No, it can't happen again," she affirmed, smiling at K. almost wistfully. "Do you mean that seriously?" K. asked. "Yes," she said quietly, "but above all, you mustn't take it too hard. So much happens in the world! Since you speak so openly with me, Mr. K., I can confess to you that I listened a bit from behind the door and that the two guards also told me some things. It concerns your well-being, and that truly matters to me, perhaps more than it should, since I am just the landlord. Well, I've heard some things, but I can't say that it was anything particularly bad. No. You are indeed under arrest, but not in the way a thief is arrested. When someone is arrested like a thief, it is serious, but this arrest— it seems to me like something scholarly, excuse me if I say something foolish, it seems to me like something scholarly that I don't understand, but that doesn't necessarily need to be understood."

"It's not at all foolish what you said, Mrs. Grubach; at least I partly share your opinion. However, I judge the whole situation even more harshly than you do and consider it simply not even something scholarly, but nothing at all. I was caught off guard, that's what it was. If I had gotten up right after waking, without being distracted by Anna's absence, and had gone straight to you without regard for anyone who might have gotten in my way, I might have had breakfast in the kitchen this time, had you bring my clothes from my room, in short, if I had acted reasonably, then nothing else would have happened; everything that wanted to happen would have been smothered. But one is so unprepared. In the bank, for example, I am prepared; something like that could never happen to me there. I have my own servant, the general telephone and the office telephone right in front of me on the table, and people, parties, and officials are constantly coming and going. Moreover, and above all, I am always in the context of work there, and therefore alert; it would actually be a pleasure for me to be confronted with such a situation there. Well, it's over now, and I didn't really want to talk about it anymore, but I did want to hear your judgment, the judgment of a sensible woman, and I'm very glad that we agree on this. Now, you must shake my hand; such an agreement needs to be confirmed with a handshake."

Would she extend her hand to me? The supervisor hadn't offered his hand, he thought, and looked at the woman differently than before, scrutinizing her. She got up because he had also stood up; she felt a bit awkward because not everything K. had said was clear to her. Due to this awkwardness, she said something she didn't mean to and which was completely out of place: "Please don't take it so hard, Mr. K.," she said, her voice trembling with tears, and of course, she forgot the handshake. "I wouldn't know that I'm taking it hard," K. said suddenly, feeling exhausted and realizing the worthlessness of all this woman's reassurances.

At the door, he asked, "Is Miss Bürstner at home?" "No," Mrs. Grubach replied, smiling at this dry response with a delayed, rational sympathy. "She is at the theater. Did you want something from her? Should I pass on a message?" "Oh, I just wanted to speak to her for a moment." "Unfortunately, I don't know when she'll be back; when she's at the theater, she usually comes home late." "That doesn't really matter," K. said, already turning his lowered head toward the door to leave, "I just wanted to apologize for using her room today." "That's not necessary, Mr. K., you're too considerate. The young lady knows nothing about it; she hasn't been home since early this morning. Everything has already been taken care of, see for yourself." And she opened the door to Miss Bürstner's room. "Thank you, I believe you," K. said, but he did go to the open door. The moon shone quietly into the dark room. As far as he could see, everything was indeed in its place; even the blouse was no longer hanging on the window latch. The cushions on the bed seemed surprisingly high, partly illuminated by the moonlight. "Miss Bürstner often comes home late," K. said, looking at Mrs. Grubach as if she bore some responsibility for it. "That's just how young people are!" Mrs. Grubach said, sounding apologetic. "Of course, of course," K. replied, "but it can go too far." "It can," Mrs. Grubach said, "you're absolutely right, Mr. K. Maybe even in this case. I certainly don't wish to slander Miss Bürstner; she is a good, kind girl—friendly, tidy, punctual, hardworking. I appreciate all of that very much. But one thing is true: she should be prouder and more reserved. I have seen her twice this month in remote streets, always with a different gentleman. It embarrasses me greatly; I am only telling you this in complete confidence, Mr. K., but I cannot avoid discussing it with the young lady herself. Besides, it's not the only thing that makes me suspicious of her." "You're on entirely the wrong track," K. said angrily, almost unable to hide it. "Besides, you've clearly misunderstood my comment about the young lady; it wasn't meant that way. I sincerely warn you against saying anything to her.

You're completely mistaken; I know the young lady very well, and none of what you said is true. By the way, maybe I'm going too far; I don't want to stop you. Say what you want to her. Good night." "Mr. K.," Mrs. Grubach said pleadingly, rushing after him to his door, which he had already opened, "I don't intend to speak to the young lady just yet; of course, I want to observe her further first. I've only confided in you about what I know. In the end, it must be in the interest of every tenant to keep the boarding house clean, and that's all I'm trying to do." "Cleanliness!" K. shouted through the crack of the door, "if you want to keep the boarding house clean, you must first evict me." Then he slammed the door shut, ignoring a soft knock that followed.

Instead, he decided, since he had no desire to sleep, to stay awake and take the opportunity to see when Miss Bürstner would arrive. Perhaps it would also be possible, however inappropriate it might be, to exchange a few words with her. As he lay in the window, pressing his tired eyes, he even briefly considered punishing Mrs. Grubach and persuading Miss Bürstner to resign together with him. But that immediately seemed terribly exaggerated to him, and he even suspected that he was looking to change apartments because of the events of the morning. Nothing could have been more nonsensical, and above all, more pointless and contemptible.

When he grew tired of looking out at the empty street, he lay down on the sofa, after slightly opening the door to the foyer so he could see anyone entering the apartment from the sofa. He lay quietly there, smoking a cigar, until about 11 o'clock. After that, he could no longer tolerate staying there and moved a bit into the foyer, as if that might hasten Miss Bürstner's arrival. He had no particular longing for her; he couldn't even remember exactly what she looked like, but now he wanted to talk to her, and it irritated him that her late arrival was causing further unrest and disorder at the end of the day. She was also to blame for the fact that he hadn't had dinner that evening and that he had skipped his planned visit to Elsa. However, he could still make up for both by going to the wine bar where Elsa worked. He intended to do that after speaking with Miss Bürstner.

It was half past eleven when someone could be heard in the stairwell. K., lost in his thoughts and pacing the waiting room as if it were his own room, retreated behind his door. It was Miss Bürstner who had arrived. Shivering, she wrapped a silk scarf around her slender shoulders while locking the door. In the next moment, she would have to go into her room, which K. certainly could not enter at midnight; so he had to speak to her now, but unfortunately, he had neglected to turn on the electric light in his room, making his emergence from the dark room look like an assault, which must have startled her quite a bit. In his helplessness and with no time to lose, he whispered through the crack of the door, "Miss Bürstner." It sounded like a plea, not like a call. "Is someone here?" Miss Bürstner asked, looking around with wide eyes. "It's me," K. said as he stepped forward. "Oh, Mr. K.!" Miss Bürstner said with a smile. "Good evening," and she offered him her hand. "I wanted to speak with you for a moment; will you allow me to do that now?" "Now?" Miss Bürstner asked, "Does it have to be now? It's a little strange, isn't it?" "I've been waiting for you since 9 o'clock." "Well, I was at the theater; I knew nothing of you." "The reason for what I want to tell you has only come up today." "Well, I don't have any fundamental objections, except that I'm too tired to fall over. So come into my room for a few minutes. We can't talk here; we'll wake everyone, and that would be even more uncomfortable for us than for the others. Wait here until I've turned on the light in my room, and then switch off the light here." K. did as she said but waited until Miss Bürstner quietly urged him to come from her room again.

"Have a seat," she said, pointing to the ottoman, while she remained upright by the bedpost despite the fatigue she had mentioned; she didn't even take off her small hat, which was adorned with an abundance of flowers. "So what did you want? I'm really curious." She crossed her legs slightly. "You might say," K. began, "that it wasn't urgent enough to be discussed now, but—" "I always skip introductions," Miss Bürstner interrupted. "That makes my job easier," K. said. "Your room was somewhat disordered this morning, in a way due to my fault; it happened through strangers against my will, and yet, as I said, it was my fault. For that, I wanted to apologize." "My room?" Miss Bürstner asked, looking at K. instead of the room. "It is so," K. said, and for the first time, they looked each other in the eyes. "The way it happened isn't worth mentioning." "But that's actually the interesting part," Miss Bürstner replied. "No," K. said. "Well," said Miss Bürstner, "I don't want to intrude into secrets; if you insist it's uninteresting, then I won't object. I gladly grant you the apology you seek, especially since I can't find any trace of disorder." She placed her flat hands on her hips and walked around the room. She stopped at the mat with the photographs. "Look," she exclaimed, "my photographs are really in disarray. That's ugly. So someone has been in my room without permission." K. nodded and silently cursed the official Kaminer, who could never tame his dull, senseless liveliness. "It's strange," Miss Bürstner said, "that I have to forbid you from doing something you should forbid yourself, namely entering my room in my absence." "I told you, Miss," K. said, walking over to the photographs, "that it wasn't me who meddled with your photographs; but since you don't believe me, I must admit that the investigation commission brought three bank officials, one of whom, whom I will have thrown out of the bank at the next opportunity, probably took the photographs." "Yes, there was an investigation commission here," K. added, as Miss Bürstner looked at him with a questioning glance. "For your sake?" she asked. "Yes," K. replied. "No," Miss Bürstner exclaimed, laughing. "Yes," K. said, "do you think I am innocent?" "Well, innocent," Miss Bürstner said, "I won't immediately make a possibly consequential judgment, and I don't know you, but it must be quite a serious criminal to whom an investigation commission is sent. But since you are free—at least I deduce from your calmness that you haven't escaped from prison—you can't have committed such a crime." "Yes," K. said, "but the investigation commission may have seen that I am innocent, or at least not as guilty as assumed." "Certainly, that could be," Miss Bürstner said very attentively. "You see," K. said, "you don't have much experience with legal matters." "No, I don't," Miss Bürstner admitted, "and I have often regretted it because I want to know everything, and legal matters interest me immensely. The court has a peculiar attraction, doesn't it? But I will surely enhance my knowledge in this regard, as I will be starting as a clerk in a law office next month." "That's very good," K. said, "then you can help me a little with my trial." "That could be," Miss Bürstner said, "why not? I like to use my knowledge." "I mean it seriously," K. said, "or at least with the half-seriousness with which you mean it. To involve a lawyer is too trivial for this matter, but I could use a counselor." "Yes, but if I am to be a counselor, I would need to know what it's about," Miss Bürstner said. "That's precisely the hitch," K. said, "I don't know that myself." "Then you have made a joke out of me," Miss Bürstner said, excessively disappointed, "it was highly unnecessary to choose this late hour for it." And she moved away from the photographs, where they had stood together for so long. "But my dear Miss," K. said, "I'm not joking. That you don't want to believe me! What I know, I've already told you. Even more than I know, because there was no investigation commission; I call it that because I don't know another name for it. Nothing was investigated; I was just arrested, but by a commission." Miss Bürstner sat on the ottoman and laughed again. "How was it?" she asked. "Terrible," K. said, but he wasn't thinking about that now; he was completely captivated by the sight of Miss Bürstner, who rested her face on one hand—the elbow resting on the cushion of the ottoman—while her other hand slowly stroked her waist. "That's too general," Miss Bürstner said. "What is too general?" K. asked. Then he remembered and asked, "Shall I show you how it was?" He wanted to move but not leave. "I'm already tired," Miss Bürstner said. "You came so late," K. replied. "Now it ends with me getting reproached, which is also justified since I shouldn't have let you in anymore. It wasn't necessary, as it turns out." "It was necessary; you will see that only now," K. said. "May I move the nightstand from your bed?" "What are you thinking?" Miss Bürstner said, "you certainly can't do that!" "Then I can't show it to you," K. said, agitated, as if an immense harm were being done to him. "Well, if you need it for the demonstration, then just go ahead and move the nightstand," Miss Bürstner said, and after a moment added with a weaker voice, "I'm so tired that I'm allowing more than is good." K. placed the nightstand in the middle of the room and sat behind it. "You have to imagine the distribution of the people correctly; it's very interesting. I'm the supervisor, there on the suitcase sit two guards, three young men are standing by the photographs. On the window handle hangs, just to mention it in passing, a white blouse. And now it begins. Yes, I forget myself; the most important person, that is me, is standing here in front of the nightstand. The supervisor is sitting extremely comfortably, legs crossed, arm hanging over the back, a real slouch. And now it really begins. The supervisor calls, as if he has to wake me, he almost shouts; unfortunately, to make it clear to you, I also have to shout; by the way, it's only my name that he shouts like that." Miss Bürstner, who was listening while laughing, placed her index finger on her mouth to silence K.'s shouting, but it was too late; K. was too much into the role, and he slowly called, "Josef K.," not as loudly as he had threatened, but loud enough that the cry, after being suddenly uttered, seemed to gradually spread through the room.

There was a strong, brief, and regular knock at the door of the adjoining room. Miss Bürstner turned pale and placed her hand over her heart. K. was particularly startled by this because he was still unable to think of anything other than the events of the morning and the girl to whom he had presented them. As soon as he composed himself, he jumped to Miss Bürstner and took her hand. "Don't be afraid," he whispered, "I'll take care of everything. But who could it be? Next door is just the living room, where no one is sleeping." "Yes," Miss Bürstner whispered in K.'s ear, "since yesterday, a nephew of Mrs. Grubach, a captain, has been sleeping here. There are no other rooms available. I had forgotten about it too. That you had to shout like that! I'm so upset about it." "There's no reason to be upset," K. said, and as she sank back onto the pillow, he kissed her forehead. "Go away, go away," she said, quickly sitting up again. "Please leave, please leave, what do you want? He's listening at the door; he hears everything. You're tormenting me!" "I won't leave," K. said, "until you are a bit calmer. Come to the other corner of the room; he won't hear us there." She allowed herself to be led there. "You don't consider," he said, "that this is an inconvenience for you, but not a danger at all. You know how Mrs. Grubach, who ultimately decides in this matter especially since the captain is her nephew, holds me in high regard and believes everything I say without question. She is also dependent on me, as she has borrowed a large sum from me. I will accept any of your suggestions for an explanation for our being together, as long as they are somewhat appropriate, and I assure you that I can persuade Mrs. Grubach to believe the explanation not only in public but truly and sincerely. You needn't spare me in this matter. If you want to spread the word that I attacked you, then Mrs. Grubach will be informed accordingly and will believe it without losing her trust in me; she is very attached to me." Miss Bürstner looked quietly and a bit slumped down at the floor. "Why shouldn't Mrs. Grubach believe that I attacked you?" K. added. He saw her hair in front of him, parted, low and voluminous, tightly held back, reddish hair. He thought she would turn her gaze to him, but she remained in her unchanged position and said, "I apologize, I was startled by the sudden knocking, not so much by the potential consequences of the captain's presence. It was so quiet after your shout, and then there was that knock; that's why I was so frightened. I was sitting close to the door, and it knocked almost right beside me. I appreciate your suggestions, but I cannot accept them. I can take responsibility for everything that happens in my room, and I do so to everyone. I am surprised you don't realize how insulting your suggestions are to me, alongside the good intentions, which I certainly acknowledge. But now please go; leave me alone, I need it now more than ever. Those few minutes you asked for have turned into half an hour or more." K. took her by the hand and then by the wrist: "You're not angry with me, are you?" he asked. She brushed his hand aside and replied, "No, no, I am never angry and never with anyone." He reached for her wrist again; she tolerated it this time and led him to the door. He was firmly resolved to leave. But before the door, as if he hadn't expected to find a door here, he hesitated. This moment was used by Miss Bürstner to free herself, open the door, slip into the anteroom, and quietly say to K., "Now please come. Look" — she pointed at the captain's door, under which a light was shining — "he has lit a lamp and is talking about us." "I'm coming," K. said, running ahead, taking her, kissing her on the mouth and then all over her face, like a thirsty animal rushing its tongue over finally found spring water. Finally, he kissed her on the neck, where the throat is, and there he kept his lips for a long time. A noise from the captain's room made him look up.

"Now I'll go," he said; he wanted to call Miss Bürstner by her first name but didn't know it. She nodded tiredly, half-turning away, offering her hand for him to kiss, as if she were unaware of it, and bent back into her room. Shortly after, K. lay in his bed. He fell asleep very quickly; before falling asleep, he thought for a while about his behavior, was satisfied with it, but wondered why he wasn't even more satisfied; because of the captain, he felt serious concern for Miss Bürstner.

## 2
# FIRST INVESTIGATION

K. had been informed by telephone that a small investigation regarding his case would take place the following Sunday. He was made aware that these investigations would now occur regularly, although perhaps not every week, but certainly more frequently. On one hand, it was in the general interest to conclude the process quickly; on the other hand, the investigations must be thorough in every respect, yet not last too long due to the associated effort. Therefore, they had chosen the approach of these rapid, but brief investigations. The decision to designate Sunday as the day for the investigation was made in order not to disrupt K.'s professional work. It was assumed that he would agree to this; if he wished for another date, they would accommodate him as much as possible. Investigations could, for instance, also take place at night, but K. would likely not be alert enough then. In any case, as long as K. did not object, they would stick with Sunday. It was taken for granted that he must appear without fail, and they felt it unnecessary to remind him of this. He was given the number of the house where he was to report, which was located in a remote suburban street that K. had never visited before.

K. hung up the phone without responding after he received the message; he was immediately determined to go on Sunday. It was certainly necessary; the trial was getting underway, and he had to confront it. This initial investigation should also be the last. He stood there, still deep in thought by the device, when he heard the voice of the deputy director behind him, who wanted to make a call but was blocked by K. "Bad news?" the deputy director asked lightly, not really wanting to know anything but to draw K. away from the phone. "No, no," K. replied, stepping aside but not leaving. The deputy director picked up the receiver and said, while waiting for the connection, over the earpiece: "A question, Mr. K.? Would you do me the pleasure of joining me for a sailing trip on my boat this Sunday morning? There will be a larger group, certainly some acquaintances of yours among them, including Prosecutor Hesterer. Will you come? Do come!" K. tried to pay attention to what the deputy director was saying. It was not unimportant for him, as this invitation from the deputy director, with whom he had never been on very good terms, represented an attempt at reconciliation from his side and showed how important K. had become at the bank, and how valuable his friendship—or at least his neutrality—appeared to the second-highest official of the bank. This invitation was a humiliation for the deputy director, even if it was uttered only while waiting for the phone connection over the earpiece.

But K. had to respond to this second humiliation; he said, "Thank you very much! But unfortunately, I have no time on Sunday; I already have a commitment." "Too bad," said the deputy director, turning to the phone conversation that had just been established. It was not a short conversation, but K. remained standing next to the device, lost in thought the entire time. Only when the deputy director hung up did he startle and said, to excuse his pointless lingering a bit: "I've just been called; I want to go somewhere, but they forgot to tell me what time." "Why don't you ask again?" said the deputy director. "It's not that important," K. replied, even though this further weakened his already inadequate excuse. The deputy director spoke about other matters as he left. K. forced himself to respond, but mainly thought that it would be best to come on Sunday at 9 AM, as all the courts started to work at that hour on weekdays.

# THE TRIAL

Sunday was overcast. K. was very tired, as he had stayed at the tavern late into the night for a regular gathering and had almost overslept. In a hurry, without time to think and organize the various plans he had devised during the week, he got dressed and ran, without having breakfast, to the suburban area designated for him. Strangely enough, despite having little time to look around, he encountered the three officials involved in his case: Rabensteiner, Kullich, and Kaminer. The first two were riding an electric tram across K.'s path, while Kaminer was sitting on the terrace of a café, leaning over the railing curiously just as K. passed by. They all watched him closely and were surprised at how their superior was walking; it was some sort of defiance that had prevented K. from taking a ride. He had a strong aversion to any, even the slightest, outside assistance in his matter, and he did not want to involve anyone or risk even the faintest disclosure. Ultimately, he also had no desire to humiliate himself by being overly punctual before the investigative committee. Nevertheless, he was now rushing to arrive by 9 o'clock, even though he hadn't been given a specific appointment time.

He had thought he would be able to recognize the house from a distance by some sign that he couldn't quite picture in his mind, or by a particular movement at the entrance. But the Julius Street, where it was supposed to be and where K. paused for a moment, was lined almost entirely with uniform houses—tall, gray tenement buildings inhabited by poor people. Now, on Sunday morning, most of the windows were occupied; men in their sleeves leaned out and smoked or carefully held small children at the window ledge. Other windows were stuffed high with bedding, above which the disheveled head of a woman occasionally appeared. People were calling out to each other across the street, and such a shout caused a great laugh at K.'s expense. Regularly spaced along the long street were small shops, situated below street level and accessible by a few steps, selling various groceries. Women were coming in and out or standing on the steps chatting. A fruit vendor, who was promoting his goods up to the windows, would have almost knocked K. down with his cart, just as oblivious as K. was. Just then, an old gramophone from better neighborhoods began to play loudly and harshly.

K. walked deeper into the alley, slowly, as if he now had time, or as if the examining magistrate could see him from some window and therefore knew that K. had arrived. It was shortly after 9 o'clock. The building was quite far back; it was unusually extensive, especially the entrance, which was high and wide. It was clearly intended for delivery trucks serving the various warehouses that now surrounded the large courtyard, all locked up and bearing the names of companies, some of which K. recognized from his banking work. Contrary to his usual habit of not paying much attention to such details, he stood for a moment at the entrance of the courtyard. Nearby, a barefoot man sat on a crate reading a newspaper. Two boys were rocking on a handcart. By a pump, a frail young girl in a nightgown stood watching K. as water flowed into her jug. In one corner of the courtyard, a rope was strung between two windows, already holding laundry that was meant to dry. A man stood below directing the work with a few shouts.

K. turned towards the staircase to get to the examination room, but then paused again, for in addition to this staircase, he saw three different stairways in the courtyard, and it also seemed that a small passage at the end of the courtyard led to a second courtyard. He was annoyed that they had not provided him with clearer directions to the room; it was, after all, a strange carelessness or indifference with which he was being treated, and he intended to point that out very loudly and clearly. Finally, he climbed the first staircase and played in his mind with a memory of the guard Willem's remark that the court was drawn to guilt, which implied that the examination room must be located at the staircase K. had randomly chosen.

As he ascended, he disturbed many children who were playing on the stairs, and they glared at him angrily as he passed through their ranks. "Next time I come through here," he thought to himself, "I either need to bring candy to win them over, or a stick to beat them." Just before reaching the first floor, he even had to wait for a while until a play ball finished its course, while two little boys with the cunning expressions of adult rascals grabbed at his trousers; if he had wanted to shake them off, he would have had to hurt them, and he feared their cries.

## THE TRIAL

On the first floor, the actual search began. Since he couldn't ask about the investigation committee, he invented a carpenter named Lanz—he thought of this name because the captain, the nephew of Mrs. Grubach, was called that—and now he wanted to inquire in all the apartments if a carpenter named Lanz lived there, so he could find the opportunity to look into the rooms. It turned out that this was usually quite easy, as almost all the doors were open, and children were running in and out. Generally, they were small single-windowed rooms where cooking also took place. Some women held infants in their arms and worked with their free hand at the stove. Adolescents, seemingly dressed only in aprons, hurried back and forth most busily. In all the rooms, the beds were still in use; there were sick people, those still asleep, or individuals stretching out in their clothes. K. knocked on the doors of the apartments that were closed and asked if a carpenter named Lanz lived there. Most of the time, a woman opened the door, listened to the question, and turned to someone getting out of bed. "The gentleman is asking if a carpenter Lanz lives here." "Carpenter Lanz?" asked the person from the bed. "Yes," K. said, even though the investigation committee was undoubtedly not there, and thus his task should have been over. Many believed that K. was very eager to find the carpenter Lanz; they thought for a long time, named a carpenter who did not have the name Lanz, or mentioned a name that bore a distant resemblance to Lanz, or they asked neighbors or accompanied K. to a distant door where, in their opinion, such a man might possibly be living in sublet, or where someone could provide better information than they could. Eventually, K. hardly needed to ask anymore; he was pulled through the floors in this manner. He regretted his plan, which had initially seemed so practical to him. Before the fifth floor, he decided to give up the search, said goodbye to a friendly young worker who wanted to take him further up, and went downstairs. But then he was annoyed again by the futility of the entire undertaking; he went back once more and knocked on the first door of the fifth floor. The first thing he saw in the small room was a large wall clock that showed it was already 10 o'clock. "Does a carpenter named Lanz live here?" he asked. "Please," said a young woman with bright black eyes, who was washing children's laundry in a bucket, and she pointed with her wet hand to the open door of the adjoining room.

K. believed he was entering a gathering. A crowd of various people filled a medium-sized room with two windows; no one paid attention to the newcomer. The room was cramped, surrounded at the ceiling by a gallery that was also completely full, where people could only stand hunched over, hitting their heads and backs against the ceiling. K., finding the air too stuffy, stepped back outside and said to the young woman, who had probably misunderstood him, "I asked for a carpenter, a certain Lanz?" "Yes," said the woman, "please go inside." K. might not have followed her if she hadn't approached him, grabbed the door handle, and said, "I have to close after you; no one else can come in." "Very sensible," said K., "but it's already too crowded." Still, he went back inside.

He maneuvered between two men who were talking right by the door —one was gesturing with both hands as if counting money, while the other looked sharply into his eyes—when a small, rosy-cheeked boy reached out for K. "Come, come," he said. K. allowed himself to be led, and it turned out that amidst the chaotic crowd, there was indeed a narrow path that possibly separated two factions; this was suggested by the fact that K. could hardly see any faces turned towards him in the front rows on either side, only the backs of people who directed their speeches and movements solely at members of their own group. Most were dressed in black, wearing old, long, and loosely hanging festive skirts. It was only this attire that puzzled K.; otherwise, he would have thought it was just a political district meeting.

At the other end of the hall, where K. was led, there stood a small table set up horizontally on a very low, also overcrowded podium. Behind it, close to the edge of the podium, sat a small, chubby, panting man who was engaged in conversation with someone standing behind him—this person had rested his elbow on the armrest of the chair and crossed his legs—amidst great laughter. Occasionally, the man would throw his arm in the air as if he were mimicking someone. The young boy who was leading K. struggled to make his report. Twice he had tried to say something while standing on his tiptoes, without being noticed by the man above. It was only when one of the people on the podium pointed out the boy that the man turned his attention to him and listened, leaning down to hear his quiet report. Then he took out his watch and quickly looked at K. "You were supposed to appear 1 hour and 5 minutes ago," he said. K. wanted to respond, but he had no time, for scarcely had the man finished speaking when a general murmur arose from the right side of the hall. "You were supposed to appear 1 hour and 5 minutes ago," the man repeated in a raised voice, now also quickly glancing down into the hall. Immediately, the murmur grew louder and then faded away as the man said nothing more, only gradually. It was now much quieter in the hall than when K. had entered. Only the people in the gallery continued to make their comments. They seemed, as far as one could distinguish anything in the dim light, haze, and dust up there, to be dressed more poorly than those below. Some had brought cushions, which they had placed between their heads and the ceiling to avoid discomfort.

K. had decided to observe more than to speak; consequently, he waived his defense regarding his alleged lateness and simply said, "I may have arrived late, but now I am here." Applause followed, again from the right side of the room. "Easily swayed people," K. thought, only disturbed by the silence in the left side of the room, which was just behind him and from which only sporadic clapping could be heard. He considered what he could say to win everyone over at once or, if that wasn't possible, at least temporarily win over the others.

"Yes," the man said, "but I am no longer obliged to question you now"—again there was murmuring, but this time it was unclear, as the man continued, waving his hand at the people, "However, I will make an exception and question you today. Such lateness must not happen again. Now step forward!" Someone jumped down from the podium, creating a space for K. to climb up. He stood pressed close to the table, the crowd behind him was so large that he had to push back against it, lest he knock the judge's table and perhaps the judge himself off the podium.

The investigating judge, however, paid no attention to that; he sat comfortably in his chair and, after giving a final word to the man behind him, reached for a small notebook, the only item on his desk. It was like a school notebook, old and warped from much handling. "So," said the investigating judge, flipping through the notebook and addressing K. in a tone of assertion, "you are a house painter?" "No," K. replied, "but rather the chief procurator of a large bank." This answer was met with laughter from the right side, so hearty that K. had to laugh along. The people leaned on their knees and shook with laughter as if suffering from a severe coughing fit. Even some individuals in the gallery were laughing. The now quite enraged investigating judge, who was likely powerless against the people below, sought to retaliate against the gallery, jumped up, threatened them, and his otherwise unremarkable eyebrows pressed together in a bushy, black, and large manner above his eyes.

The left side of the room, however, remained silent; the people stood there in rows, their faces turned toward the podium, listening to the words exchanged above just as calmly as they absorbed the noise from the other side. They even tolerated the occasional mingling of individuals from their ranks with those from the other side. The people on the left, who were also less numerous, might have been just as insignificant as those on the right, but the calmness of their demeanor made them appear more significant. As K. began to speak now, he was convinced he was speaking in their interest.

"Your question, Mr. Investigating Judge, about whether I am a house painter—rather, you did not actually ask, but rather stated it outright—is indicative of the entire nature of the proceedings against me. You might object that this is not a proceeding at all, and you would be quite right, as it is only a proceeding if I acknowledge it as such. However, for the moment, I do acknowledge it, somewhat out of pity. One cannot help but feel pity when one considers it at all. I do not say that it is a disgraceful process, but I would like to offer you that designation for your self-reflection."

K. paused and looked down into the hall. What he had said was sharp, sharper than he had intended, but still true. It deserved applause here or there, yet everything was silent; everyone was apparently waiting with bated breath for what would come next, perhaps a breakthrough was brewing in the silence that would put an end to everything. It was distracting that at that moment, the door at the end of the hall opened, and the young laundress, likely finished with her work, entered and, despite all her caution, drew some glances. Only the investigating judge brought immediate joy to K., for he seemed to be struck by the words right away. Until now, he had been listening while standing, surprised by K.'s speech as he had straightened up for the gallery. Now, during the pause, he gradually sat down, as if he did not want it to be noticed. Probably to calm his expression, he took out the little booklet again.

"It does no good," K. continued, "even your little booklet, Mr. Examining Magistrate, confirms what I am saying." Satisfied to hear only his calm words in the foreign assembly, K. even dared to take the booklet from the magistrate and, as if he were shy to lift it from the middle page, he held it up with his fingertips so that the densely written, stained, and yellowed pages hung down on either side. "These are the magistrate's records," he said, dropping the booklet onto the table. "Feel free to continue reading, Mr. Examining Magistrate; I truly do not fear this book of guilt, even though it is inaccessible to me, as I can only touch it with two fingertips and cannot take it in my hand." It could only be a sign of deep humiliation, or it had to be interpreted that way, as the magistrate reached for the booklet, which had fallen on the table, tried to organize it a bit, and picked it up again to read.

The faces of the people in the front row were so intently focused on K. that he looked down at them for a while. They were all older men, some with white beards. Perhaps they were the decisive ones who could influence the entire assembly, which, despite the magistrate's humiliation, remained unmoved in the stillness into which they had sunk since K.'s speech.

"What has happened to me," K. continued, somewhat quieter than before, and kept scanning the faces in the front row, which gave his speech a somewhat distracted air, "what has happened to me is just an isolated case and, as such, not very important, since I don't take it too seriously. However, it is a sign of a process that is practiced against many. I stand here for them, not for myself."

He had unconsciously raised his voice. Somewhere, someone clapped their hands and shouted, "Bravo! Why not? Bravo! And again, Bravo!" Those in the front row occasionally stroked their beards; no one turned around in response to the shout. K. also paid it no mind, but he felt encouraged; he no longer thought it necessary for everyone to applaud; it was enough if the public began to reflect on the matter, and now and then, someone was won over through persuasion.

"I do not want to succeed as a speaker," K. said, considering this, "that would probably not be achievable for me anyway. The examining magistrate likely speaks much better; it's part of his profession. What I want is merely a public discussion of a public issue. Listen: I was arrested about ten days ago; I laugh at the fact of my arrest itself, but that's not relevant here. I was ambushed early in bed; perhaps — as the examining magistrate suggested, it's not impossible — there was an order to arrest some room painter who is just as innocent as I am, but they chose me. The next room was occupied by two rough guards. If I were a dangerous robber, they couldn't have been more cautious. Moreover, these guards were demoralized scum; they kept talking my ears off, trying to be bribed, wanting to trick me into giving them laundry and clothes, wanting money to supposedly bring me breakfast after they shamelessly devoured my own breakfast before my eyes. That wasn't enough. I was taken to a third room in front of the supervisor. It was the room of a lady I hold in high regard, and I had to watch as this room, because of me but without my fault, was somewhat tainted by the presence of the guards and the supervisor. It was not easy to remain calm. However, I succeeded, and I asked the supervisor, completely calmly — if he were here, he would have to confirm it — why I was arrested. What did this supervisor, whom I still see before me sitting in the chair of the aforementioned lady like a representation of the dullest arrogance, reply? My gentlemen, he essentially said nothing; perhaps he really knew nothing. He had arrested me and was satisfied with that. He even went a step further and brought three lowly employees from my bank into the lady's room, who busied themselves touching and disarranging her photographs. The presence of these employees had, of course, another purpose; they were to spread the news of my arrest, damage my public reputation, and especially undermine my position at the bank. Now none of that succeeded, not even in the slightest; even my landlady, a very simple person — I want to mention her name here in a respectful sense; her name is Mrs. Grubach — even Mrs. Grubach was sensible enough to realize that such an arrest means no more than a prank executed by inadequately supervised boys on the street. I reiterate, the whole thing has only caused me inconveniences and temporary annoyance; but could it not have had worse consequences?"

When K. interrupted himself and looked at the silent examining magistrate, he thought he noticed that the magistrate was just signaling someone in the crowd with a glance. K. smiled and said, "Right next to me, the examining magistrate is giving someone in your midst a secret sign. So there are people among you who are being directed from up here. I don't know if the signal is meant to prompt hissing or applause, and by choosing not to reveal this matter prematurely, I consciously forgo learning the meaning of the sign. I am completely indifferent to it, and I publicly authorize the examining magistrate to command his paid employees down there not with secret signs, but with loud words, saying perhaps once: Now hiss, and the next time: Now clap."

Flustered or impatient, the examining magistrate shifted in his seat. The man behind him, with whom he had spoken earlier, leaned toward him again, either to encourage him in general or to give him specific advice. The people below were conversing quietly but animatedly. The two parties, which had seemed to hold such opposing views earlier, mingled; some individuals pointed at K., others at the examining magistrate. The misty haze in the room was extremely bothersome, even preventing a closer observation of those further away. It must have been particularly disruptive for the gallery visitors, who were forced to cast shy glances at the examining magistrate while quietly asking questions of the assembly participants to gather more information. The answers were given just as quietly, shielded by hands held up.

"I'm almost done," K. said, and since there was no bell, he banged his fist on the table. The suddenness of it made the heads of the examining judge and his advisor jerk apart. "This whole matter is remote to me, so I can assess it calmly, and you can, provided that you care about this so-called trial, gain a lot by listening to me. I ask you to postpone your discussions about what I present for later, as I have no time and will be leaving soon."

Immediately, there was silence; K. had already taken control of the meeting. No one shouted over each other like at the beginning, and there was not even applause anymore, but they seemed already convinced or on their way to being so.

"It is without a doubt," K. said very quietly, for he took pleasure in the tense attention of the entire assembly; in this silence arose a hum that was more provocative than the most ecstatic applause, "it is without a doubt that behind all the statements of this court, in my case thus behind my arrest and today's examination, there is a large organization at work. An organization that employs not only corrupt guards, foolish supervisors, and examining magistrates, who, at best, are modest, but that also maintains a judiciary of high and highest rank, along with the countless essential attendants, clerks, gendarmes, and other support staff, perhaps even executioners—I'm not shying away from that word. And what is the purpose of this large organization, gentlemen? It is to arrest innocent people and initiate a senseless and mostly, as in my case, fruitless procedure against them. How could one conceal the worst corruption of the officials amidst the senselessness of it all? It is impossible; even the highest judge couldn't manage that for himself. That is why the guards seek to strip the arrested of their clothes, why supervisors break into strangers' homes, and why the innocent are preferred to be publicly humiliated rather than interrogated. The guards have only talked about depots where the property of the arrested is taken; I once wished to see these depot sites where the hard-earned wealth of the arrested decays, unless it has already been stolen by thieving depot officials."

K. was interrupted by a shriek from the back of the hall. He shaded his eyes to see, as the dim daylight made the mist appear whitish and blinding. It was the laundress, whom K. had immediately recognized as a significant disturbance upon her entrance. Whether she was guilty or not could not be determined. K. only saw that a man had pulled her into a corner by the door and was pressing himself against her. But it was not she who screamed; it was the man, his mouth wide open as he looked up at the ceiling. A small circle had formed around them, and the gallery visitors nearby seemed delighted that the seriousness K. had brought to the assembly was interrupted in this way. K. wanted to rush over immediately, thinking everyone would be eager to restore order and at least escort the couple out of the hall, but the first rows in front of him remained firmly seated, none moved, and no one let K. pass. On the contrary, they obstructed him, and some hand—he didn't have time to turn around—gripped him by the collar from behind, while old men held their arms out in front of him. K. no longer thought about the couple; it felt as if his freedom was being restricted, as if they were taking the arrest seriously, and he jumped recklessly down from the podium. Now he stood face to face with the crowd. Had he misjudged the people? Had he overestimated the impact of his speech? Had they pretended while he spoke, and now, as he reached his conclusions, were they tired of the pretense? What faces surrounded him! Little black eyes flitted back and forth, their cheeks sagged like those of drunks, the long beards were stiff and sparse, and if one reached into them, it felt as if one were grasping merely claws, not beards. But beneath the beards—and this was the real discovery K. made—badges of various sizes and colors shimmered at their coat collars. Everyone had these badges, as far as he could see. They all belonged together, the apparent parties on the right and left, and when he suddenly turned around, he saw the same badges on the collar of the examining magistrate, who was calmly looking down with his hands in his lap. "So," K. shouted, throwing his arms up, the sudden realization demanding space, "you are all officials, as I see, you are the corrupt gang I was speaking against, you crowded here as listeners and snoopers, pretended to form parties, and one applauded to test me, you wanted to learn how to deceive the innocent. Well, I hope you have been utterly useless here; either you discussed that someone expected the defense of innocence from you, or—let me go, or I'll hit you," K. shouted at a trembling old man who had pushed particularly close to him—"or you actually learned something. And with that, I wish you good luck in your trade." He quickly grabbed his hat, which lay on the edge of the table, and pushed his way toward the exit amid a complete silence, at least one of total surprise. However, the examining magistrate seemed to have been even quicker than K., for he awaited him at the door. "One moment," he said. K. stopped but did not look at the examining magistrate; instead, he focused on the door, the handle of which he had already grasped. "I just wanted to point out to you," the examining magistrate said, "that today—you may not have realized it yet—you have deprived yourself of the advantage that an interrogation offers to the arrested person in any case." K. laughed at the door. "You scoundrels, I give you all the interrogations," he shouted, opened the door, and hurried down the stairs. Behind him, the noise of the assembly coming back to life rose, as they began to discuss the events like students.

## 3

# IN THE EMPTY COURTROOM ·
# THE STUDENT · THE OFFICES

K. waited day by day during the next week for another communication. He couldn't believe that his refusal to be questioned had been taken literally, and when the expected communication did not arrive by Sunday evening, he assumed he had been quietly summoned back to the same place for the same duration. Therefore, he went back on Sunday, this time going straight up the stairs and down the hall; a few people who remembered him greeted him at their doors, but he didn't have to ask anyone and soon arrived at the correct door. When he knocked, the door was opened immediately, and without looking at the familiar woman who stood by the door, he wanted to go straight into the adjoining room. "There is no session today," said the woman. "Why shouldn't there be a session?" he asked, unwilling to believe it. But the woman convinced him by opening the door to the adjoining room. It was indeed empty and looked even more miserable in its emptiness than it had the previous Sunday. On the table, which stood unchanged on the podium, lay some books. "Can I have a look at the books?" K. asked, not out of particular curiosity, but just to avoid feeling completely useless for being there. "No," said the woman, closing the door again, "that's not allowed. The books belong to the investigating judge." "Oh, I see," K. nodded, "the

41

books are probably law books, and it's part of this court system that one can be convicted not only for being innocent but also for being ignorant." "That seems to be the case," said the woman, who hadn't understood him exactly. "Well, then I'll leave," K. said. "Should I report something to the investigating judge?" asked the woman. "You know him?" K. asked. "Of course," said the woman, "my husband is a court clerk." Only then did K. notice that the room, which had only had a washbasin in it last time, was now a fully furnished living room. The woman noticed his astonishment and said, "Yes, we have free accommodation, but we have to clear the room on session days. My husband's position has its disadvantages." "I'm not so much surprised by the room," K. said, looking at her angrily, "but rather by the fact that you are married." "Are you perhaps referring to the incident in the last session when I interrupted your speech?" asked the woman. "Of course," said K., "it has almost passed and is nearly forgotten now, but at the time it made me downright furious. And now you say yourself that you are a married woman." "It wasn't to your disadvantage that your speech was interrupted. It was judged very unfavorably afterward." "That may be," K. said, diverting the topic, "but that doesn't excuse you." "I'm excused in front of everyone who knows me," said the woman. "The one who embraced me back then has been pursuing me for a long time. I may not generally be alluring, but I am to him. There's no protection against this; my husband has already come to terms with it. If he wants to keep his position, he has to endure it because that man is a student and will probably gain more power in the future. He is constantly after me; he left just before you arrived." "It fits with everything else," K. said, "it doesn't surprise me." "You want to improve some things here," the woman asked slowly and cautiously, as if she were saying something dangerous for both herself and K. "I inferred that from your speech, which I personally liked very much. However, I only heard part of it; I missed the beginning and during the end, I was on the floor with the student. — It's so disgusting here," she said after a pause, taking K.'s hand. "Do you believe you will succeed in achieving an improvement?" K. smiled and turned his hand slightly in her soft hands. "Actually," he said, "I'm not assigned to achieve improvements here, as you put it, and if you were to tell the investigating judge, you would be laughed at or punished. In fact, I wouldn't have involved myself in these matters of my own free will, and the need for improvement in this court system would never have disturbed my sleep. But I have been forced to intervene here, supposedly because I was arrested — I am indeed arrested — for my own sake. However, if I can be of any use to you in the process, I will gladly do so. Not only out of goodwill but also because you can help me." "How could I do that?" the woman asked. "By showing me, for example, the books on the table right now." "Of course," the woman exclaimed, hastily pulling him along. They were old, worn-out books; one cover was almost torn in the middle, the pages were only held together by fibers. "How dirty everything is here," K. said, shaking his head, while the woman wiped away the dust with her apron before K. could reach for the books, at least superficially. K. opened the first book; it revealed an indecent picture. A man and a woman sat naked on a sofa, the vile intention of the artist was clearly recognizable, but his clumsiness had been so great that in the end, only a man and a woman could be seen, who protruded too physically from the picture, sitting too upright and, due to the false perspective, could only awkwardly turn towards each other. K. did not flip through any further but merely opened the title page of the second book; it was a novel titled: "The Torments Grete Suffered from Her Husband Hans." "These are the law books that are studied here," K. said, "by such people I am to be judged." "I will help you," said the woman. "Will you?" "Could you really do that without putting yourself in danger? You said earlier that your husband is very dependent on superiors." "Nevertheless, I want to help you," said the woman. "Come, we need to discuss it. Don't speak of my danger anymore; I only fear danger where I want to fear it. Come." She pointed to the podium and invited him to sit with her on the step. "You have beautiful dark eyes," she said after they had sat down, looking up at K.'s face, "they say I have beautiful eyes too, but yours are much more beautiful. By the way, you caught my attention right when you first entered here. You were also the reason I later went into the meeting room, which I never do otherwise and which is even somewhat forbidden for me." 'So that's it,' thought K., 'she is offering herself to me, she is as corrupted as everyone else around here, she is fed up with the court officials, which is understandable, and therefore welcomes any random stranger with a compliment about his eyes.' And K. stood up silently as if he had spoken his thoughts out loud, thereby explaining his behavior to the woman. "I don't believe you could help me," he said, "to truly help me, one would need connections to high officials. But you surely only know the low-ranking employees who swarm around here. You must be very familiar with them and could achieve quite a bit with them; I have no doubt about that, but the most significant thing you could accomplish with them would be entirely irrelevant to the final outcome of the process. However, you would lose some friends in the process. I do not want that. Maintain your previous relationship with these people; it seems to me that it is essential for you. I say this not without regret because, to reciprocate your compliment in some way, I also find you appealing, especially when you look at me so sadly as you do now, for which, by the way, there is no reason at all. You belong to the society I must fight against, yet you seem very comfortable in it, you even love the student, and if you don't love him, you at least prefer him to your husband. That could be easily inferred from your words." "No," she exclaimed, remaining seated and reaching for K.'s hand, which he could not withdraw quickly enough. "You must not leave now; you must not go with a false judgment of me. Would you really be able to leave now? Am I really so worthless that you won't even do me the favor of staying here a little longer?" "You misunderstand me," K. said, sitting down. "If you truly want me to stay, I will gladly stay; I have time after all; I came here expecting there to be a hearing today. With what I said earlier, I only wanted to ask you not to undertake anything for me in my trial. But that need not offend you when you consider that I do not care about the outcome of the trial at all and that I will only laugh at a conviction. Provided that there is even going to be a real conclusion to the trial, which I highly doubt. I rather believe that the proceedings have already been abandoned due to laziness or forgetfulness, or perhaps even out of fear on the part of the officials, or will be abandoned in the near future. However, it is also possible that they will seemingly continue the trial in hopes of some greater bribery, completely in vain, as I can already say today, because I will not bribe anyone. It would still be a favor you could do for me if you would inform the investigating judge or anyone else who likes to spread important news that I will never, by any tricks that the gentlemen are certainly rich in, be moved to bribery. It would be completely hopeless; you can tell them that openly. Moreover, they may have already noticed it themselves, and even if they haven't, I don't care much whether it is known now or later. It would only save the gentlemen some work, but it would also spare me some inconveniences, which I am happy to endure if I know that each one is a blow against the others. And I will ensure that it will be this way. Do you actually know the investigating judge?" "Of course," said the woman, "I even thought of him first when I offered you help. I didn't know he was just a low-ranking official, but since you say so, it is probably correct. Nonetheless, I believe that the reports he submits upstairs have some influence. And he writes a lot of reports. Last Sunday, for example, the session lasted until evening. Everyone left, but the investigating judge stayed in the hall; I had to bring him a lamp. I only had a small kitchen lamp, but he was satisfied with it and immediately started writing. Meanwhile, my husband also arrived, who happened to have a day off that Sunday; we fetched the furniture, set our room up again, and some neighbors came over; we chatted by candlelight, in short, we forgot about the investigating judge and went to sleep. Suddenly, in the night, it must have been deep into the night, I woke up to find the investigating judge standing by the bed, shielding the lamp with his hand so that no light fell on my husband; it was unnecessary caution, my husband sleeps so soundly that even the light wouldn't have woken him. I was so startled that I almost screamed, but the investigating judge was very friendly; he warned me to be careful, whispered to me that he had been writing until now, that he was now returning the lamp, and that he would never forget how he had found me asleep. With all this, I just wanted to tell you that the investigating judge indeed writes many reports, especially about you, since your interrogation was certainly one of the main topics of the two-day session. Such long reports cannot be entirely meaningless. Moreover, you can see from the incident that the investigating judge is courting me and that I can now have a significant influence on him, especially since he must have just now noticed me. That he cares a lot about me,

I have more evidence for now. He sent me silk stockings yesterday through the student, whom he trusts a lot and who is his assistant, supposedly as a thank you for cleaning up the meeting room, but that is just a pretext, as this work is only my duty and my husband gets paid for it. They are beautiful stockings, see — she stretched her legs, pulled her skirt up to her knees, and looked at the stockings herself — they are beautiful stockings, but actually too fine and not suitable for me."

Suddenly, she interrupted herself, placed her hand on K.'s hand as if to calm him, and whispered, "Quiet, Bertold is watching us." K. slowly raised his gaze. In the doorway of the meeting room stood a young man; he was short, had slightly crooked legs, and was trying to give himself an air of dignity through a short, shaggy reddish beard that he continually stroked with his fingers. K. looked at him curiously; this was the first student of the unknown law he had encountered in a somewhat human manner, a man who would likely one day attain higher official positions. The student, however, seemed to pay no attention to K.; he merely waved a finger, which he pulled for a moment out of his beard, at the woman and walked over to the window. The woman leaned toward K. and whispered, "Please don't be angry with me; I beg you, don't think badly of me. I must go to him now, to that horrible man. Just look at his crooked legs. But I'll be back right away, and then I'll go with you, if you'll take me. I'll go wherever you want; you can do whatever you want with me. I will be happy if I can leave here for as long as possible, preferably forever." She caressed K.'s hand, jumped up, and ran to the window. Instinctively, K. reached out for her hand, but found only emptiness. The woman truly tempted him; despite all his thoughts, he could not find a solid reason not to give in to that temptation. He easily dismissed the fleeting objection that she might be trying to trap him for the court. How could she trap him? Wasn't he always free enough to dismantle the entire court, at least as far as he was concerned? Couldn't he have just a little confidence in himself? And her offer of help sounded sincere and might not be worthless. Furthermore, there might be no better revenge against the examining magistrate and his entourage than to take this woman away from them and keep her for himself. It could happen that the examining magistrate, after laboriously crafting false reports about K. late at night, found the woman's bed empty. And empty because it belonged to K., because this woman at the window, this lush, supple, warm body in a dark dress made of coarse, heavy fabric, truly belonged to K.

After he had addressed the woman's concerns in this way, he found the quiet conversation at the window to be too long. He knocked on the podium with his knuckles and then with his fist. The student briefly glanced over the woman's shoulder at K., but did not seem disturbed; in fact, he pressed himself closer to the woman and embraced her. She lowered her head deeply as if she were listening to him attentively. He kissed her loudly on the neck as she bent down, without significantly interrupting his speech. K. saw this as a confirmation of the tyranny the student exercised over her, according to her complaints, and he stood up and began to pace the room. He considered, while casting sidelong glances at the student, how he could quickly remove him, and therefore did not mind when the student, evidently disturbed by K.'s pacing, which had started to resemble stomping, remarked, "If you're impatient, you can leave. You could have left earlier; no one would have missed you. In fact, you should have left when I arrived, and you should have done so quickly." This remark could have contained all sorts of rage, but it also carried the arrogance of a future court official speaking to an unwanted defendant. K. stood very close to him and said with a smile, "I am impatient, that's true, but the easiest way to alleviate this impatience is for you to leave us. However, if you have come to study — I heard you are a student — I will gladly make room for you and leave with the woman. By the way, you still have much studying to do before you become a judge. Although I am not very familiar with your court system, I assume it is not just about crude speeches, which you certainly know how to deliver quite shamelessly." "He shouldn't have been allowed to walk around so freely," said the student, as if he wanted to explain K.'s insulting words to the woman, "it was a mistake. I told the investigating judge. They should have kept him in his room at least between interrogations. The investigating judge can be incomprehensible at times." "Useless talk," K. said, reaching out his hand to the woman, "come with me." "Oh, no," said the student, "you can't have her," and with a strength one wouldn't have expected from him, he lifted her into his arms and ran to the door with a bent back, looking tenderly at her. A certain fear of K. was unmistakable in this, yet he dared to provoke K. further by stroking and squeezing the woman's arm with his free hand. K. walked a few steps beside him, ready to grab him and, if necessary, choke him, when the woman said, "It's no use, the investigating judge is sending for me, I can't go with you, this little monster," she swiped her hand across the student's face as she said this, "this little monster won't let me." "And you don't want to be freed," K. shouted, placing his hand on the student's shoulder, who snapped at her with his teeth. "No," the woman cried, pushing K. away with both hands, "no, no, not that! What are you thinking? That would be my ruin. Please, let him go. He's only carrying out the investigating judge's orders and taking me to him." "Then let him run, and I never want to see you again," K. said angrily, disappointed, and gave the student a shove in the back that made him stumble for a moment, only to immediately jump higher with his burden in delight at not having fallen. K. followed them slowly, realizing that this was the first undeniable defeat he had experienced at the hands of these people. It was, of course, no reason to be anxious; he suffered this defeat only because he sought the fight. If he stayed at home and lived his usual life, he was vastly superior to any of these people and could easily clear them from his path with a kick. He imagined the most ridiculous scene, for example, if this pitiful student, this puffed-up child, this crooked-bearded man were to kneel before Elsa's bed and plead for mercy with folded hands. K. found this idea so amusing that he resolved to take the student to Elsa if any opportunity arose.

Out of curiosity, K. hurried to the door; he wanted to see where the woman was being taken. Surely the student wouldn't carry her through the streets in his arms. It turned out that the route was much shorter. Directly opposite the apartment door, a narrow wooden staircase probably led to the attic, making a turn so that its end was not visible. The student was carrying the woman up this staircase, already very slowly and groaning, as he had been weakened by the earlier walking. The woman waved her hand down to K. and tried to indicate through

THE TRIAL

the movement of her shoulders that she was innocent in the abduction, although there was not much regret in that gesture. K. looked at her expressionlessly, like a stranger, not wanting to reveal that he was disappointed, nor that he could easily overcome the disappointment.

The two had already disappeared, but K. still stood in the doorway. He had to assume that the woman had not only deceived him but had also lied to him by claiming that she was being taken to the investigating magistrate. After all, the magistrate wouldn't be sitting in the attic waiting. The wooden staircase explained nothing, no matter how long he looked at it. Then K. noticed a small note next to the staircase, walked over, and read in a childish, unpracticed handwriting: "Stairs to the court offices." So, the court offices were in the attic of this tenement? That was not an arrangement that inspired much respect, and it was reassuring for a defendant to imagine how little financial means this court must have if it housed its offices where tenants, who were among the poorest, tossed their useless junk. However, it was not impossible that there was enough money, but that the officials squandered it before it could be used for court purposes. Based on K.'s previous experiences, that was even very likely; but then such a degradation of the court was humiliating for a defendant, yet fundamentally more reassuring than the court's poverty would have been. Now K. could also understand why they felt embarrassed to summon the defendant to the attic for the first hearing and preferred to disturb him in his own apartment. What position was K. in compared to the judge sitting in the attic, while he himself had a large room with an anteroom at the bank and could look down through a huge window onto the bustling city square? However, he had no additional income from bribes or embezzlement, nor could he have a woman carried into the office by the servant. But K. was willing to forgo that, at least in this life.

K. was still standing in front of the notice board when a man came up the stairs, looked through the open door into the living room, from which one could also see into the meeting room, and finally asked K. if he had seen a woman here recently. "You're the court usher, aren't you?" K. asked. "Yes," said the man, "oh, so you are the defendant K., now I recognize you; welcome." He extended his hand to K., who had not expected this at all. "But there is no session scheduled for today," the court usher said when K. remained silent. "I know," K. replied, examining the civil coat of the court usher, which, besides some ordinary buttons, had two gilded buttons that seemed to have been removed from an old officer's coat. "I spoke with your wife a little while ago. She's not here anymore. The student took her to the investigating judge." "You see," said the court usher, "they always take her away from me. Today is Sunday, and I'm not obliged to work, but just to get me out of here, they send me away with a useless message. And they don't send me far, so I have hope that if I hurry, I might return just in time. So, I run as fast as I can, shout my message through the crack of the door to the office I was sent to, breathless, so that they probably barely understood me, then run back, but the student hurried even more than I did; he had a shorter way, he just had to run down the basement stairs. If I weren't so dependent, I would have crushed the student against the wall here long ago. Right here next to the notice board. I always dream about that. Here, just above the floor, he is pinned down, arms stretched out, fingers splayed, crooked legs twisted into a circle, and blood splatters all around. So far, though, it has only been a dream." "Is there no other help?" K. asked with a smile. "I wouldn't know of any," said the court usher. "And now it's even worse; until now, he only took her to himself, but now he's taking her, which I had long expected, to the investigating judge as well." "Does your wife bear no guilt in this?" K. asked, having to restrain himself at this question, as he now felt jealousy too. "But of course," said the court usher, "she bears the greatest guilt. She has clung to him. As for him, he chases after all women. In this house alone, he has been thrown out of five apartments he sneaked into. My wife is, however, the most beautiful in the entire house, and I, of all people, cannot fight back." "If that's the case, then there is indeed no help," K. said. "Why not?" asked the court usher. "One should really beat the student, who is a coward, so badly that he would never dare to touch my wife again. But I can't do it, and others won't help me either, because everyone fears his power. Only a man like you could do it." "Why me?" K. asked, astonished. "You are on trial," the court usher said. "Yes," K. replied, "but that only makes me fear even more that he might have some influence, if not on the outcome of the trial, then probably on the preliminary investigation." "Yes, certainly," said the court usher, as if K.'s viewpoint was just as valid as his own. "However, generally, no hopeless trials are conducted here." "I disagree with you," K. said, "but that shouldn't stop me from occasionally dealing with the student." "I would be very grateful to you," said the court usher somewhat formally, though he seemed not to truly believe in the fulfillment of his highest wish. "Perhaps," K. continued, "other officials of yours and maybe even all of them deserve the same." "Yes, yes," said the court usher, as if it were something self-evident. Then he looked at K. with a trusting gaze, which he hadn't done before, despite all the friendliness, and added, "One always rebels." However, the conversation seemed to have become somewhat uncomfortable for him, as he cut it short by saying, "Now I have to report to the office. Would you like to come along?" "I have nothing to do there," K. said. "You could take a look at the offices. No one will pay attention to you." "Are they worth seeing?" K. asked hesitantly, but he had a strong desire to go. "Well," said the court usher, "I thought you might find it interesting." "Alright," K. finally said, "I'll go with you." And he hurried up the stairs faster than the court usher.

As he entered, he nearly stumbled, for there was a step behind the door. "They don't pay much attention to the audience," he said. "They don't pay any attention at all," replied the court usher, "just look at the waiting room here." It was a long corridor with rough wooden doors leading to the various departments of the attic. Although there was no direct light coming in, it was not completely dark, as some departments had not solid wooden walls but rather bare wooden grilles reaching up to the ceiling, through which some light filtered and through which one could also see individual officials writing at tables or standing at the grilles, observing the people in the corridor through the gaps. There were only a few people in the corridor, probably because it was Sunday. They made a very modest impression. They sat at almost regular intervals on two rows of long wooden benches placed on either side of the corridor. All were dressed in a neglected manner, although most, judging by their facial expressions, posture, beard styles, and many barely distinguishable small details, belonged to the higher classes. Since there were no coat hooks available, they had placed their hats under the benches, probably following each other's example. When those sitting closest to the door saw K. and the court usher, they stood up to greet them. When the others saw this, they felt they should also greet, so that everyone stood up as K. and the usher walked by. They never stood completely upright; their backs were hunched, their knees bent, they looked like street beggars. K. waited for the court usher, who was walking a bit behind him, and said, "How humbled they must feel." "Yes," replied the usher, "all those you see here are defendants." "Really!" K. said. "Then they are my colleagues." He turned to the next person, a tall, slender man who was already almost gray-haired. "What are you waiting for?" K. asked politely. The unexpected question confused the man, which was all the more embarrassing since he was evidently a worldly-wise person who surely knew how to hold himself together elsewhere and was not quick to give up the superiority he had gained over many. Here, however, he did not know how to answer such a simple question and looked at the others as if they were obliged to help him, feeling that no one could demand an answer from him if that help was lacking. Then the court usher stepped in and said to calm and encourage the man, "The gentleman here is only asking what you are waiting for. Please answer." The usher's voice, which the man probably recognized, had a better effect: "I am waiting—" he began, but hesitated. Clearly, he had chosen that beginning to answer the question precisely but now could not find a continuation. Some of the others waiting had approached and surrounded the group, and the court usher said to them, "Step back, clear the corridor." They backed away a little but not to their previous seats. Meanwhile, the questioned man had collected himself and even replied with a small smile, "I submitted some evidence requests in my case a month ago and am waiting for them to be addressed." "You seem to be making a lot of effort," K. said. "Yes," said the man, "it is my case." "Not everyone thinks like you," K. said, "I, for example, am also a defendant, but as sure as I want to be saved, I have neither submitted an evidence request nor undertaken anything of the sort. Do you think that's necessary?" "I'm not sure," the man said again, completely uncertain; he evidently thought K. was joking with him, so he would have preferred to repeat his earlier answer entirely, but under K.'s impatient gaze, he only said, "As for me, I have submitted evidence requests." "You probably don't believe that I am a defendant," K. asked. "Oh, certainly," said the man, stepping aside a little, but there was no belief in his answer, just fear. "So you don't believe me?" K. asked and, unconsciously prompted by the man's humble demeanor, grabbed him by the arm as if to force him to believe. He did not want to hurt him, having only touched him lightly, yet the man screamed as if K. had grabbed him with a red-hot tongs instead of just two fingers. This ridiculous scream finally made K. weary; if they did not believe he was a defendant, so much the better; he might even have thought him a judge. He then actually grasped him more firmly as a farewell, pushed him back onto the bench, and walked on. "Most defendants are so sensitive," said the court usher. Behind them, almost all the waiting people gathered around the man, who had already stopped screaming, seeming to question him closely about the incident. Now a guard approached K., identifiable mainly by a saber, whose scabbard, at least in color, was made of aluminum. K. marveled at this and even reached out to touch it. The guard, who had come because of the scream, inquired about what had happened. The court usher tried to calm him with a few words, but the guard insisted on looking into it himself, saluted, and walked on with very urgent but very short steps, probably measured out by gout.

K. did not concern himself for long with the man and the people in the hallway, especially since he saw an opportunity to turn right into an opening without a door about halfway down the corridor. He communicated with the court usher to confirm whether this was the right way, and the usher nodded, so K. actually turned in there. It annoyed him that he always had to walk one or two steps ahead of the usher; at least in this place, it could seem like he was being led in as a prisoner. He waited for the usher several times, but he kept falling behind. Finally, to put an end to his discomfort, K. said, "I've seen how it looks here, I want to leave now."

. . .

"You haven't seen everything yet," the usher replied completely innocuously.

"I don't want to see everything," K. said, who actually felt quite tired, "I want to go. How do you get to the exit?"

"Have you really lost your way already?" the usher asked in surprise. "You go to the corner, then turn right and go straight down the corridor to the door."

"Come with me," K. said, "show me the way; I'll miss it—there are so many paths here."

"It's the only way," the usher said reproachfully now, "I can't go back with you; I have to make my report and I've already wasted a lot of time because of you."

"Come with me," K. repeated now more sharply, as if he had finally caught the usher in a lie.

"Don't shout like that," the usher whispered, "there are offices everywhere here. If you don't want to go back alone, you can walk a little further with me or wait here until I've completed my report, then I'll gladly go back with you."

"No, no," K. said, "I won't wait, and you must come with me now." K. had not even looked around the room he was in until one of the many wooden doors standing around opened. A girl, who must have been summoned by K.'s loud speaking, entered and asked, "What does the

## THE TRIAL

gentleman wish?" In the distance behind her, a man was approaching in the dim light. K. looked at the usher. The usher had said that no one would care about K., and now two people were coming; it wouldn't take much for the officials to pay attention to him and want an explanation for his presence. The only understandable and acceptable explanation was that he was the accused and wanted to know the date of the next hearing. However, he did not want to provide this explanation, especially since it was not truthful; he had come out of curiosity or, which was an even less plausible explanation, out of a desire to confirm that the interior of this judicial system was just as repulsive as its exterior. And it seemed he was right in this assumption; he did not want to delve further. He was already cramped enough by what he had seen so far; he was not in the mood to confront a higher official, who could appear behind any door. He wanted to leave, either with the usher or alone, if necessary.

But his silent standing out had to be striking, and indeed, the girl and the court attendant looked at him as if some great transformation must happen to him in the next minute, which they did not want to miss observing. And in the doorway stood the man whom K. had noticed earlier from a distance; he held onto the beam of the low door and swayed a little on his toes, like an impatient spectator. The girl, however, was the first to realize that K.'s behavior stemmed from a slight discomfort. She brought a chair and asked, "Would you like to sit down?" K. immediately sat down and, to get a better grip, rested his elbows on the armrests. "You feel a bit dizzy, don't you?" she asked him. Now he had her face close before him; it had a stern expression, like that of some women in their most beautiful youth. "Don't worry about it," she said, "this is nothing unusual; almost everyone gets such a spell when they come here for the first time. This is your first time here? Well, that's nothing extraordinary. The sun beats down on the roof structure, and the hot wood makes the air so stuffy and heavy. Because of that, this place is not very suitable for office spaces, despite the advantages it offers otherwise. But as for the air, on days with a lot of traffic—which is almost every day—it's hardly breathable. And if you consider that laundry is often hung out to dry here—you can't completely forbid the tenants from doing that—you won't be surprised that you felt a bit unwell. But you eventually get used to the air very well. When you come for the second or third time, you will hardly feel the heaviness here anymore. Do you feel any better?" K. did not answer; it was too embarrassing for him to be at the mercy of the people here due to this sudden weakness. Moreover, now that he had learned the causes of his discomfort, he did not feel better, but rather a little worse. The girl noticed this immediately, took a hook stick that was leaning against the wall, and pushed open a small hatch that was just above K. and led outside. But so much soot came in that the girl had to close the hatch right away and clean K.'s hands of soot with her handkerchief, as he was too tired to do it himself. He would have liked to sit quietly here until he felt strong enough to leave, but this had to happen all the sooner the less they would care for him. Now the girl added, "You can't stay here; we're disturbing the traffic." K. asked with his eyes what traffic he was disturbing here. "I'll take you to the sick room if you want," she said. "Please help me," she said to the man in the doorway, who immediately came closer. But K. did not want to go to the sick room; that was exactly what he wanted to avoid. The further he was taken, the worse it must get. "I can go on my own," he said, and stood up, trembling from being spoiled by the comfortable sitting. But then he could not keep himself upright. "It's not working," he said, shaking his head, and sighed as he sat back down. He remembered the court attendant, who could easily take him out despite everything, but he seemed to have been gone for a long time. K. looked through the girl and the man standing before him but could not find the court attendant.

"I believe," said the man, who was elegantly dressed and particularly noticeable for his gray vest that ended in two long, sharply cut points, "that the gentleman's discomfort is due to the atmosphere here. It would therefore be best, and also most agreeable for him, if we do not lead him to the sick room, but rather out of the offices altogether."

"That's it," K. exclaimed, almost interrupting the man's speech out of sheer joy. "I'll surely feel better right away; I'm not so weak, I just need a little support under my arms. I won't cause you much trouble; it's not

## THE TRIAL

a long way. Just lead me to the door, and I'll sit on the steps for a bit and I'll be refreshed in no time. I'm really not suffering from such attacks; it comes as a surprise to me. After all, I'm a civil servant and used to office air, but it does seem quite severe here, as you say. Would you be so kind as to help me a little? I'm feeling dizzy, and I'll feel worse if I try to get up on my own." He lifted his shoulders to make it easier for the two to help him under his arms.

But the man did not follow the request; instead, he kept his hands calmly in his pockets and laughed loudly. "You see," he said to the girl, "I did hit the mark after all. The gentleman is just not well here, not in general." The girl smiled too, but lightly tapped the man on the arm with her fingertips, as if he had made too much of a joke with K. "But what do you think," the man continued laughing, "I really do want to lead the gentleman out." "Then that's good," said the girl, tilting her delicate head for a moment. "Don't attach too much importance to laughter," she said to K., who had once again stared blankly ahead, looking as if he didn't need an explanation, "this gentleman — may I introduce you?" (the gentleman granted permission with a hand gesture) — "so this gentleman is the informer. He provides all the information that the waiting parties need, and since our judicial system is not very well known among the public, many inquiries are made. He knows the answer to every question; you can test him on that whenever you feel like it. But that's not his only virtue; his second virtue is his elegant clothing. We, that is, the officials, once thought it necessary to dress the informer elegantly since he is always the first to negotiate with the parties, in order to make a worthy first impression. We others, as you can see from my appearance, are unfortunately dressed very poorly and out of fashion; it doesn't make much sense to invest in clothing since we are almost constantly in the offices and even sleep here. But as I said, we once considered nice clothing necessary for the informer. However, since it was not available from our administration, which is a bit peculiar in this regard, we held a collection — even the parties contributed — and we bought him this nice outfit and others. Everything is now prepared to make a good impression, but he ruins it again with his laughter and frightens people." "That's true," the gentleman said mockingly, "but I don't understand, Miss, why you are sharing all our intimacies with the gentleman, or rather imposing them on him, since he doesn't want to know them at all. Just look at him, clearly preoccupied with his own affairs." K. didn't even feel like arguing; the girl's intention might have been good, perhaps aimed at distracting him or giving him a chance to collect himself, but the approach was misguided. "I had to explain your laughter to him," the girl said. "It was indeed insulting." "I believe he would forgive even worse insults if I finally lead him out," K. said nothing, didn't even look up; he tolerated the two discussing him as if he were an object, and in fact preferred it that way. But suddenly he felt the informer's hand on one arm and the girl's hand on the other. "So come on, you weak man," said the informer. "Thank you both very much," K. said, pleasantly surprised, slowly getting up and guiding the foreign hands to the places where he needed support the most. "It seems," the girl whispered softly in K.'s ear as they approached the corridor, "as if I particularly care about presenting the informer in a good light, but believe me, I want to speak the truth. He doesn't have a hard heart. He is not obligated to lead sick parties out, yet he does, as you can see. Perhaps none of us are hard-hearted; we would all like to help, but as court officials, we easily give the impression that we are hard-hearted and unwilling to help anyone. I actually suffer from it." "Would you like to sit down here for a moment?" the informer asked, as they were already in the corridor and just in front of the accused whom K. had approached earlier. K. almost felt ashamed in front of him; he had stood so upright before him before, but now he had to be supported by two people, the informer balanced his hat on splayed fingers, and his hair was disheveled, hanging in sweat-drenched strands on his forehead. But the accused seemed not to notice anything; he stood humbly before the informer, who looked past him, and only sought to excuse his presence. "I know," he said, "that the resolution of my requests cannot be given today. But I have come anyway; I thought I could wait here, it's Sunday, I have time, and I'm not bothering anyone." "You don't have to apologize so much," said the informer, "your diligence is quite commendable; though you are unnecessarily taking up space here, I will not hinder you from closely following the progress of your case, as long as it doesn't become bothersome for me. When you've seen people who shamefully neglect their duties, you learn to be patient with people like you. Please, sit down." "How he knows how to speak to the parties," whispered the girl. K. nodded but immediately stopped when the informer asked again, "Would you not like to sit down here?" "No," K. said, "I don't want to rest." He had said this with as much determination as possible, but in reality, it would have been very beneficial for him to sit down. He felt like he was seasick. He believed he was on a ship that was in heavy seas. It felt as if the water was crashing against the wooden walls, as if a roar was coming from the depths of the corridor like rushing water, as if the corridor was swaying sideways and the waiting parties were being lifted and lowered on either side. The calmness of the girl and the man leading him was all the more incomprehensible. He was at their mercy; if they let go of him, he would fall like a plank. Sharp glances exchanged between their small eyes, he felt their steady steps without being able to match them, as he was almost carried from step to step. Finally, he noticed that they were speaking to him, but he didn't understand them; he only heard the noise that filled everything, through which an unchanging high tone seemed to resonate like that of a siren. "Louder," he whispered with his head down, feeling ashamed because he knew they had spoken loudly enough, even if it was unintelligible to him. Then finally, as if the wall before them had been torn down, a fresh breeze met him, and he heard beside him say: "At first, he wants to leave, but then you can tell him a hundred times that this is the exit, and he won't budge." K. realized he was standing before the exit door that the girl had opened. It felt as if all his strength returned at once; eager for a taste of freedom, he stepped onto a stair and bid farewell to his companions from there as they leaned down to him. "Thank you very much," he repeated, shook both their hands repeatedly, and only stopped when he thought he saw that they, accustomed to the office air, were struggling to endure the relatively fresh air coming from the stairs. They could hardly respond, and the girl might have stumbled if K. hadn't closed the door extremely quickly. K. then stood still for a moment, adjusted his hair with the help of a pocket mirror, picked up his hat, which lay on the next stair — the informer had presumably thrown it — and then ran down the stairs so briskly and in such long leaps that he almost felt afraid of this sudden change. Such surprises had never occurred to him before, not even with his otherwise quite stable health. Did his body perhaps want to revolt and give him a new trial, now that he was enduring the old one so effortlessly? He didn't completely reject the idea of seeing a doctor at the next opportunity; in any case, he decided — he could reason this out himself — to spend all future Sunday mornings better than this one.

## 4
# THE FRIEND OF MISS BÜRSTNER

In the following days, K. found it impossible to speak even a few words with Miss Bürstner. He tried in various ways to approach her, but she always managed to prevent it. He came home right after work, stayed in his room without turning on the light, sitting on the sofa and occupied himself solely with watching the anteroom. If the maid passed by and closed the door to the seemingly empty room, he would eventually get up and open it again. In the mornings, he woke up an hour earlier than usual in hopes of meeting Miss Bürstner alone as she left for work. However, none of these attempts were successful. He then wrote her a letter, both at the office and at her apartment, in which he tried again to justify his behavior, offered to make amends for everything, promised never to cross the boundaries she set for him, and only asked for the chance to speak with her, especially since he could not do anything with Mrs. Grubach without first consulting her. Ultimately, he informed her that he would be waiting in his room all day the following Sunday for a sign from her that would indicate whether his request could be fulfilled or at least explain why it could not, despite his promise to comply with her wishes. The letters were not returned, but there was also no response. However, on Sunday, there was a sign that was clear enough. Early in the morning, K. noticed unusual movement in the anteroom through the keyhole, which soon became clear. A French teacher, who was actually German and named Montag, a weak, pale girl with a slight limp who had previously had her own room, was moving into Miss Bürstner's room. For hours, she was seen shuffling through the anteroom, always forgetting a piece of laundry, a cover, or a book that had to be retrieved and carried over to the new apartment.

When Mrs. Grubach brought K. his breakfast — since she had angered him so much, she no longer entrusted even the slightest task to the maid — K. could not hold back and spoke to her for the first time. "Why is there such a noise in the anteroom today?" he asked while pouring his coffee. "Couldn't that be stopped? Is it necessary to clean up on a Sunday?" Although K. did not look up at Mrs. Grubach, he noticed that she sighed with relief. Even these stern questions from K. she interpreted as an apology or the start of one. "They aren't cleaning up, Mr. K.," she said, "Miss Montag is merely moving to Miss Bürstner's and is taking her things over." She said nothing more but waited to see how K. would respond and whether he would allow her to continue speaking. However, K. tested her; he thoughtfully stirred his coffee with the spoon and remained silent. Then he looked up at her and said, "Have you given up your earlier suspicion regarding Miss Bürstner?" "Mr. K.," Mrs. Grubach exclaimed, who had been waiting for this question and held out her folded hands to K. "You took a casual remark I made the other day too seriously. I never meant to offend you or anyone else. You've known me long enough, Mr. K., to be convinced of that. You have no idea how I've suffered these last few days! I should slander my tenants! And you, Mr. K., believed it! And said I should give you notice! Give you notice!" The last exclamation was already choked with tears; she lifted her apron to her face and sobbed loudly.

"Please don't cry, Mrs. Grubach," K. said, looking out the window. He was only thinking about Miss Bürstner and the fact that she had taken a strange girl into her room. "Please don't cry," he repeated as he turned back into the room and saw that Mrs. Grubach was still crying. "It wasn't meant so badly by me back then. We simply misunderstood each other. That can happen even among old friends." Mrs. Grubach adjusted her apron under her eyes to see if K. was truly reconciled. "Well, it is as it is," K. said, and now, judging by Mrs. Grubach's behavior, he dared to add, since the captain had revealed nothing, "Do you really think I could become hostile with you over a strange girl?"

"That's exactly it, Mr. K.," said Mrs. Grubach. It was her misfortune that whenever she felt even a little freer, she would say something awkward. "I kept asking myself: Why does Mr. K. care so much about Miss Bürstner? Why does he argue with me over her, even though he knows that every harsh word from him keeps me awake at night? I haven't said anything about the young lady that I haven't seen with my own eyes." K. said nothing in response; he would have had to throw her out of the room with his first word, and he didn't want that. He contented himself with drinking his coffee and making Mrs. Grubach feel unnecessary.

Outside, they could hear the slow footsteps of Miss Montag crossing the entire foyer. "Do you hear that?" K. asked, pointing toward the door. "Yes," Mrs. Grubach sighed, "I wanted to help her and also have the maid help her, but she's stubborn; she wants to move everything herself. I'm surprised by Miss Bürstner. It's often a nuisance for me to have Miss Montag as a tenant, but Miss Bürstner even takes her into her room." "You shouldn't worry about that," K. said, crushing the sugar remnants in his cup. "Have you suffered any loss because of it?"

"No," said Mrs. Grubach. "In itself, it's quite welcome; I get a room freed up and can accommodate my nephew, the captain, there. I've long feared that he might have disturbed you in the last few days while I had to let him stay in the living room next door. He doesn't consider others much." "What ideas!" K. said, standing up. "That's out of the question. You seem to think I'm overly sensitive because I can't stand these wanderings of Miss Montag — she's going back again now." Mrs. Grubach felt quite powerless. "Should I, Mr. K., say that she should postpone the rest of the move? If you want, I can do it right away." "But she should be moving to Miss Bürstner!" K. said. "Yes," Mrs. Grubach replied, not fully understanding what K. meant. "Well then," K. said, "she must take her things over." Mrs. Grubach merely nodded. This silent helplessness, which looked no different from defiance on the outside, irritated K. even more. He began to pace in the room from the window to the door, thereby denying Mrs. Grubach the opportunity to leave, which she likely would have done otherwise.

Just as K. had made it to the door again, there was a knock. It was the maid, who announced that Miss Montag would like to speak with Mr. K. and requested that he come to the dining room, where she was waiting for him. K. listened thoughtfully to the maid, then turned to the startled Mrs. Grubach with an almost mocking look. This glance seemed to suggest that K. had long anticipated this invitation from Miss Montag and that it fit perfectly with the torment he had experienced that Sunday morning from Mrs. Grubach's tenants. He sent the maid back with the message that he would come immediately, then went to the wardrobe to change his jacket, responding to Mrs. Grubach, who was quietly lamenting the annoying visitor, with only the request that she should clear away the breakfast dishes. "You hardly touched anything," said Mrs. Grubach. "Oh, just take it away," K. shouted; it felt to him as if Miss Montag had somehow tainted everything, making it repulsive.

As he walked through the foyer, he glanced at the closed door of Miss Bürstner's room. But he was not invited there; instead, he burst open the door to the dining room without knocking.

It was a very long but narrow room with a single window. There was just enough space to awkwardly fit two cabinets in the corners by the door, while the rest of the room was completely taken up by the long dining table, which started near the door and almost reached the large window, making it nearly inaccessible. The table was already set, and it was prepared for many people, as almost all the tenants ate lunch here on Sundays.

When K. entered, Miss Montag came towards him along one side of the table from the window. They greeted each other silently. Then Miss Montag, as always with her head unusually held high, said, "I don't know if you know me." K. looked at her with narrowed eyes. "Of course," he said, "you've been living with Mrs. Grubach for quite a while." "But I believe you don't care much about the boarding house," Miss Montag remarked. "No," K. replied. "Would you like to sit down?" Miss Montag asked. They both silently pulled out two chairs at the far end of the table and sat across from each other. However, Miss Montag quickly got up again because she had left her handbag on the windowsill and went to retrieve it; she dragged it through the entire room. When she returned, lightly swinging her handbag, she said, "I would like to speak a few words with you on behalf of my friend. She wanted to come herself, but she's feeling a bit unwell today. Please excuse her and listen to me instead. She wouldn't have been able to say anything different than what I will tell you. On the contrary, I believe I can even tell you more since I am relatively uninvolved. Don't you think?"

"What would there be to say?" replied K., who was tired of seeing Miss Montag's eyes constantly fixed on his lips. She was already asserting some control over what he wanted to say. "Miss Bürstner clearly does not want to grant me the personal conversation I requested."

"That's it," said Miss Montag, "or rather, that's not it at all; you express it rather sharply. Generally speaking, conversations are neither granted nor denied. But it can happen that one considers conversations unnecessary, and that is indeed the case here. Now, after your remark, I can speak openly. You have asked my friend, either in writing or verbally, for a meeting. Now my friend knows—at least I must assume—what this meeting is supposed to be about, and therefore, for reasons I do not know, she is convinced that it would not benefit anyone if the meeting were to actually take place. Furthermore, she mentioned to me just yesterday, only very briefly, that you probably do not care much about the meeting either, as you came up with such an idea purely by chance and would, without further explanation, if not already now, then very soon recognize the pointlessness of it all. I replied that this may be correct, but that I would still consider it advantageous to provide you with a clear response for the sake of complete clarification. I offered to take on this task, and after some hesitation, my friend agreed. I hope I have acted in your best interest as well, because even the slightest uncertainty in the most trivial matter is always tormenting, and if one can easily eliminate it, as in this case, it is better to do so immediately."


"Thank you," K. said right away, slowly standing up, looking at Miss Montag, then across the table, then out the window—the house across the street was bathed in sunlight—and went to the door. Miss Montag followed him a few steps, as if she did not fully trust him. However, both had to step back as the door opened, revealing Captain Lanz. K. saw him up close for the first time. He was a tall man, around 40 years old, with a tanned, fleshy face. He made a slight bow, which was also directed at K., then approached Miss Montag and respectfully kissed her hand. He was very graceful in his movements. His politeness towards Miss Montag stood in stark contrast to the treatment she had received from K. Nevertheless, Miss Montag did not seem to be angry with K., as she even wanted, as K. thought he noticed, to introduce him to the captain. But K. did not want to be introduced; he would not have been able to be friendly to either the captain or Miss Montag in any way. The kiss on the hand had, for him, connected her to a group that sought to keep him away from Miss Bürstner under the guise of utmost innocence and selflessness. However, K. not only recognized this, but he also saw that Miss Montag had chosen a clever, albeit double-edged, approach. She exaggerated the significance of the relationship between Miss Bürstner and K., particularly inflating the importance of the requested conversation, and simultaneously tried to turn it around as if it were K. who was exaggerating everything. She was mistaken; K. did not want to exaggerate anything; he knew that Miss Bürstner was a little typist who would not be able to resist him for long. In doing so, he deliberately did not take into account what he had learned from Mrs. Grubach about Miss Bürstner. He considered all this while barely acknowledging the others as he left the room. He intended to go straight to his room, but a small laugh from Miss Montag that he heard behind him from the dining room made him think he might be able to surprise both her and the captain. He looked around and listened to see if any disturbance could be expected from the surrounding rooms; everything was quiet, only the conversation from the dining room could be heard along with the voice of Mrs. Grubach from the hallway leading to the kitchen. The opportunity seemed favorable, so K. went to Miss Bürstner's door and knocked softly. When nothing stirred, he knocked again, but still received no response. Was she sleeping? Or was she really unwell? Or was she just pretending not to be there because she sensed it could only be K. knocking so quietly? K. assumed that she was hiding and knocked harder, finally, since the knocking was unsuccessful, carefully opened the door, not without feeling that he was doing something wrong and moreover pointless. The room was empty. It hardly resembled the room as K. had known it. There were now two beds placed back to back against the wall, three chairs near the door were piled high with clothes and laundry, and a wardrobe stood open. Miss Bürstner had probably left while Miss Montag had been talking to K. in the dining room. K. was not very disturbed by this; he had hardly expected to easily meet Miss Bürstner, and had made this attempt almost out of spite against Miss Montag. Nevertheless, it was all the more embarrassing for him when, as he closed the door, he saw Miss Montag and the captain talking in the open doorway of the dining room. They had probably been standing there since K. had opened the door; they avoided any appearance of having been watching K. and were conversing quietly, glancing around only in a distracted manner as one does during a conversation. But those looks weighed heavily on K., and he hurried along the wall to his room.

## 5

# THE BULLY

As K. passed through the corridor that separated his office from the main staircase one of the next evenings—he was going home almost last this time, with only two servants working in the small light of a bulb in the reception area—he heard sighs coming from behind a door he had always assumed was just a storage room, without ever having seen inside. He stopped in astonishment and listened again to confirm he wasn't mistaken; it was quiet for a moment, but then the sighs returned. At first, he wanted to fetch one of the servants, as a witness might be needed, but then he was overcome by such an uncontrollable curiosity that he flung the door open. It was indeed a storage room, as he had suspected. Useless old printing materials and overturned empty clay ink bottles lay just inside the threshold. Inside the room stood three men, hunched over in the low space. A candle fixed on a shelf provided them with light. "What are you doing here?" K. asked, his excitement bubbling over but not loud. One man, who clearly dominated the others and turned their attention to himself first, was dressed in a kind of dark leather outfit that left his neck down to his chest and his arms completely bare. He did not respond. But the other two called out, "Sir! We are to be beaten because you complained about us to the investigating magistrate." Only then did K. realize that it was indeed the guards Franz and Willem, and that the third man was holding a switch to beat them. "Well," K. said, staring at them, "I did not complain; I merely stated what happened in my apartment. And you certainly did not behave properly." "Sir," Willem said, while Franz evidently tried to protect himself behind him from the third man, "if you knew how poorly we are paid, you would judge us better. I have a family to feed, and Franz here wanted to get married; one seeks to enrich oneself as best as one can, for mere labor does not suffice, not even through the most strenuous efforts. Your fine laundry tempted me; it is, of course, forbidden for the guards to act in such a way, it was wrong, but it is a tradition that the laundry belongs to the guards; it has always been so, believe me. It is also understandable what such things mean for someone who is so unfortunate as to be arrested. However, if he speaks of it publicly, then punishment must follow." "What you are saying now, I did not know; I certainly did not demand your punishment; I was concerned about a principle." "Franz," Willem turned to the other guard, "didn't I tell you that the sir did not demand our punishment? Now you hear that he didn't even know we had to be punished." "Don't let such talk affect you," the third man said to K., "the punishment is as just as it is inevitable." "Don't listen to him," Willem said, pausing only to quickly bring his hand, which had just received a blow from the switch, to his mouth. "We are only being punished because you reported us. Otherwise, nothing would have happened to us, even if it became known what we did. Can that be called justice? We two, especially I, had proven ourselves as guards for a long time—you must admit that from the point of view of the authority, we guarded well—we had prospects for advancement and would surely have soon become beaters like this one, who happened to be lucky enough not to have been reported by anyone, as such reports are indeed quite rare. And now, sir, everything is lost; our careers are over, we will have to do much more subordinate work than guarding, and besides, we are now getting these terribly painful beatings." "Can a switch really cause such pain?" K. asked, testing the switch that the beater was swinging before him. "We will have to strip completely naked," Willem said. "Oh, I see," K. said, looking closely at the beater; he was tanned like a sailor and had a wild, fresh face. "Is there no way to spare the two of them from the beating?" he asked him. "No," said the beater, shaking his head with a smile. "Strip," he ordered the guards. And to K. he said, "You must not believe everything they say; they have become a bit irrational from the fear of the beatings. What this one here,"—he pointed at Willem—"has said about his possible career is downright ridiculous. Look at how fat he is—the first strokes of the switch would be completely lost in that fat. Do you know how he got so fat? He has the habit of eating all the breakfast of the detainees. Didn't he also eat your breakfast? There, I told you. But a man with such a belly can never become a beater, that is entirely out of the question." "There are such beaters," Willem claimed, as he loosened his belt. "No," said the beater, brushing his switch across Willem's neck in such a way that he flinched. "You are not to listen but to strip." "I would reward you well if you let them go," K. said, drawing his wallet without looking at the beater again—such matters are best handled with downcast eyes on both sides. "You probably want to report me too," said the beater, "and then get me beaten as well. No, no!" "Be reasonable," said K., "if I had wanted these two punished, I wouldn't want to buy them off now. I could just slam the door here, not want to see or hear anything further, and go home; but I am not doing that; rather, I seriously want to free them. Had I known they were to be punished, or even that they could be punished, I would never have mentioned their names. I do not consider them guilty; the organization is guilty; the high officials are guilty." "That's right," the guards shouted and immediately received a blow across their already bare backs. "If you had a high judge under your switch," K. said, pressing down the switch that was trying to rise again as he spoke, "I would truly not stop you from striking; on the contrary, I would even give you money to strengthen yourself for the good cause." "What you say sounds credible," said the beater, "but I will not be bribed. I am employed to beat, so I will beat." The guard Franz, who had perhaps been relatively reserved until now, waiting for K.'s intervention to yield a good outcome, now stepped forward to the door dressed only in his trousers, knelt down, clung to K.'s arm, and whispered, "If you cannot secure mercy for both of us, at least try to free me. Willem is older than I, less sensitive in every respect, and he has already received a light beating a few years ago. I, however, have not yet been dishonored, and I was only led to my actions by Willem, who is my teacher in both good and bad. My poor fiancée is waiting outside in front of the bank for the outcome; I am so terribly ashamed." He dried his tear-streaked face on K.'s coat. "I won't wait any longer," said the beater, grabbing the switch with both hands and striking Franz, while Willem crouched in a corner and secretly watched, not daring to turn his head. The scream that Franz let out was unbroken and unchanged; it seemed not to come from a human but from a tortured instrument. The whole corridor groaned with it; the entire building must have heard it. "Don't scream," K. shouted; he could not hold back, and while he anxiously looked toward where the servants must be coming from, he pushed Franz—not hard but just strongly enough that the unconscious man fell and searched the ground with his hands in a spasm; however, he could not escape the blows; the switch found him on the ground; while he writhed under it, its tip swung up and down regularly. And already a servant appeared in the distance and a second one a few steps behind him. K. quickly slammed the door, went to a nearby window, and opened it. The screaming had completely stopped. To keep the servants from coming closer, he called out, "It's me." "Good evening, Mr. Prosecutor," came the reply. "Is something happening?" "No, no," K. answered. "It's just a dog barking in the courtyard." When the servants did not move, he added, "You can continue with your work." To avoid having to engage in conversation with the servants, he leaned out of the window. When he looked back into the corridor after a while, they were already gone. K., however, remained by the window, as he did not dare to go back into the storage room, and he did not want to go home either. It was a small square courtyard he looked down into; surrounding it were office rooms, all the windows were dark now, only the uppermost ones caught a reflection of the moon. K. strained his eyes to penetrate the darkness of a corner of the courtyard where several handcarts had collided. He was tormented by the fact that he had not managed to prevent the beating, but it was not his fault that he had failed—if Franz had not screamed—certainly, it must have hurt a lot, but at a decisive moment, one must maintain control—had he not screamed, K. would have likely found a way to persuade the beater.

If the entire lower ranks of officials were scum, why would the beater, who had the most inhumane job, be an exception? K. also observed well how the beater's eyes had lit up at the sight of the banknote; he was evidently just serious about the beating to increase the bribe a little more. And K. would not have held back; he truly cared about freeing the guards; once he had begun to combat the corruption of this judicial system, it was only natural that he intervened from this side as well. But at the moment Franz began to scream, of course, everything was over. K. could not allow the servants and perhaps all sorts of people to come and catch him in negotiations with the group in the storage room. No one could truly demand such a sacrifice from K. If he had intended to do that, it would have almost been simpler for K. to strip himself and offer himself to the beater as a substitute for the guards. Moreover, the beater would certainly not have accepted such a substitution, as he would have severely violated his duty without gaining any advantage, and likely would have violated it doubly, for K. must be inviolable for all court employees as long as he was in proceedings. However, special regulations might apply here too. In any case, K. could do nothing else but slam the door, even though that did not eliminate all danger for him. It was regrettable that he had pushed Franz in the end, and only his agitation could excuse it.

In the distance, he heard the footsteps of the servants; to avoid drawing attention, he closed the window and made his way toward the main staircase. He paused briefly at the door to the utility room and listened. It was completely silent. The man could have beaten the guards to death, as they were entirely at his mercy. K. had already reached for the doorknob but then pulled his hand back. He could no longer help anyone, and the servants would be coming soon; however, he promised himself that he would bring up the matter and punish the truly guilty parties—the high officials—who had yet to show themselves to him, as far as he was able. As he descended the outdoor steps of the bank, he carefully observed all the passersby, but even in the wider vicinity, there was no girl to be seen waiting for anyone. Franz's remark that his fiancée was waiting for him turned out to be a somewhat forgivable lie, intended solely to evoke greater sympathy.

Even the next day, K. couldn't get the guards out of his mind; he was distracted at work and had to stay in the office a little longer than the day before to get through his tasks. As he walked home and passed by the storeroom again, he opened it out of habit. What he saw instead of the expected darkness left him speechless. Everything was unchanged, just as he had found it the evening before when he opened the door. The printed materials and ink bottles right behind the threshold, the enforcer with the rod, the fully dressed guards, the candle on the shelf, and the guards began to complain and called out: "Sir!" Immediately, K. slammed the door shut and pounded on it with his fists as if that would make it more securely locked. Almost in tears, he ran to the servants, who were calmly working at the copying machines and paused in their tasks, surprised. "Please finally clear out the storeroom," he shouted. "We are drowning in filth." The servants were willing to do it the next day; K. nodded, realizing that he couldn't force them to work late at night as he had originally intended. He sat down for a moment to keep the servants nearby, threw some copies around, creating the impression that he was checking them, and then, understanding that the servants wouldn't dare leave at the same time as him, tired and lost in thought, he went home.

## 6

# THE UNCLE · LENI

One afternoon—K. was very busy just before the post office closed—K.'s uncle Karl, a small landowner from the countryside, pushed his way into the room between two servants who were bringing in documents. K. was less startled by the sight than he had been when he had previously imagined the uncle's arrival some time ago. It had been clear to K. for about a month that the uncle would come. Back then, he had already believed he could see him, slightly hunched over, holding his dented Panama hat in his left hand, his right hand outstretched to him from a distance, rushing it across the desk and knocking over anything in his way. The uncle was always in a hurry because he was plagued by the unhappy thought that during his brief one-day stay in the capital, he had to accomplish everything he had planned, and he must not miss any spontaneous conversation, business, or pleasure that might arise. K. had to assist him in every possible way, especially since he had been his former guardian, and he also had to let him stay overnight. "The ghost from the countryside," he used to call him.

Right after the greeting — he had no time to sit down in the armchair to which K. invited him — he asked K. for a brief conversation alone. "It is necessary," he said, swallowing hard, "for my peace of mind, it is necessary." K. immediately sent the servants out of the room with instructions not to let anyone in. "What have I heard, Josef?" exclaimed the uncle, when they were alone, sitting on the table and stuffing various papers under himself to sit better. K. remained silent; he knew what was coming, but suddenly relaxed from the exhausting work he had been doing, he indulged in a pleasant lethargy and looked out the window at the opposite street, from which only a small triangular slice was visible from his seat, a piece of empty wall between two shop displays. "You're looking out the window," the uncle exclaimed with raised arms, "for heaven's sake, Josef, please answer me. Is it true, can it really be true?" "Dear Uncle," K. said, pulling himself from his distraction, "I don't even know what you want from me." "Josef," the uncle warned, "you have always told the truth, as far as I know. Should I take your last words as a bad omen?" "I suspect I know what you want," K. replied obediently, "you have probably heard about my trial." "That's right," the uncle answered, nodding slowly, "I have heard about your trial." "From whom?" K. asked. "Erna wrote to me," the uncle said, "she has no contact with you, unfortunately you don't care much about her, yet she found out. I received the letter today and came right away. For no other reason, but it seems a sufficient reason. I can read you the part of the letter that concerns you." He took the letter out of his wallet. "Here it is. She writes: I haven't seen Josef in a long time; last week I was at the bank, but Josef was so busy that I wasn't let in; I waited almost an hour, but had to go home because I had a piano lesson. I would have liked to speak with him; maybe there will be another opportunity soon. For my name day, he sent me a large box of chocolates; it was very kind and thoughtful. I had forgotten to mention it to you at that time; only now, as you ask me, do I remember. You must know that chocolates disappear immediately in the boarding house; hardly have you come to your senses that you have been gifted chocolate, and it's already gone. But regarding Josef, I wanted to tell you something else. As I mentioned, I wasn't let in at the bank because he was negotiating with a gentleman at that moment. After I had waited quietly for some time, I asked a servant if the negotiation would take long. He said it probably would, since it was likely about the trial against the gentleman prosecutor. I asked what kind of trial it was, if he wasn't mistaken, but he said he wasn't mistaken; it was a trial, and indeed a serious trial, but he didn't know more. He himself would like to help the gentleman prosecutor, for he is a good and fair man, but he doesn't know how to start, and he only wishes that influential gentlemen would take care of him. This will surely happen, and it will eventually have a good ending, but for now, according to the mood of the gentleman prosecutor, it doesn't look good at all, as he could gather. Of course, I didn't attach much importance to these words; I also tried to calm the simple servant, forbidding him to speak of it to anyone else, and I considered the whole thing to be nonsense. Still, it might be good if you, dear father, would look into the matter on your next visit; it would be easy for you to find out more details, and if it should really be necessary, to intervene through your influential acquaintances. But if it's not necessary, which is the most likely scenario, at least your daughter will soon have the chance to embrace you, which would make her happy." "A good child," the uncle said, as he finished reading the letter, wiping a few tears from his eyes. K. nodded; he had completely forgotten Erna due to the various disturbances of recent times, even forgetting her birthday, and the story about the chocolates was clearly invented to protect him from his uncle and aunt. It was very touching and certainly not enough reward for the theater tickets he now intended to regularly send her, but he felt unfit for visits to the boarding house and conversations with a little 18-year-old schoolgirl. "And what do you say now?" the uncle asked, having forgotten all haste and excitement through the letter and seeming to read it again. "Yes, uncle," K. said, "it is true." "True?" the uncle exclaimed, "What is true? How can it be true? What trial? It's not a criminal trial, is it?" "A criminal trial," K. replied. "And you sit calmly here with a criminal trial hanging over your head?" the uncle shouted, becoming louder. "The calmer I am, the better it is for the outcome," K. said tiredly. "Don't be afraid." "That doesn't reassure me," the uncle shouted, "Josef, dear Josef, think of yourself, of your relatives, of our good name. You have been our honor so far; you must not become our shame. Your attitude," he looked at K. with his head tilted, "does not please me; no innocent accused behaves like that when he is still in good spirits. Just tell me quickly what it's about, so that I can help you. It's about the bank, isn't it?" "No," K. said, standing up, "but you're speaking too loudly, dear uncle; the servant is probably at the door listening. That makes me uncomfortable. We better leave. I will then answer all your questions as best as I can. I know very well that I owe the family an explanation." "Right," the uncle shouted, "very right, hurry up, Josef, hurry up." "I just need to give a few orders," K. said and called his representative to him by phone, who entered in a few moments. The uncle, in his agitation, gestured to him that K. had called him, which would have otherwise left no doubt. K., standing at the desk, explained to the young man, who listened coolly but attentively, in a low voice, using various documents, what needed to be completed during his absence today. The uncle interrupted, first standing with wide eyes and nervously biting his lips, without actually listening, but the mere appearance of this was already disturbing enough. Then he began to pace the room, stopping here and there in front of the window or a picture, where he would break out into various exclamations, such as: "I find it completely incomprehensible" or "Now just tell me, what will come of this?" The young man pretended not to notice any of this, listened calmly to K.'s instructions until the end, noted some things down, and after bowing to K. as well as to the uncle, who had just turned his back, he left, looking out the window and crumpling the curtains with outstretched hands. The door had scarcely closed when the uncle exclaimed: "Finally, the puppet has left; now we can go too. Finally!" Unfortunately, there was no way to persuade the uncle to refrain from asking about the trial in the hall, where several clerks and servants were standing, and where the deputy director crossed their path, as they were also instructed not to ask about the trial. "So, Josef," the uncle began, while he answered the greetings of those present with a light salute, "now tell me openly, what kind of trial is it?" K. made some vague remarks, laughed a little, and only on the stairs did he explain to the uncle that he did not want to speak openly in front of people. "Right," the uncle said, "but now speak." With his head lowered, smoking a cigar in short, hurried puffs, he listened. "Above all, uncle," K. said, "it is not even a trial before a regular court." "That's bad," the uncle said. "What?" K. replied, looking at the uncle. "That it's bad, I mean," the uncle repeated. They stood on the staircase leading to the street; since the porter seemed to be listening, K. pulled the uncle down; the lively street traffic swept them along. The uncle, who had hooked his arm in K.'s, did not ask so urgently about the trial anymore; they even walked on in silence for a while. "But how did it happen?" the uncle finally asked, stopping so suddenly that the people behind him had to step aside in surprise. "Such things don't happen suddenly; they prepare for a long time; there must have been signs. Why didn't you write to me? You know that I would do anything for you; I am, in a way, still your guardian and have been proud of it until today. Of course, I will help you now; it is just very difficult now that the trial is already underway. It would be best if you took a little vacation and came to us in the countryside. You have lost a bit of weight; I notice it now. In the countryside, you will regain your strength; that will be good, as you will certainly have exertions ahead of you. Moreover, you will also be somewhat removed from the court. Here, they have all kinds of means of power, which they will necessarily apply to you as well; but in the countryside, they would first have to delegate organs or try to influence you only by letter, telegram, or telephone. That of course weakens the effect, doesn't free you, but allows you to breathe." "They could forbid me to leave," K. said, somewhat drawn into the uncle's reasoning. "I don't think they will do that," the uncle said thoughtfully, "the loss of power they would suffer from your departure isn't that great." "I thought," K. said, taking the uncle by the arm to keep him from stopping, "that you would attach even less importance to it than I do, and now you are taking it so hard yourself." "Josef," the uncle exclaimed, trying to free himself to be able to stop, but K. wouldn't let him, "you have changed; you always had such a proper understanding, and just now it's leaving you? Do you want to lose the trial? Do you know what that means? It means that you will simply be wiped off the map. And that the whole family will be dragged down or at least humiliated to the ground. Josef, pull yourself together. Your indifference is driving me mad. When one looks at you, one might almost believe the proverb: 'To have such a trial means to have already lost it.'" "Dear uncle," K. said, "the excitement is so pointless; it is on your side, and it would be on mine too. You don't win trials with excitement; let my practical experiences count a little, just as I always and even now greatly respect yours, even if they surprise me. Since you say that the family would also be affected by the trial — which I certainly cannot understand, but that is beside the point — I will gladly follow you in everything. Only I don't believe that a stay in the countryside would be advantageous even in your interest, for that would mean flight and guilt. Moreover, while I am more pursued here, I can also manage the matter better myself." "Right," the uncle said in a tone that seemed to bring them finally closer together, "I only made the suggestion because I feared that your indifference would jeopardize the matter if you stayed here, and I thought it would be better if I worked for you instead of you. But if you want to pursue it with all your might yourself, that is, of course, far better." "So we agree on that," K. said. "And do you now have a suggestion for what I should do first?" "I must of course think about the matter," the uncle said, "you must consider that I have been on the land almost uninterrupted for 20 years, and my instincts in these matters are declining. Various important connections with individuals who might know better here have loosened by themselves. I am a bit isolated in the countryside, you know that. One only really notices it in such situations. Partly, your situation also caught me by surprise, although I strangely sensed something like this after Erna's letter, and today, seeing you, I almost knew it for certain. But that is irrelevant; the most important thing now is not to lose any time." Even while he was speaking, he stood on his tiptoes, waving at a car, and now, while simultaneously shouting a destination to the driver, he pulled K. behind him into the car. "We are going to lawyer Huld now," he said, "he was my schoolmate. You surely know the name? No? That's strange. He has quite a reputation as a defender and public lawyer. But I have particularly great trust in him as a person." "I'm fine with whatever you undertake," K. said, although the urgent and pressing manner in which the uncle was treating the matter made him uneasy. It was not very pleasant to go to a public lawyer as an accused person. "I didn't know," he said, "that one could also engage a lawyer in such a case." "But of course," the uncle said, "that is self-evident. Why not? And now tell me everything that has happened so far, so that I am fully informed about the matter." K.

began to tell immediately, without omitting anything; his complete openness was the only protest he could allow himself against his uncle's view that the trial was a great shame. He only mentioned Miss Bürstner's name once and fleetingly, but that did not affect his openness, for Miss Bürstner was not connected to the trial. While he was talking, he looked out the window and observed how they were approaching the suburb where the court offices were located; he pointed this out to the uncle, who did not find the encounter particularly striking. The car stopped in front of a dark house. The uncle rang the bell at the first door on the ground floor; while they were waiting, he smiled broadly, showing his large teeth, and whispered, "8 o'clock, an unusual time for parties to visit. Huld won't hold it against me." Two large black eyes appeared in the peephole of the door, looked at the two guests for a while, and then disappeared; however, the door did not open. The uncle and K. confirmed to each other the fact of having seen the two eyes. "A new maid who is afraid of strangers," the uncle said and knocked again. The eyes appeared once more, and one could almost consider them sad; perhaps that was only an illusion caused by the open gas flame, which burned strongly hissing just above their heads but gave off little light. "Open up," the uncle shouted, banging his fist against the door, "we are friends of the lawyer." "The lawyer is ill," came a whisper from behind them. In a door at the other end of the small hallway stood a gentleman in a bathrobe, making this announcement in an exceedingly quiet voice. The uncle, who was already furious from the long wait, turned around abruptly, shouted, "Ill? You say he is ill?" and approached him almost threateningly, as if the gentleman were the illness itself. "They have already opened," the gentleman said, pointing to the lawyer's door, gathered his bathrobe together, and disappeared. The door had indeed been opened; a young girl — K. recognized the dark, slightly bulging eyes again — stood in a long white apron in the anteroom, holding a candle in her hand. "Next time, open earlier," the uncle said instead of a greeting, while the girl made a small curtsy. "Come, Josef," he then said to K., who slowly passed by the girl. "The lawyer is ill," the girl said as the uncle hurried towards a door. K. continued to look at the girl while she had already turned around to lock the apartment door again; she had a doll-like rounded face; not only the pale cheeks and chin were rounded, but also the temples and the edges of the forehead. "Josef," the uncle called again, and he asked the girl: "Is it heart trouble?" "I believe so," the girl said, having had time to go ahead with the candle and open the bedroom door. In a corner of the room, where the candlelight had not yet reached, a face with a long beard rose from the bed. "Leni, who is coming?" asked the lawyer, who, blinded by the candle, did not recognize the guests. "Albert, your old friend," said the uncle. "Oh, Albert," said the lawyer, falling back onto the pillows, as if this visit required no pretense. "Is it really that bad?" the uncle asked, sitting on the edge of the bed. "I don't believe it. It's an attack of your heart trouble and will pass, just like the previous ones." "Maybe," the lawyer said softly, "but it's worse than it has ever been. I breathe heavily, don't sleep at all, and lose strength daily." "So," the uncle said, pressing his Panama hat firmly onto his knee with his large hand. "Those are bad news. By the way, are you receiving the proper care? It's so sad here, so dark. It's been a long time since I was last here; it seemed friendlier then. Your little girl here also doesn't seem very cheerful, or she is pretending." The girl still stood with the candle near the door; as far as her vague gaze could tell, she seemed to be looking at K. rather than at the uncle, even when he was now speaking of her. K. leaned against a chair that he had moved closer to the girl. "When one is as sick as I am," the lawyer said, "one must have peace. I am not sad." After a short pause, he added, "And Leni takes good care of me; she is kind." However, this did not convince the uncle; he was visibly biased against the nurse, and although he did not reply to the sick man, he watched the nurse with stern eyes as she now leaned over the sick man, placed the candle on the nightstand, leaned over him, and whispered while arranging the pillows. He almost forgot the consideration for the sick man, stood up, walked back and forth behind the nurse, and K. would not have been surprised if he had grabbed her by the skirts and dragged her away from the bed. K. himself watched everything calmly; the lawyer's illness was even somewhat welcome to him; he could not resist the fervor that the uncle had developed for his case; the distraction that this fervor now experienced without his intervention he accepted gladly. Then the uncle said, perhaps only with the intention of offending the nurse: "Miss, please, leave us alone for a while; I have a personal matter to discuss with my friend." The nurse, who was still leaning far over the sick man and just smoothing the sheet on the wall, merely turned her head and calmly said, which formed a striking contrast to the uncle's furious and then overflowing speeches: "You see, the gentleman is so sick, he cannot discuss matters." She probably only repeated the uncle's words out of convenience; still, even from an uninvolved person, it could have been interpreted as mocking, but the uncle naturally reacted like one stung. "You damned one," he said, still somewhat incomprehensibly in the first surge of excitement; K. was startled, even though he had expected something similar, and rushed towards the uncle with the firm intention of covering his mouth with both hands. Fortunately, however, the sick man rose up behind the girl, the uncle made a grim face as if he were swallowing something disgusting, and then said more calmly: "We certainly have not lost our minds; if what I am demanding were not possible, I would not demand it. Please go now." The nurse stood upright at the bed, fully facing the uncle, with one hand caressing the lawyer's hand. "You can say anything in front of Leni," the sick man said, undoubtedly in a tone of urgent request. "It does not concern me," said the uncle, "it is not my secret." And he turned around as if he intended not to enter into negotiations anymore but would still give a little time for consideration. "Who does it concern then?" the lawyer asked with a fading voice, lying back down. "My nephew," the uncle said, "I brought him along too." And he introduced: "Prokurist Josef K." "Oh," said the sick man much livelier, stretching his hand toward K., "forgive me, I didn't notice you at all. Go, Leni," he then said to the nurse, who also did not resist anymore, and reached out his hand to her as if it were a farewell for a long time. "So you have come," the lawyer finally said to the uncle, who had stepped closer in reconciliation, "not to pay me a sick visit, but you come in business." It was as if the idea of a sick visit had paralyzed the lawyer until now; he looked much more vigorous now, constantly propped up on one elbow, which must have been quite tiring, and kept pulling at a strand of hair in the middle of his beard. "You look much healthier now," said the uncle, "since that witch is out." He interrupted himself, whispered, "I bet she is eavesdropping," and jumped to the door. But there was no one behind the door; the uncle came back, not disappointed, for their absence of eavesdropping seemed to him an even greater malice, but rather embittered. "You misunderstand her," said the lawyer, without further defending the nurse; perhaps he wanted to express that she was not in need of protection. But in a much more sympathetic tone, he continued: "As for the matter of your nephew, I would actually be glad if my strength were sufficient for this extremely difficult task; I am very much afraid it will not be enough, but I will leave no stone unturned; if I am not enough, we could still involve someone else. To be honest, I am too interested in the matter to bring myself to abstain from any involvement. If my heart doesn't hold out, at least here it will find a worthy opportunity to fail completely." K. believed he understood none of this entire speech; he looked at the uncle to find an explanation, but he was sitting with the candle in his hand on the nightstand, from which a medicine bottle had already rolled onto the carpet, nodding at everything the lawyer said, agreeing with everything and occasionally looking at K. with a request for the same agreement. Had the uncle perhaps already told the lawyer about the trial? But that was impossible; everything that had happened before spoke against it. "I don't understand," he said therefore. "Yes, have I possibly misunderstood you?" the lawyer asked, equally astonished and embarrassed as K. "I might have been hasty. What did you want to discuss with me? I thought it was about your trial?" "Of course," said the uncle and then asked K.: "What do you want?" "Yes, but how do you know something about me and my trial?" K. asked. "Ah, I see," the lawyer said with a smile, "I am a lawyer after all; I mingle in court circles; they talk about various trials, and especially when it concerns the nephew of a friend, one remembers it. That's nothing strange." "What do you want?" the uncle asked K. again. "You are so restless." "You mingle in these court circles," K. asked. "Yes," said the lawyer. "You ask like a child," the uncle said. "With whom should I mingle if not with people of my profession?" the lawyer added. It sounded so irrefutable that K. did not answer at all. "You work at the court in the justice palace, not in the attic," he had wanted to say but could not bring himself to actually say it. "You must consider," the lawyer continued, in a tone as if he were explaining something obvious, unnecessarily and as a side note, "you must consider that I also derive great benefits for my clientele from such mingling, and in many ways; one should not always talk about it. Of course, now due to my illness, I am a bit hindered, but I still receive visits from good friends at the court and learn something. Perhaps I even learn more than many who spend the whole day at the court in perfect health. For example, I have a dear visit right now." And he pointed to a dark corner of the room. "Where?" K. asked, almost rudely in his first surprise. He looked around uncertainly; the light of the small candle did not reach to the opposite wall at all. And indeed, something began to stir in that corner. In the candlelight, which the uncle was now holding high, one could see an older gentleman sitting at a small table. He had probably not even breathed, so unnoticed had he remained for so long. Now he stood up awkwardly, apparently dissatisfied that he had been noticed. It was as if he wanted to fend off all greetings and introductions with his hands, which he moved like short wings, as if he wanted to disturb no one by his presence and as if he were urgently requesting to be reassigned to the darkness and to be forgotten. But that could no longer be granted to him. "You surprised us," the lawyer explained, waving encouragingly to the gentleman to come closer, which he did slowly, hesitantly, glancing around and yet with a certain dignity, "the gentleman clerk director — oh, pardon, I didn't introduce you — here is my friend Albert K., here is his nephew Prokurist Josef K. and here is the gentleman clerk director — so the gentleman clerk director was kind enough to visit me. The value of such a visit can only be appreciated by the initiated, who know how overburdened the dear clerk director is with work. Well, he came nonetheless; we were having a peaceful conversation, as far as my weakness allowed, we hadn't forbidden Leni to let in visitors, for none were expected, but we thought we should be alone; then however came your pounding, Albert, the gentleman clerk director moved the chair and table into the corner, but now it turns out that we may possibly, that is, if there is a desire for it, have a joint matter to discuss and can very well move closer together. — Mr. Clerk Director," he said with a nod and submissive smile, indicating an armchair near the bed. "I can unfortunately only stay a few minutes longer," said the clerk director kindly, sitting broadly in the armchair and looking at his watch, "business calls me. In any case, I do not want to miss the opportunity to meet a friend of my friend." He nodded slightly to the uncle, who seemed very pleased with the new acquaintance but, due to his nature, could not express feelings of submission and accompanied the clerk director's words with embarrassed yet loud laughter. A hideous sight! K. could calmly observe everything, for no one cared about him; the clerk director took, as was his habit, control of the conversation; the lawyer, whose first weakness might only have served to drive away the new visitor, listened attentively, hand to ear; the uncle, as the candle bearer — balancing the candle on his lap, the lawyer often looked concerned — was soon free from embarrassment and only delighted, both by the way the clerk director spoke and by the gentle wavy hand movements with which he accompanied his speech. K., leaning against the bedpost, was perhaps even intentionally completely neglected by the clerk director and served only as a listener for the old gentlemen. Besides, he hardly knew what the conversation was about and soon thought of the nurse and the bad treatment she had received from the uncle, and soon wondered if he had already seen the clerk director before, perhaps even at the assembly during his first investigation. Even if he was mistaken, the clerk director would have fit in quite well among the participants in the front row, the old gentlemen with the thinning beards.

A noise from the anteroom, like breaking porcelain, made everyone stop and listen. "I'll go see what happened," said K., slowly stepping outside as if giving the others a chance to stop him. Hardly had he entered the anteroom and tried to find his way in the dark when a small hand, much smaller than K.'s, placed itself on the hand he was using to hold the door, and the door closed quietly. It was the caregiver who had been waiting there. "Nothing happened," she whispered, "I just threw a plate against the wall to get you out." In his embarrassment, K. said, "I was thinking of you, too." "All the better," said the caregiver, "come." After a few steps, they reached a door made of frosted glass, which the caregiver opened for K. "Please, step inside," she said. It was clearly the lawyer's office; as far as could be seen in the moonlight, which now only illuminated a small square patch of the floor at each of the two large windows, it was furnished with heavy old furniture. "Over here," said the caregiver, pointing to a dark chest with a carved backrest. Even as he sat down, K. looked around the room; it was a high, large room, and the clients of the public lawyer must have felt lost here. K. imagined the small steps with which the visitors approached the massive desk. But then he forgot about that and had eyes only for the caregiver, who was sitting very close to him and pressing him against the side rest. "I thought," she said, "that you would come out to me on your own, without me having to call you first. It was strange, really. First, you looked at me steadily as soon as you entered, and then you made me wait. By the way, you can call me Leni," she added quickly and abruptly, as if no moment of this conversation should be wasted. "Gladly," said K. "But as for the strangeness, Leni, it's easy to explain. First, I had to listen to the chatter of the old gentlemen and couldn't just run away for no reason; secondly, I'm not rude, but rather shy, and you, Leni, didn't exactly seem like someone I could easily approach." "That's not it," said Leni, resting her arm on the backrest and looking at K., "but you didn't like me, and you probably still don't." "Like isn't much," K. replied evasively. "Oh!" she said with a smile, gaining a certain superiority from K.'s remark and this small exclamation. K. remained silent for a while. As he had already gotten used to the darkness in the room, he was able to distinguish various details of the furnishings. He particularly noticed a large painting hanging to the right of the door; he leaned forward to see it better. It depicted a man in a judge's robe; he was sitting in a high throne chair, the gilding of which stood out prominently from the painting. What was unusual was that this judge was not sitting there in peace and dignity but was pressing his left arm firmly against the back and side rest, while his right arm was completely free, only grasping the side rest with his hand, as if he were about to leap up violently and perhaps indignantly to say something decisive or even announce a verdict. The accused could well be imagined at the foot of the stairs, the topmost steps covered with a yellow carpet still visible in the painting. "Perhaps that's my judge," said K., pointing at the painting with his finger. "I know him," said Leni, looking up at the painting too, "he comes here often. The painting is from his youth, but he could never have looked even remotely like that because he is almost tiny. Still, he has let himself be stretched out in the painting because he is absurdly vain, like everyone here. But I too am vain and very dissatisfied that I don't appeal to you at all." To her last remark, K. responded only by embracing Leni and pulling her close; she quietly leaned her head against his shoulder. However, regarding the rest, he said, "What rank does he have?" "He is an investigating judge," she said, taking K.'s hand, which he was still holding, and playing with his fingers. "Just an investigating judge again," said K., disappointed, "the high officials are hiding. But he is sitting on a throne." "That's all an invention," Leni said, her face bent over K.'s hand, "in reality, he sits on a kitchen stool, with an old horse blanket folded over it. But must you always think about your trial?" she added slowly. "No, not at all," said K., "I probably think too little about it." "That's not the mistake you're making," said Leni, "you are too unyielding, that's what I've heard." "Who said that?" asked K., feeling her body against his chest and looking down at her rich, dark, tightly curled hair. "I would give away too much if I said," Leni replied. "Please, don't ask for names, but correct your mistake; don't be so unyielding anymore, you can't fight against this court, you have to make the confession. Do make the confession at the next opportunity. Only then is there a chance to escape, only then. However, even that is not possible without outside help, but you need not worry about that help; I will provide it myself." "You understand a lot about this court and the tricks necessary here," said K., lifting her onto his lap as she pressed too closely against him. "That's good," she said, settling herself on his lap, smoothing her skirt and adjusting her blouse. Then she hung both hands around his neck, leaned back, and looked at him for a long time. "And if I don't make the confession, then you can't help me?" K. asked tentatively. I am recruiting helpers, he thought, almost astonished, first Miss Bürstner, then the wife of the court attendant, and finally this little caregiver, who seems to have an incomprehensible need for me. She sits on my lap as if it were her only rightful place! "No," Leni replied, shaking her head slowly, "then I can't help you. But you don't really want my help; you don't care, you're stubborn and refuse to be convinced." "Do you have a lover?" she asked after a while. "No," said K. "Oh yes," she said. "Yes, really," said

K., "just think, I have denied her and yet I even carry her photograph with me." At her urging, he showed her a photograph of Elsa, and curled up on his lap, she studied the picture. It was a candid shot; Elsa was captured after a whirl dance that she liked to perform in the wine tavern, her skirt still flying in the folds of the spin around her, her hands placed on her solid hips, and she was looking sideways with a taut neck, laughing; who her laughter was directed at could not be discerned from the picture. "She is tightly laced," said Leni, pointing to where she thought it was visible. "I don't like her; she is clumsy and coarse. But perhaps she is gentle and kind towards you; one could infer that from the picture. Such tall, strong girls often know nothing else but to be gentle and kind. But could she sacrifice herself for you?" "No," said K., "she is neither gentle nor kind, nor could she sacrifice herself for me. I haven't asked for either from her so far. In fact, I haven't even looked at the picture as closely as you have." "So you don't care much for her," said Leni, "she isn't really your lover." "Yes," said K. "I don't take back my word." "So she may now be your lover," said Leni, "but you wouldn't miss her much if you lost her or exchanged her for someone else, for example, for me." "Certainly," said K. with a smile, "that would be conceivable, but she has a significant advantage over you; she knows nothing about my trial, and even if she knew something about it, she wouldn't think about it. She wouldn't try to persuade me to be more yielding." "That's not an advantage," said Leni. "If she has no other advantages, I won't lose courage. Does she have any physical flaws?" "A physical flaw?" asked K. "Yes," said Leni, "I have such a small flaw, you see." She spread the middle and ring fingers of her right hand apart, between which the webbing almost reached the top joint of the short fingers. K. didn't immediately realize what she was trying to show him in the dark, so she guided his hand there for him to feel it. "What a natural play," said K., and added, as he took in the whole hand, "What a pretty claw!" With a kind of pride, Leni watched as K. stared in wonder, repeatedly pulling her two fingers apart and together until he finally kissed them lightly and let go. "Oh!" she immediately exclaimed, "You kissed me!" Eagerly, with her mouth open, she climbed onto his lap with her knees; K. looked up at her almost in shock; now that she was so close, a bitter, exciting smell like pepper emanated from her, she took his head in her hands, leaned over him, and bit and kissed his neck, even biting into his hair. "You have exchanged me," she cried from time to time, "look, now you have really exchanged me!" Then her knee slipped, and with a little scream, she nearly fell onto the carpet; K. caught her to hold her back, and was pulled down towards her. "Now you belong to me," she said.

"Here is the house key, come whenever you want," were her last words, and a aimless kiss brushed against his back as she walked away. As he stepped out of the front gate, a light rain began to fall. He wanted to walk to the middle of the street, hoping to catch a glimpse of Leni at the window, when suddenly his uncle, who had been waiting in a car that K. hadn't noticed in his distraction, jumped out, grabbed him by the arms, and shoved him against the front door as if to pin him there. "Boy," he shouted, "how could you do this? You have caused terrible damage to your situation, which was on a good path. You hide away with some little dirty thing who is obviously the lawyer's mistress, and you stay away for hours. You don't even try to make an excuse, you hide nothing, no, you are completely open, you run to her and stay with her. Meanwhile, we sit here together—the uncle who is working hard for you, the lawyer who is supposed to be won over for you, the director of the office, above all, this important gentleman who is currently in charge of your case. We want to discuss how we can help you; I have to handle the lawyer carefully, and he in turn has to deal with the director, and you should at least have reason to support me. Instead, you just stay away. Ultimately, it can't be hidden any longer; well, they are polite, refined men, they don't speak of it, they spare my feelings, but in the end, they too can no longer bring themselves to overcome it, and since they can't talk about the matter, they fall silent. We sat there in silence for minutes, listening to see if you would finally arrive. All in vain. Finally, the director, who stayed much longer than he originally intended, stood up, said his goodbyes, visibly regretted my situation without being able to help me, waited in inexplicable kindness for a while longer at the door, then left. Of course, I was relieved that he was gone; I was already struggling to breathe. The sick lawyer was even more affected by it all; the poor man could hardly speak when I bid him farewell. You have likely contributed to his complete breakdown and are thus hastening the death of a man on whom you depend. And you, your uncle, leave me here in the rain; feel this, I am completely soaked, waiting for hours."

## ❦ 7 ❦
# LAWYER · MANUFACTURER · PAINTER

On a winter morning—outside, snow was falling in the dull light—K. sat in his office, already extremely tired despite the early hour. To protect himself at least from the lower clerks, he had instructed the servant not to let any of them in, as he was busy with a larger task. But instead of working, he turned in his chair, slowly rearranged some items on the table, and then, without realizing it, left his entire arm stretched out on the tabletop and remained motionless with his head bowed.

The thought of the trial never left him. He had often considered whether it would be beneficial to draft a defense statement and submit it to the court. He wanted to provide a brief life history and explain, for every significant event, the reasons behind his actions, whether those actions should be judged negatively or positively according to his current understanding, and what justifications he could offer for one thing or another. The advantages of such a defense statement compared to relying solely on the otherwise imperfect lawyer were undeniable. K. had no idea what the lawyer was doing; it certainly wasn't much. He hadn't summoned him for a month, and during none of the earlier discussions had K. had the impression that this man could achieve much for him. Above all, the lawyer had hardly asked him anything. Yet there was so much to ask. Asking was the main thing. K. felt he could pose all the necessary questions himself. The lawyer, on the other hand, instead of asking, would tell stories or sit silently across from him, leaning slightly over the desk, probably due to his poor hearing, pulling on a strand of his beard and staring down at the carpet, perhaps precisely at the spot where K. had lain with Leni. Now and then, he would give K. some empty admonitions, similar to those given to children. Such useless and boring speeches, which K. intended to pay for with not a single heller in the end. After believing he had sufficiently humiliated K., the lawyer usually started to uplift him a bit. He would recount how he had already won many similar cases, either entirely or partially. Cases that, while perhaps not as difficult as this one in reality, appeared outwardly even more hopeless. He had a list of these cases in his drawer—at this point, he tapped on some drawer of the desk—but he regretted that he couldn't show the documents, as they were matters of official secrecy. Nevertheless, K. would benefit from the vast experience he had gained through all these cases. He had, of course, immediately begun working, and the first submission was almost finished. It was very important because the first impression that the defense made often determined the entire direction of the proceedings. Unfortunately, he had to make K. aware that sometimes the first submissions were not even read by the court. They would simply be added to the case files and it would be pointed out that, for the time being, the interrogation and observation of the accused were more important than anything written down. If the petitioner became insistent, it would be added that before a decision could be made, all materials would be reviewed in connection, including that first submission, once all materials had been gathered. Unfortunately, this was often not correct either; the first submission would usually be misplaced or completely lost, and even if it remained until the end, it was, as the lawyer had only heard by rumor, hardly read. All of this was regrettable but not entirely unjustified. K. should not overlook that the proceedings were not public; they could become public if the court deemed it necessary, but the law did not mandate publicity. Consequently, the court's documents, particularly the indictment, were inaccessible to the accused and their defense. Thus, one generally did not know or at least not precisely what the first submission needed to address; it could, therefore, only accidentally contain something of significance to the case. Truly accurate and evidentiary submissions could only be drafted later once the various charges and their justifications became clearer or could be inferred during the interrogations of the accused. Under these circumstances, the defense found itself in a very unfavorable and difficult position. But this was also intended. The defense was not actually permitted by law but only tolerated, and there was even dispute about whether at least some tolerance could be read from the relevant legal provision. Therefore, strictly speaking, there were no lawyers recognized by the court; everyone appearing as a lawyer in this court was essentially just a corner lawyer. This certainly had a degrading effect on the entire profession, and when K. next went to the court offices, he could, for the sake of seeing it, look at the lawyers' room. He would likely be shocked by the company gathered there. Even the cramped, low chamber assigned to them showed the contempt the court had for these people. The chamber only received light through a small window, which was positioned so high that one had to find a colleague to lift them up if they wanted to look outside, where the smoke from a nearby chimney would inevitably blow into their face and darken it. The floor of this chamber—just to give another example of these conditions—had had a hole for over a year, not so large that a person could fall through, but big enough that one could sink a leg in completely. The lawyers' room was located on the second attic; if someone sank in, their leg would dangle down into the first attic and right into the corridor where the parties waited. It is no exaggeration to say that such conditions are considered disgraceful among lawyer circles. Complaints to the administration have no success whatsoever, but the lawyers are strictly prohibited from making any changes to the room at their own expense. However, this treatment of lawyers has its justification. The aim is to minimize the role of the defense; everything should rest solely on the accused themselves. A not bad standpoint fundamentally, but nothing could be more misguided than to conclude that lawyers were unnecessary for the accused in this court. On the contrary, no other court requires them as much as this one. The proceedings, in general, are not only secret from the public but also from the accused. Of course, only to the extent that this is possible, but it is possible to a very great extent. The accused also have no insight into the court documents, and inferring from the interrogations about the documents underlying them is very difficult, particularly for the accused, who is under stress and has all sorts of worries that distract him. Here, the defense intervenes. In general, defenders are not allowed to be present during interrogations, so they must question the accused about the interrogation immediately after it, preferably still at the door of the interrogation room, and extract usable information for the defense from these often very muddied reports. But this is not the most important thing, as one cannot learn much this way, although, as everywhere, a capable person learns more than others. The most important factor remains the personal relationships of the lawyer; therein lies the main value of the defense. K. has likely already learned from his own experiences that the lowest organization of the court is far from perfect, featuring negligent and corrupt officials, which somewhat creates gaps in the strict closure of the court. Here, the majority of lawyers squeeze in, bribing and eavesdropping; indeed, in earlier times, there were even cases of theft of files. It cannot be denied that, in this way, some surprisingly favorable results for the accused can be achieved in the short term, and these small lawyers strut around, attracting new clients. However, for the further progress of the trial, it means either nothing or nothing good. Only honest personal relationships, especially with higher officials, have real value, and only officials of the lower grades are meant here. Only through such relationships can the progress of the trial, albeit initially only imperceptibly, later become more and more influenced. Naturally, only a few lawyers can manage this, and K.'s choice was very fortunate in this regard. Only perhaps one or two lawyers could demonstrate similar relationships as Dr. Huld. These, however, do not concern themselves with the company in the lawyers' room and have nothing to do with it. However, their connection with the court officials is much closer. It is not even always necessary for Dr. Huld to go to court; he waits in the anterooms of the investigating judges for their incidental appearances and, depending on their mood, achieves a mostly only apparent success or perhaps not even that. No, K. has seen it himself;

the officials, including quite high-ranking ones, come themselves, willingly provide information, open or at least easily interpretable, discuss the next steps of the proceedings, and even in some cases, they can be convinced and readily adopt foreign views. However, one should not trust them too much in this last respect; just as they express their new, favorable intentions for the defense, they might indeed go straight to their office and issue a court decision for the next day that contradicts it and is perhaps even much stricter for the accused than their first intention, from which they claimed to have completely departed. One cannot defend oneself against this, of course, for what they said in private remains private and does not allow for public conclusions, even if the defense must strive to maintain the favor of these gentlemen. On the other hand, it is also true that these gentlemen do not engage with the defense, naturally only with a competent defense, out of mere human kindness or friendly feelings; rather, they are, in a sense, dependent on them. Here, the disadvantage of a court organization comes into play that establishes the secret report even in its beginnings. The officials lack a connection to the populace; they are well-equipped for the ordinary standard cases; such a case almost rolls itself along its path and only needs a nudge here and there, but against very simple cases or particularly difficult ones, they are often at a loss; they do not have the right sense for human relationships because they are constantly constrained by the law day and night, and they suffer greatly from this lack in such cases. Then they come to the lawyer for advice, with a servant carrying the files that are otherwise so secret. At this window, one could have encountered many gentlemen, whom one would least expect, as they stared hopelessly out into the street while the lawyer studied the files at his desk to provide them with good advice. Moreover, one can see, especially on such occasions, how seriously these gentlemen take their profession and how they can fall into great despair over obstacles that they cannot overcome by nature. Their position is not easy either, and one should not do them wrong or regard their position lightly. The hierarchy and the escalation of the court are infinite and not foreseeable even for the initiated. The proceedings in the courts are generally also secret for the lower officials; thus, they can hardly ever follow the matters they are dealing with completely in their further progress. The court case appears in their court circle without them often knowing where it is coming from, and it continues without them knowing where it is going. The insights one can gain from studying the individual stages of the trial, the final decision, and its reasons are thus lost on these officials. They may only deal with that part of the trial which the law has delineated for them and know less about the progress beyond that, thus the results of their own work than the defense, which generally remains in contact with the accused almost until the end of the trial. In this respect as well, they can learn quite a bit of value from the defense. Does K. still wonder, keeping all this in mind, about the irritability of the officials, which sometimes manifests itself in—everyone has this experience—offensive ways towards the parties? All officials are irritable, even if they seem calm. Naturally, small lawyers particularly suffer from this. For example, there is a story that has a strong appearance of truth. An old official, a good quiet gentleman, studied a difficult court case, which had been particularly complicated by the lawyer's submissions, for a day and a night without interruption—these officials are indeed diligent, more so than anyone else. Toward morning, after 24 hours of likely not very fruitful work, he went to the entrance door, hid there, and threw every lawyer who tried to enter down the stairs. The lawyers gathered at the bottom on the landing and deliberated on what to do; on one hand, they have no real claim to be let in, so they can hardly take legal action against the official, and they must, as mentioned, also be careful not to provoke the officials against themselves. On the other hand, every day spent not in court is a loss for them, so they had a strong interest in getting in. Eventually, they agreed to tire out the old gentleman. Again and again, a lawyer was sent up the stairs who then allowed himself to be thrown down with as much passive resistance as possible, whereupon he was caught by his colleagues. This went on for about an hour, and then the old gentleman, having been exhausted by the night work, truly became tired and returned to his office. The ones below could hardly believe it at first and sent someone to check behind the door to see if it was truly empty. Only then did they venture in and likely did not even dare to complain. For the lawyers—and even the smallest among them can at least partially oversee the conditions—it is completely foreign to them to want to introduce or implement any improvements in court, while —and this is very significant—almost every accused person, even completely simple individuals, immediately begins to think of suggestions for improvement upon their very first entrance into the proceedings and often wastes time and energy that could be far better used elsewhere. The only right thing is to come to terms with the existing conditions. Even if it were possible to improve details—and it is a nonsensical superstition—one would at best achieve something for future cases but would harm oneself immeasurably by attracting the special attention of the ever vindictive officials. Just don't attract attention! Behave calmly, even if it goes completely against one's nature! Try to see that this great court organism remains, in a sense, eternally in suspension and that if one independently changes something in one's place, one risks losing the ground under one's feet and can fall while the large organism easily compensates for the small disturbance elsewhere—everything is interconnected—and remains unchanged unless it, perhaps, which is even likely, becomes even more closed, more attentive, stricter, and more malicious. Let the lawyer do the work instead of disturbing it. Accusations are not of much use, especially when one cannot explain their cause in all its significance, but it must still be said how much K. has harmed his case through his behavior towards the office director. This influential man was already almost to be crossed off the list of those from whom something could be done for K. Even fleeting mentions of the trial he clearly ignores. In some respects, the officials are like children. Often they can be so hurt by harmlessness, which unfortunately does not include K.'s behavior, that they stop talking even to good friends, turn away from them when they encounter them, and work against them in every possible way. Yet, surprisingly, once, without any particular reason, they can be brought to laughter by a small joke, which one only dares because everything seems hopeless, and are reconciled. It is simultaneously difficult and easy to deal with them; there are hardly any principles for this. Sometimes it is astonishing that a single average life is enough to grasp so much that one can work with some success here. However, there come gloomy hours, as everyone has, where one believes they have achieved nothing at all, where it seems to them that only those cases that were destined for a good outcome from the very beginning have ended well, as they would have without any assistance, while all others have been lost despite all the side efforts, all the toil, and all the small apparent successes that had brought such joy. Then nothing seems secure anymore, and one would not even dare to deny in response to specific questions that they might have led processes that were inherently favorable to a good outcome astray through their involvement. This, too, is a kind of self-confidence, but it is the only thing that remains at that moment. Such attacks—of course, they are merely attacks, nothing more—are particularly common for lawyers when a case they have conducted far enough and satisfactorily is suddenly taken from them. This is perhaps the worst thing that can happen to a lawyer. It is not the accused who takes the case from them; that never happens. An accused person who has once taken a certain lawyer must stay with them, no matter what happens. How could they manage alone if they have once sought help? Thus, this does not happen, but sometimes the case takes a direction where the lawyer can no longer follow. The case and the accused and everything is simply taken from the lawyer; then even the best relationships with the officials can no longer help, for they themselves know nothing. The case has entered a stage where no assistance may be rendered, where inaccessible courts are dealing with it, and where even the accused is no longer reachable for the lawyer. One then comes home one day and finds on their desk all the many submissions they have crafted with great diligence and the brightest hopes for this case, returned because they cannot be carried over into the new stage of the proceedings; they are worthless scraps. Yet the case does not have to be lost; certainly not, at least there is no decisive reason for this assumption; one simply knows nothing more about the case and will not learn anything more about it. Fortunately, such cases are exceptions, and even if K.'s case should be such a case, it is still far from such a stage for now. There is still ample opportunity for legal work, and K. can be sure that it will be utilized. The submission, as mentioned, has not yet been delivered, but that is not urgent; much more important are the preliminary discussions with key officials, and these have already taken place. With varying success, as should be openly acknowledged. It is much better not to reveal details for now, which could only negatively influence K. or make him overly hopeful or overly anxious; only that much can be said that some individuals have expressed themselves very favorably and have shown themselves very willing, while others have expressed themselves less favorably but have not refused their assistance at all. The overall result is very promising; however, one should not draw any special conclusions from it, as all preliminary negotiations start similarly, and only the further development will reveal the value of these preliminary negotiations. In any case, nothing is lost yet, and if it should still be possible to win over the office director despite everything—various initiatives have already been undertaken for this purpose—then the whole thing, as the surgeons say, is a simple wound, and one can confidently expect the following.

In such and similar conversations, the lawyer was inexhaustible. They repeated themselves with every visit. There were always advancements, but the nature of these advancements could never be shared. Work was constantly being done on the initial submission, yet it was never completed; this often turned out to be a certain advantage during the next visit, as circumstances had, unexpectedly, been very unfavorable for the submission recently. When K. sometimes remarked, exhausted by the discussions, that progress was indeed very slow, he was told that it was not slow at all, but rather that they would have been much further along if K. had approached the lawyer in a timely manner. Unfortunately, he had neglected to do so, and this oversight would lead to further disadvantages, not only in terms of time.

The only welcome interruption during these visits was Leni, who always managed to bring tea to the lawyer in K.'s presence. She would stand behind K., seemingly watching as the lawyer eagerly bent down to pour the tea and drink it, while secretly allowing K. to hold her hand. There was complete silence. The lawyer drank, K. squeezed Leni's hand, and Leni sometimes dared to gently stroke K.'s hair. "Are you still here?" the lawyer asked after finishing. "I wanted to take away the dishes," Leni replied, and there was one last handshake; the lawyer wiped his mouth and began to talk to K. with renewed vigor.

Was the lawyer seeking comfort or despair? K. didn't know, but he soon believed it was clear that his defense was not in good hands. Everything the lawyer said might have been correct, but it was obvious that he wanted to present himself prominently and had probably never handled such a significant case as K.'s, at least in his own opinion. However, the constantly emphasized personal connections to the officials remained suspicious. Did they have to be exploited solely for K.'s benefit? The lawyer never failed to point out that these were just low-ranking officials, meaning they were in a very dependent position, for whom certain developments in the case could potentially be significant. Were they perhaps using the lawyer to achieve outcomes that would always be unfavorable for the accused? Maybe they didn't do this in every case, certainly that was unlikely; there were probably cases where they offered advantages to the lawyer for his services, as they must have been interested in maintaining his unblemished reputation. But if that was indeed the case, how would they intervene in K.'s trial, which, as the lawyer explained, was very difficult and thus important, and had initially attracted significant attention from the court? It could hardly be in doubt what they would do. Signs of this could already be seen in the fact that the first submission had still not been delivered, despite the trial having lasted for months, and that everything, according to the lawyer, was still in its early stages, which was, of course, very likely to put the accused into a state of lethargy and helplessness, only to then suddenly overwhelm him with the decision or at least with the announcement that the investigation, concluded to his detriment, would be forwarded to the higher authorities.

It was absolutely necessary for K. to intervene himself. Especially in states of great fatigue, like on that winter morning when everything flowed through his mind without will, this conviction was undeniable. The disdain he once had for the trial no longer applied. If he had been alone in the world, he could have easily disregarded the trial, though it was certain that it would not have arisen at all in that case. But now his uncle had already drawn him into hiring a lawyer, family considerations were at play; his position was no longer entirely independent of the course of the trial. He had, recklessly, mentioned the trial with a certain inexplicable satisfaction in front of acquaintances, and others

THE TRIAL

had learned about it in unknown ways. His relationship with Miss Bürstner seemed to fluctuate according to the trial — in short, he hardly had the choice to accept or reject the trial; he was right in the middle of it and had to defend himself. When he was tired, it was even worse.

However, there was no reason for excessive worry, at least for the time being. He had managed to work his way up to a high position in the bank in a relatively short time and had maintained that position with the recognition of all. Now he just needed to apply the skills that had enabled him to do this to the process at hand, and there was no doubt that it would turn out well. Above all, if anything was to be achieved, it was essential to reject any thoughts of possible guilt from the outset. There was no guilt. The trial was nothing more than a major business deal, similar to those he had often concluded with great benefit to the bank, a deal in which, as was customary, various dangers lurked that needed to be warded off. For this purpose, one could not entertain thoughts of any guilt but rather should hold onto the idea of one's own advantage as firmly as possible. From this perspective, it was also inevitable to relieve the lawyer of his representation very soon, preferably that very evening. Although it was something unprecedented and likely very insulting according to his accounts, K. could not tolerate obstacles to his efforts in the trial that might be caused by his own lawyer. However, once the lawyer was shaken off, the submission had to be handed over immediately and, if possible, pressed every day thereafter to ensure it was considered. For this purpose, it would obviously not suffice for K. to sit in the corridor like the others with his hat placed under the bench. He himself, or the women, or other messengers, had to run after the officials day by day, forcing them to sit at their table and study K.'s submission instead of looking through the grating into the corridor. One must not relent in these efforts; everything had to be organized and monitored; the court should eventually encounter a defendant who knew how to defend his rights.

However, even if K. dared to carry out all of this, the difficulty of drafting the submission was overwhelming. Previously, just about a week ago, he could only think of the idea of being forced to make such a submission himself with a feeling of shame; he had never considered that it could also be difficult. He remembered how, one morning when he was overwhelmed with work, he suddenly pushed everything aside and took out the writing pad to tentatively outline the thought process for such a submission, perhaps to provide it to the cumbersome lawyer. Just at that moment, the door to the director's office opened, and the deputy director entered with great laughter. It had been very embarrassing for K. at the time, although the deputy director was, of course, not laughing about the submission, of which he knew nothing, but about a stock market joke he had just heard—a joke that required a drawing for understanding, which the deputy director executed over K.'s desk with K.'s pencil, which he took from K.'s hand, on the writing pad that was meant for the submission.

Today, K. felt no shame; the submission had to be made. If he couldn't find time for it at the office, which was very likely, then he would have to do it at home during the nights. If the nights wouldn't be enough, he would need to take a vacation. He must not stop halfway; that was not only the most nonsensical thing in business but in everything, everywhere. The submission meant almost endless work, of course. One didn't need to be a particularly anxious person to easily come to the belief that it was impossible to ever finish the submission. Not out of laziness or cunning, which could only hinder the lawyer's completion, but because, in ignorance of the existing charges and even their potential extensions, his entire life had to be recalled, represented, and scrutinized from all sides in the smallest actions and events. And how sad such work was, besides. It might be suitable to occupy a childish mind after retirement and help pass the long days. But now, when K. needed all his thoughts for his work, when every hour, as he was still on the rise and already posed a threat for the deputy director, was passing with the utmost speed, and when he wanted to enjoy the short evenings and nights as a young man, he was now supposed to start drafting this submission. Once again, his thoughts turned to complaints. Almost involuntarily, just to put an end to it, he reached for the button of the electric bell that led to the waiting room. As he pressed it, he glanced at the clock. It was 11 o'clock; he had wasted two hours, a long precious time, and was of course even more exhausted than before. Nevertheless, the time was not lost; he had made decisions that could be valuable. The servants brought, in addition to various pieces of mail, two business cards from gentlemen who had been waiting for K. for some time. They were, in fact, very important clients of the bank, whom one should never have kept waiting. Why did they come at such an inconvenient time? — and why, the gentlemen seemed to ask again from behind the closed door, was the diligent K. using the best business hours for personal matters? Tired from the previous events and anticipating fatigue from what was to come, K. stood up to receive the first visitor.

He was a small, lively gentleman, a manufacturer whom K. knew well. He expressed regret for disturbing K. during important work, and K. in turn regretted having kept the manufacturer waiting for so long. However, this regret was conveyed in such a mechanical manner and with almost incorrect emphasis that the manufacturer, if he hadn't been completely absorbed in business matters, should have noticed it. Instead, he quickly pulled out invoices and spreadsheets from all his pockets, spread them out before K., explained various items, corrected a small calculation error that he had noticed even during this cursory review, reminded K. of a similar business deal they had concluded about a year ago, casually mentioned that this time another bank was competing for the business with great sacrifices, and finally fell silent, waiting to hear K.'s opinion. K. had indeed followed the manufacturer's speech well at first; the thought of the important business had also engaged him, but unfortunately not for long. He soon lost focus, nodded along to the louder remarks of the manufacturer for a while, but eventually stopped even that and limited himself to looking at the bald head bent over the papers, wondering when the manufacturer would finally realize that his entire speech was useless. When he fell silent, K. initially believed it was to give him the opportunity to admit that he was unable to listen. However, he soon realized with regret from the tense look of the obviously prepared manufacturer that the business discussion had to continue. He inclined his head as if in response to a command and began to slowly move his pencil back and forth over the papers, occasionally pausing to stare at a figure. The manufacturer suspected objections; perhaps the figures were not fixed after all, maybe they were not decisive. In any case, he covered the papers with his hand and began anew, moving closer to K. to give a general overview of the business. "It's difficult," K. said, pursing his lips and sinking into the side of his chair, since the papers, the only tangible thing, were now covered. He barely looked up when the door to the director's office opened, and the deputy director appeared, not clearly, almost as if behind a gauze veil. K. didn't think much about it but only noted the immediate effect, which was very pleasant for him. For the manufacturer immediately jumped up from his chair and hurried to meet the deputy director, but K. wished he had moved even ten times faster, for he feared the deputy director might disappear again. It was an unnecessary fear; the gentlemen met, shook hands, and approached K.'s desk together. The manufacturer complained that he had found very little inclination for the business from the procurator and pointed at K., who, under the deputy director's gaze, again bent over the papers. When the two leaned against the desk and the manufacturer began to win over the deputy director, K. felt as if two men, whose size he exaggerated in his imagination, were negotiating over him. Slowly, he tried to cautiously glance upward to see what was happening above, took one of the papers from the desk without looking, placed it in his flat hand, and gradually raised it toward the gentlemen while he stood up. He didn't think of anything specific but acted solely on the feeling that he should behave this way once he had completed the important submission that should entirely relieve him. The deputy director, who participated in the conversation with full attention, glanced only briefly at the paper, did not even read what was written there, for what was important to the procurator was unimportant to him, took it from K.'s hand, said, "Thank you, I already know everything," and calmly placed it back on the table. K. looked at him bitterly from the side. The deputy director, however, didn't notice or, if he did, was only encouraged by it, laughing loudly several times, and once embarrassed the manufacturer with a quick retort, but immediately pulled him out of it by making an objection of his own, and finally invited him to come over to his office, where they could finish the matter. "It's a very important issue," he said to the manufacturer, "I completely understand that. And the procurator,"—even with this

## THE TRIAL

remark, he was really only speaking to the manufacturer—"will surely be glad if we take it off his hands. The matter requires careful consideration. He seems to be quite overwhelmed today, and some people have already been waiting for him in the anteroom for hours." K. barely managed to turn away from the deputy director and direct his friendly but stiff smile only at the manufacturer; otherwise, he did not intervene at all, leaning slightly forward with both hands on the desk like an office clerk behind the counter, and watched as the two gentlemen, amid further conversation, took the papers from the table and disappeared into the director's office. At the door, the manufacturer turned around, said he was not saying goodbye yet, but would of course report to the procurator about the outcome of the discussion, and also had another small message to convey to him.

Finally, K. was alone. He didn't even think about allowing any other party to enter, and it only vaguely crossed his mind how pleasant it was that the people outside believed he was still negotiating with the manufacturer, which meant no one— not even the servant—could come in. He went to the window, sat on the ledge, held onto the handle with one hand, and looked out at the square. The snow was still falling; it hadn't brightened up at all.

He sat there for a long time, unsure of what was truly bothering him. Every now and then, he glanced nervously over his shoulder at the door to the anteroom, where he mistakenly thought he had heard a noise. However, when no one came, he became calmer, went to the washstand, splashed his face with cold water, and returned to his window seat with a clearer mind. The decision to take his defense into his own hands now seemed more serious than he had originally thought. As long as he had delegated his defense to the lawyer, he had remained largely unaffected by the trial; he had observed it from a distance and had not been able to be directly reached. He could have looked in whenever he wanted to see how his case was progressing, but he could also have pulled back his head whenever he chose. Now, however, if he were to conduct his own defense, he would have to fully expose himself to the court, and the outcome should ultimately lead to his complete and final liberation. But to achieve that, he would have to put himself in much greater danger than he had so far. If he had any doubts, today's meeting with the acting director and the manufacturer could have easily convinced him otherwise. How had he sat there, completely dazed by the mere decision to defend himself? How would it be later? What days lay ahead of him! Would he find the path that led through everything to a good conclusion? Did a meticulous defense not mean—since everything else was pointless—that he would need to isolate himself from everything else as much as possible? Would he manage to endure that successfully? And how would he manage the execution at the bank? It wasn't just about the submission, for which a leave of absence might have sufficed, even though requesting a leave right now would have been a significant risk; it concerned a whole trial, the duration of which was unpredictable. What an obstacle had suddenly been thrown in K.'s path!

And now he was supposed to work for the bank? — He looked down at the desk. — Now he was supposed to prioritize parties and negotiate with them? While his trial continued to roll on, while the court officials were up in the attic poring over the documents of this trial, was he expected to handle the bank's affairs? Didn't it look like a form of torture, one that was recognized by the court and accompanied him throughout the process? And would they take his unique situation into account when assessing his work at the bank? No one ever would. His trial was not completely unknown, even if it wasn't entirely clear who knew about it and how much. However, hopefully, the rumor had not reached the deputy director yet; otherwise, one would have had to see clearly how he would exploit K. without any collegiality or humanity. And the director? Surely, he was well-disposed towards K., and he would probably have wanted to create some relief for K. as soon as he learned about the trial, but he certainly wouldn't have succeeded, because he was increasingly falling under the influence of the deputy director, especially now that the counterbalance K. had previously provided was starting to weaken, and the deputy director was also exploiting the director's suffering to strengthen his own power. So what did K. have to hope for? Perhaps he was weakening his resistance with such thoughts, but it was necessary to avoid self-deception and to see everything as clearly as possible at the moment.

Without any particular reason, just to avoid returning to his desk for the time being, he opened the window. It was difficult to open; he had to turn the handle with both hands. Then the fog mixed with smoke blew into the room through the entire width and height of the window, filling it with a faint smell of burning. A few snowflakes were blown in as well. "A nasty autumn," said the manufacturer behind K., who had entered the room unnoticed after coming from the deputy director. K. nodded and anxiously looked at the manufacturer's briefcase, from which he expected the manufacturer would soon pull out the papers to inform him of the outcome of the discussions with the deputy director. However, the manufacturer followed K.'s gaze, tapped his briefcase, and said, without opening it, "You want to hear how it turned out. I almost have the business deal in my pocket. A charming man, your deputy director, but certainly not harmless." He laughed, shook K.'s hand, and tried to make him laugh as well. But K. found it suspicious that the manufacturer did not want to show him the papers and found nothing funny about the manufacturer's remark. "Mr. Procurator," said the manufacturer, "you seem to be suffering from the weather. You look rather gloomy today." "Yes," said K., touching his temple, "headache, family worries." "Quite right," said the manufacturer, who was a hurried man and could not listen to anyone calmly, "everyone has their cross to bear." Unconsciously, K. took a step toward the door, as if he intended to escort the manufacturer out, but the manufacturer said, "I have a small message for you, Mr. Procurator. I'm very afraid that I might be bothering you with this today, but I have already been to see you twice recently and forgot each time. If I keep postponing it, it will probably lose its purpose entirely. That would be a pity, because my message is perhaps not completely worthless." Before K. had time to respond, the manufacturer stepped closer to him, lightly tapped his knuckles against his chest, and said quietly, "You have a trial, don't you?" K. stepped back and immediately exclaimed, "The deputy director told you that." "Oh no," said the manufacturer, "how could the deputy director know?" "Through you?" K. asked, now much calmer. "I hear a few things about the court from time to time," said the manufacturer, "which is related to the message I wanted to give you." "So many people are connected with the court!"

said K., lowering his head, and led the manufacturer to the desk. They sat down again as before, and the manufacturer said, "Unfortunately, there's not much I can tell you. But in such matters, one should not neglect even the smallest details. Besides, I felt compelled to help you in some way, no matter how modest my help may be. We have been good business friends so far, haven't we? Well then." K. wanted to apologize for his behavior during today's meeting, but the manufacturer would not tolerate any interruption, pushed the briefcase up under his arm to show that he was in a hurry, and continued: "I know about your trial from a certain Titorelli. He's a painter; Titorelli is just his artist name, I don't even know his real name. He has been coming to my office from time to time for years, bringing small paintings for which I — he's almost a beggar — always give him some sort of alms. By the way, they are nice paintings, heath landscapes and the like. These sales — we had both gotten used to them — went quite smoothly. However, at one point, his visits started to happen too frequently; I scolded him, we got into a conversation, and I was interested to learn how he could support himself just by painting. To my astonishment, I found out that his main source of income was portrait painting. He said he works for the court. For which court, I asked. And then he told me about the court. You can imagine how astonished I was by these stories. Since then, I hear some news about the court during each of his visits and gradually gain a great insight into the matter. However, Titorelli is quite loquacious, and I often have to fend him off, not only because he certainly also lies, but primarily because a businessman like me, who is nearly collapsing under his own business worries, can hardly take care of foreign matters as well. But that's just a side note. Perhaps — I thought now — Titorelli can be of some help to you; he knows many judges, and even if he doesn't have much influence himself, he can still give you advice on how to approach various influential people. And even if this advice may not be decisive in itself, I believe it will be of great importance in your possession. You are almost an attorney. I always say: Procurator K. is almost an attorney. Oh, I'm not worried about your trial. But will you go to Titorelli? On my recommendation, he will certainly do everything he can. I really think you should go. It doesn't have to be today, just sometime, occasionally. However, I must say — by my giving you this advice, you are in no way obliged to go to Titorelli. No, if you think you can do without Titorelli, it's certainly better to leave him aside completely. Perhaps you already have a very precise plan, and Titorelli could interfere with it. No, then you certainly should not go. It surely takes some courage to ask such a fellow for advice. Well, it's up to you. Here is the recommendation letter, and here is the address."

Disappointed, K. took the letter and put it in his pocket. Even in the best-case scenario, the advantage that the recommendation could bring him was relatively smaller than the damage caused by the fact that the manufacturer knew about his trial and that the painter was spreading the news further. He could hardly bring himself to thank the manufacturer, who was already on his way to the door, with a few words. "I will go," he said as he bid farewell to the manufacturer at the door, "or, since I am very busy right now, I will write to him and ask him to come to my office." "I knew," said the manufacturer, "that you would find the best solution. However, I thought you would prefer to avoid inviting someone like that Titorelli to the bank to discuss the trial with him here. It is not always advantageous to hand over letters to such people. But you have certainly thought everything through and know what you are allowed to do." K. nodded and accompanied the manufacturer through the anteroom. But despite his outward calm, he was very shaken inside. The thought of writing to Titorelli was something he had only said to show the manufacturer that he appreciated the recommendation and was immediately considering the possibilities of meeting with Titorelli. But if he had truly regarded Titorelli's assistance as valuable, he would not have hesitated to write to him for real. The dangers that could result from this had only become clear to him through the manufacturer's remark. Could he really rely so little on his own judgment? If it was possible that he could invite a questionable person to the bank with a clear letter to seek advice about his trial, separated only by a door from the deputy director, was it not also possible—and even very likely—that he overlooked other dangers or walked right into them? There was not always someone beside him to warn him. And just now, when he wanted to present himself with all his strength, such previously unfamiliar doubts about his own vigilance had to arise! Should the difficulties he felt in carrying out his office work now also begin in the trial? Now, however, he could not understand at all how it had been possible for him to want to write to Titorelli and invite him to the bank.

He was still shaking his head when the servant approached him and pointed out three gentlemen sitting on a bench in the waiting room. They had been waiting a long time to be admitted to K. Now that the servant was speaking with K., they had stood up, each wanting to take the opportunity to get closer to K. without regard for the others. Since the gentlemen had been so inconsiderate as to make them waste their time in the waiting room, they decided to stop being polite themselves. "Mr. Procurator," one of them began. But K. had asked the servant to bring him his winter coat and, while he was putting it on with the servant's help, said to all three, "I apologize, gentlemen, but unfortunately I do not have time to meet with you right now. I must ask for your understanding, as I have an urgent business matter to attend to and must leave immediately. You have seen for yourselves how long I have been delayed. Would you be so kind as to come back tomorrow or whenever is convenient for you? Or shall we perhaps discuss this over the phone? Or would you like to briefly tell me what this is about now, and I can provide you with a detailed written response later? However, it would be best if you could come back another time." K.'s suggestions left the gentlemen, who had apparently waited in vain, so astonished that they looked at each other in silence. "So we are agreed?" K. asked, turning to the servant, who was now bringing him his hat. Through the open door to K.'s room, one could see that the snowfall outside had intensified. Therefore, K. pulled up the collar of his coat and buttoned it tightly under his chin.

Just then, the deputy director came in from the adjoining room, smiled at K. negotiating with the gentlemen in his winter coat, and asked, "Are you leaving now, Mr. Prokurist?" "Yes," said K., sitting up, "I have business to attend to." But the deputy director had already turned his attention to the gentlemen. "And the gentlemen?" he asked. "I believe they have been waiting for a long time." "We have already come to an agreement," K. stated. However, the gentlemen would no longer be held back; they surrounded K. and explained that they would not have waited for hours if their matters were not important and needed to be discussed thoroughly and privately. The deputy director listened to them for a while, also observing K., who was holding his hat and cleaning it of dust in places, and then said, "Gentlemen, there is a very simple solution. If you are willing to settle for me, I would be happy to take over the negotiations in place of Mr. Prokurist. Your matters must of course be discussed immediately. We are business people just like you and know how to properly value a businessman's time. Would you like to step in here?" And he opened the door that led to the anteroom of his office.

How the deputy director managed to appropriate everything that K. was now forced to give up! But was K. really giving up more than absolutely necessary? While he hurried, with vague and, as he had to admit, very slim hopes, to an unknown painter, his reputation here suffered an irreparable blow. It would probably have been much better to take off his winter coat again and at least win back the two gentlemen who had to be waiting next door. K. might have even tried that if he hadn't seen the deputy director in his room, searching through the bookstand as if it were his own. As K. approached the door in agitation, he called out, "Oh, you haven't left yet." He turned his face towards him, whose many taut wrinkles seemed to attest to strength rather than age, and immediately began searching again. "I'm looking for a copy of the contract," he said, "which, according to the company representative, should be with you. Won't you help me look for it?" K. took a step forward, but the deputy director said, "Thank you, I've already found it," and returned to his room with a large bundle of documents that contained not only the contract copy but surely much more.

Now I am no match for him, K. thought to himself, but once my personal difficulties are resolved, he will truly be the first to feel it, and it will be as bitter as possible. A bit reassured by this thought, K. instructed the servant, who had been holding the door to the corridor open for him for quite some time, to occasionally inform the director that he was on business. Almost happy to be able to fully devote himself to his matters for a while, he left the bank.

He immediately went to the painter who lived in a suburb that was completely opposite to the one where the court offices were located. It was an even poorer area, with darker houses, and the streets were full of dirt that slowly drifted on the melted snow. In the building where the painter lived, only one wing of the large gate was open, while in the other, there was a gap broken in the wall, from which, just as K. approached, a disgusting yellow, smoking liquid spewed out, causing a rat to flee into the nearby sewer. At the bottom of the stairs, a small child lay face down on the ground crying, but it was hardly audible due to the overwhelming noise coming from a plumbing workshop on the other side of the gate. The workshop door was open, and three assistants stood in a semicircle around some workpiece, striking it with hammers. A large sheet of tin hanging on the wall cast a pale light that penetrated between two assistants, illuminating their faces and work aprons. K. only took a fleeting glance at everything; he wanted to finish here as quickly as possible, just ask the painter a few questions, and then return to the bank. If he had even the slightest success here, it would positively affect his work at the bank today. On the third floor, he had to slow his pace; he was completely out of breath, the stairs as well as the floors were excessively high, and the painter was supposed to live at the very top in an attic room. The air was also very stifling; there was no courtyard, the narrow staircase was enclosed on both sides by walls, with only a few small windows placed almost at the top. Just as K. paused for a moment, a few little girls ran out of an apartment and laughed as they hurried up the stairs. K. followed them slowly, caught up with one of the girls who had stumbled and lagged behind the others, and asked her as they continued to climb, "Does a painter named Titorelli live here?" The girl, a slightly hunchbacked child of no more than thirteen, nudged him with her elbow and looked up at him sideways. Neither her youth nor her physical defect had prevented her from being completely corrupted. She didn't even smile but looked at K. seriously with a sharp, challenging gaze. K. pretended not to notice her behavior and asked, "Do you know the painter Titorelli?" She nodded and asked in return, "What do you want from him?" K. thought it beneficial to quickly learn a little about Titorelli: "I want to have a portrait painted by him," he said. "Have a portrait painted?" she asked, opening her mouth wide, lightly hitting K. with her hand as if he had said something extraordinarily surprising or awkward, lifting her already very short skirt with both hands, and ran as fast as she could after the other girls, whose shouting was already fading into the distance. At the next turn of the staircase, however, K. encountered all the girls again. They had evidently been informed by the hunchbacked girl of K.'s intention and were waiting for him. They stood on either side of the staircase, pressing themselves against the wall so that K. could pass comfortably between them, smoothing their aprons with their hands. All their faces, as well as this formation, presented a mixture of childishness and depravity. At the head of the girls, who now gathered behind K. laughing, was the hunchback, who took the lead. He owed it to her that he found the right way straight away. He wanted to continue straight up, but she indicated to him that he needed to take a turn in the staircase to reach Titorelli. The staircase leading to him was particularly narrow, very long, straight without any bends, visible in its entirety, and directly closed off by Titorelli's door at the top. This door, which was illuminated relatively brightly by a small, crookedly placed transom window, was made of unplastered beams, on which the name Titorelli was painted in broad red strokes. K. and his entourage had hardly reached the middle of the staircase when, apparently prompted by the noise of many footsteps, the door opened slightly, and a man, probably only dressed in a nightshirt, appeared in the doorway. "Oh!" he exclaimed when he saw the crowd coming and then disappeared. The hunchback clapped her hands in delight, and the other girls pushed behind K. to hurry him along.

They hadn't even made it upstairs when the painter flung the door wide open, bowed deeply, and invited K. to enter. He turned away the girls, not allowing any of them inside, no matter how much they begged or tried to enter against his will, if not with his permission. Only the hunchback managed to slip through his outstretched arm, but the painter chased after her, grabbed her by her skirts, spun her around, and then set her down in front of the door with the other girls, who, while the painter had left his post, had not dared to cross the threshold. K. didn't know how to assess the situation; it seemed as though everything was happening in friendly agreement. The girls at the door stretched their necks one after another, calling out various joking words to the painter that K. didn't understand, and the painter laughed while the hunchback nearly flew in his hand. Then he closed the door, bowed again to K., extended his hand, and introduced himself: "Art painter Titorelli." K. pointed to the door behind which the girls were whispering and said, "They seem to be very popular in the house." "Oh, those faces!" said the painter, trying in vain to fasten his nightshirt at the neck. He was otherwise barefoot and dressed only in a wide, yellowish linen pair of trousers held up by a strap, the long end of which flapped freely. "These faces are truly a burden to me," he continued, letting go of the nightshirt, which had just lost its last button, fetched a chair, and insisted that K. sit down. "I once painted one of them — she isn't even here today — and since then they all have been following me. When I'm here, they only come in if I allow it, but if I'm away, there's always at least one present. They've had a key made for my door, which they lend to each other. You can hardly imagine how annoying that is. For example, I come home with a lady I'm supposed to paint, open the door with my key, and find the hunchback sitting at the little table, painting her lips red with a brush while her little siblings, whom she's supposed to supervise, are running around and messing up the room in every corner. Or I come home late at night — please excuse my state and the disorder in the room — I come home late at night and want to get into bed, and something pinches my leg; I look under the bed and pull out another one of those things. I don't know why they crowd around me; you must have noticed that I'm not trying to lure them to me. Naturally, this also disturbs my work. If this studio weren't provided to me for free, I would have moved out long ago." Just then, a delicate, anxious voice called from behind the door, "Titorelli, may we come in already?" "No," replied the painter. "Not even me?" it asked again. "Not even you," said the painter, went to the door, and locked it.

K. had meanwhile looked around the room; he would never have thought to call this miserable little space an atelier. One could hardly take more than two long steps in length or width here. Everything—floor, walls, and ceiling—was made of wood, and between the beams, there were narrow cracks. Facing K. stood the bed against the wall, overloaded with bedding in various colors. In the middle of the room, on an easel, was a painting covered with a shirt, the sleeves dangling down to the floor. Behind K. was the window, through which one could see no further in the fog than the snow-covered roof of the neighboring house.

The turning of the key in the lock reminded K. that he had intended to leave soon. He took the manufacturer's letter out of his pocket, handed it to the painter, and said, "I learned about you from this gentleman, your acquaintance, and I came on his advice." The painter glanced through the letter quickly and tossed it onto the bed. If the manufacturer had not specifically referred to Titorelli as his acquaintance, as a poor man reliant on charity, one might have thought that Titorelli genuinely did not know the manufacturer or at least could not remember him. Moreover, the painter now asked, "Do you want to buy paintings or have a portrait made of yourself?" K. looked at the painter in surprise. What did the letter actually say? K. had assumed it was obvious that the manufacturer had informed the painter that K. only wanted to inquire about his trial. He had rushed here far too hastily and thoughtlessly! But now he had to respond to the painter somehow, and he said, glancing at the easel, "You're currently working on a painting?" "Yes," said the painter, throwing the shirt that had been draped over the easel onto the bed after the letter. "It's a portrait. A good piece of work, but not quite finished." Fortune favored K.; the opportunity to discuss the court was practically offered to him, as it was clearly a portrait of a judge. Moreover, it was strikingly similar to the painting in the lawyer's office. However, this depicted a completely different judge, a stout man with a black bushy beard that extended widely up the sides of his cheeks; that painting was an oil painting, while this one was weakly and vaguely done in pastels. Nevertheless, everything else was similar, as the judge in this painting also seemed about to rise threateningly from his throne, which he was firmly holding onto. "That's a judge," K. had wanted to say immediately, but he held back for the moment and approached the painting as if he wanted to study its details. He couldn't explain a large figure standing above the backrest of the throne and asked the painter about it. "It still needs a bit of work," the painter replied, retrieving a pastel pencil from a small table and lightly stroking the edges of the figure, though this did not clarify it for K. "It's Justice," the painter finally said. "Now I can see it," K. remarked, "here is the blindfold, and here are the scales. But aren't there wings at her heels, and isn't she in motion?" "Yes," said the painter, "I had to paint it that way on commission; it's actually Justice and the Goddess of Victory combined." "That's not a good combination," K. said with a smile, "Justice must be at rest, otherwise the scales tilt and a fair judgment is impossible." "I comply with my client's wishes," said the painter. "Of course," K. replied, not wanting to offend anyone with his remark. "You've painted the figure just as she actually sits on the throne." "No," said the painter, "I've neither seen the figure nor the throne; it's all an invention, but I was told what I was to paint." "What?" K. asked, deliberately pretending not to fully understand the painter, "Isn't it a judge sitting on the judge's bench?" "Yes," said the painter, "but he's not a high judge and has never sat on such a throne." "And yet he allows himself to be painted in such a solemn pose? He sits there like a court president." "Yes, the gentlemen are vain," said the painter. "But they have the higher permission to be painted this way. Each one is exactly instructed on how he may be portrayed. Unfortunately, one cannot judge the details of the attire and posture from this painting; pastel colors are not suitable for such representations." "Yes," K. said, "it is strange that it is painted in pastels." "The judge wanted it that way," said the painter, "it's intended for a lady." The sight of the painting seemed to have inspired him to work; he rolled up his shirt sleeves, took several pencils in hand, and K. watched as a reddish shadow formed under the trembling tips of the pencils, radiating outward towards the edge of the painting. Gradually, this play of shadow surrounded the head like an ornament or a high distinction. However, the figure of Justice remained light except for an imperceptible hue, and in that brightness, the figure seemed to stand out particularly, hardly reminding one of the goddess of Justice, nor of Victory; it now looked entirely like the goddess of the Hunt. The painter's work drew K. in more than he intended; yet he finally reproached himself for having been there so long and, in essence, not having done anything for his own case. "What is this judge's name?" he suddenly asked. "I can't tell you that," the painter replied, deeply bent over the painting and clearly neglecting his guest, whom he had initially received so considerately. K. took this as a whim and was annoyed because he was losing time. "You must be a confidant of the court?" he asked. Immediately, the painter set his pencils aside, straightened up, rubbed his hands together, and looked at K. with a smile. "Just come out with the truth," he said, "you want to learn something about the court, as stated in your letter of recommendation, and you initially talked about my paintings to win me over. But I don't take offense; you couldn't know that this is inappropriate for me. Oh please!" he said sharply, as K. tried to interject. He then continued, "Besides, you are completely right with your remark; I am a confidant of the court." He paused, as if to give K. time to come to terms with this fact. Behind the door, the girls could be heard again. They were likely crowding around the keyhole; perhaps one could even peek through the cracks into the room. K. refrained from excusing himself in any way, as he did not want to distract the painter; however, he did not want the painter to become too lofty and thereby somewhat unreachable, so he asked, "Is this a publicly recognized position?" "No," said the painter curtly, as if further discussion on the subject was cut off. But K. did not want to let him remain silent and said, "Well, often such unrecognized positions are more influential than the recognized ones." "That is indeed the case for me," said the painter, nodding with a furrowed brow. "I spoke with the manufacturer about your case yesterday; he asked me if I would help you, and I replied, 'The man can come to me,' and now I'm glad to see you here so soon. This matter seems to concern you very much, which of course doesn't surprise me. Would you like to take off your coat first?" Although K. intended to stay only a very short time, he found the painter's invitation quite welcome. The air in the room had gradually become oppressive; he had often looked curiously at a small, undoubtedly unheated iron stove in the corner, as the stuffiness in the room was inexplicable. While he took off his winter coat and also unbuttoned his jacket, the painter said apologetically, "I have to have warmth. It's quite cozy in here, isn't it? The room is well situated in this regard." K. said nothing in response, but it was not warmth that bothered him; rather, it was the stale air, almost hindering his breathing; the room had probably not been aired out for a long time. This discomfort was further heightened for K. as the painter asked him to sit on the bed while he himself took the only chair in the room in front of the easel. Moreover, the painter seemed to misunderstand why K. only stayed at the edge of the bed; rather, he insisted that K. make himself comfortable, and since K. hesitated, he went over and pushed him deep into the bedding and cushions. Then he returned to his seat and finally asked the first substantive question that made K. forget everything else. "Are you innocent?" he asked. "Yes," K. replied. Answering this question genuinely pleased him, especially since it was directed at a private individual, thus without any responsibility. No one had ever asked him so openly before. To savor this pleasure, he added, "I am completely innocent." "Oh," said the painter, lowering his head and seeming to think. Suddenly he lifted his head again and said, "If you are innocent, then the matter is very simple." K.'s gaze clouded; this alleged confidant of the court spoke like an ignorant child. "My innocence does not simplify the matter," K. said. He had to smile despite everything and slowly shook his head. "It depends on many subtleties in which the court gets lost. In the end, it draws a great guilt from somewhere where originally there was nothing." "Yes, yes, certainly," said the painter, as if K. unnecessarily disturbed his line of thought. "But you are innocent, aren't you?" "Well, yes," K. said. "That is the main thing," said the painter. He was not swayed by counterarguments, but despite his decisiveness, it was unclear whether he spoke out of conviction or merely indifference. K. wanted to ascertain this initially and said, "You surely know the court much better than I do; I don't know much more than what I have heard about it, admittedly from very different people. However, they all agreed that careless accusations are not made, and that the court, once it accuses, is firmly convinced of the accused's guilt and can hardly be dissuaded from this conviction." "Hardly?" asked the painter, raising a hand. "The court can never be dissuaded from it. If I were to paint all the judges side by side on a canvas and you had to defend yourself before this canvas, you would have more success than before the actual court." "Yes," K. said to himself, forgetting that he had only wanted to probe the painter.

# THE TRIAL

Once again, a girl started asking from behind the door: "Titorelli, won't he be leaving soon?" "Be quiet," the painter shouted towards the door, "can't you see that I'm having a meeting with the gentleman?" But the girl was not satisfied with that and asked, "You're going to paint him?" And when the painter didn't respond, she added, "Please don't paint such an ugly man." A confusing mix of incomprehensible agreeing shouts followed. The painter jumped to the door, opened it just a crack — one could see the pleading, clasped hands of the girls — and said, "If you don't be quiet, I'll throw you all down the stairs. Sit down on the steps and behave yourselves." They probably didn't comply right away, so he had to command, "Down on the steps!" Only then did it become quiet.

"Excuse me," said the painter as he returned to K. K. had barely turned toward the door; he had completely left it up to the painter whether and how he wanted to protect him. He barely moved now either when the painter leaned down to him and whispered in his ear, so as not to be overheard outside, "Those girls are also part of the court." "What?" K. asked, tilting his head to the side and looking at the painter. However, the painter sat back down in his chair and said, half jokingly, half as an explanation, "Everything is part of the court." "I haven't noticed that," K. replied shortly, the painter's general remark took away any concern he had about the mention of the girls. Nevertheless, K. looked toward the door for a while, behind which the girls were now sitting quietly on the steps. Only one had stretched a straw through a crack between the beams and was slowly moving it up and down.

"You still seem to have no overview of the court," said the painter, stretching his legs wide and tapping his toes on the floor. "But since you are innocent, you won't need one. I'll get you out."

"How do you plan to do that?" K. asked. "You just said that the court is completely inaccessible for evidence."

. . .

"Inaccessible only for evidence presented before the court," the painter replied, raising his index finger as if K. had missed a fine distinction. "However, things are different when it comes to what one tries behind the public court, in the consultation rooms, in the corridors, or, for example, right here in the studio."

What the painter said now seemed less unbelievable to K.; it actually aligned well with what he had heard from others. In fact, it was quite hopeful. If the judge could really be so easily influenced by personal connections, as the lawyer had suggested, then the painter's connections to the vain judges were particularly important and certainly not to be underestimated. The painter fit quite well into the circle of helpers that K. was gradually gathering around him. At the bank, his organizational talent had once been praised; here, where he was entirely on his own, a good opportunity arose to put it to the ultimate test. The painter observed the effect his explanation had on K. and then said with a certain anxiety, "Don't you notice that I speak almost like a lawyer? It's the constant interaction with the gentlemen of the court that influences me so much. I certainly gain a lot from it, but the artistic flair is largely lost."

"How did you first come into contact with the judges?" K. asked, wanting to gain the painter's trust before directly enlisting his services.

"That was very simple," said the painter. "I inherited this connection. My father was a court painter. It's a position that is always passed down. New people can't be used for it. There are so many different, varied, and above all secret rules for painting the various ranks of officials that they become known only within certain families. For example, in that drawer, I have my father's records, which I don't show to anyone. But only those who know them are qualified to paint judges. However, even if I lost them, I still have so many rules that I carry only in my head that no one could challenge my position. Every judge wants to be painted like the great old judges were, and only I can do that."

"That's enviable," K. said, thinking of his position at the bank. "So your position is unshakable?"

"Yes, unshakable," the painter said, proudly shrugging his shoulders. "That's why I can also afford to help a poor man who has a case from time to time."

"And how do you do that?" K. asked, as if he were not the man the painter had just called poor. The painter, however, did not get distracted and said, "In your case, for example, since you are completely innocent, I will undertake the following."

The repeated mention of his innocence was becoming tiresome for K. Sometimes it seemed to him that the painter, by making such remarks, was making a favorable outcome of the trial a prerequisite for his help, which, of course, negated the help itself. Despite these doubts, however, K. restrained himself and did not interrupt the painter. He was determined not to forgo the painter's assistance; it seemed to him that this help was certainly no more questionable than that of the lawyer. In fact, he preferred it by far to the lawyer's, as it was offered in a more harmless and straightforward manner.

The painter had pulled his chair closer to the bed and continued in a low voice: "I forgot to ask you first what kind of release you desire. There are three options: actual acquittal, apparent acquittal, and postponement. The actual acquittal is, of course, the best, but I have not the slightest influence over this kind of solution. In my opinion, there is no single person who has any influence on actual acquittal. Here, only the innocence of the accused probably matters. Since you are innocent, it would indeed be possible for you to rely solely on your innocence. In that case, you would need neither me nor any other assistance."

This ordered presentation initially astonished K., but then he quietly said, just like the painter: "I believe you are contradicting yourself." "How so?" asked the painter patiently, leaning back with a smile. This smile made K. feel as if he were about to discover contradictions not in the painter's words, but in the trial itself. Nevertheless, he did not back down and said: "Earlier, you remarked that the court is inaccessible for evidence, later you restricted this to the public court, and now you even say that the innocent do not need help before the court. That alone is already a contradiction. Furthermore, you previously stated that one can personally influence the judges, yet now you deny that a real acquittal, as you call it, can ever be achieved through personal influence. That is the second contradiction." "These contradictions are easy to clarify," said the painter. "We are talking about two different things here: what is written in the law and what I have personally experienced; you must not confuse them. The law, which I have not read, states, of course, that the innocent are acquitted; however, it does not say that the judges can be influenced. Yet I have experienced just the opposite. I know of no actual acquittals, but of many influences. It is certainly possible that in all the cases I know of, there was no innocence. But isn't that unlikely? Not a single innocence in so many cases? Even as a child, I listened closely to my father when he talked about trials at home; even the judges who came to his studio spoke of the court; in our circles, we hardly talk about anything else. As soon as I got the chance to go to court myself, I took it every time. I have listened to countless trials at important stages and, as far as they are visible, I have followed them, and—I must admit—I have not witnessed a single real acquittal." "Not a single acquittal, then," K. said, as if speaking to himself and his hopes. "That confirms the opinion I already have of the court. It is therefore pointless from this side as well. A single executioner could replace the entire court." "You must not generalize," said the painter, dissatisfied. "I was only speaking from my experiences." "That is sufficient," K. said, "or have you heard of acquittals from earlier times?" "Such acquittals," replied the painter, "are said to have existed. However, it is very difficult to ascertain this.

The final decisions of the court are not published; they are not even accessible to the judges, so only legends have survived about old court cases. These do contain, in the majority, real acquittals, one can believe them, but they are not verifiable. Nevertheless, they should not be entirely neglected; they surely contain a certain truth, and they are very beautiful. I myself have painted some pictures that depict such legends." "Pure legends do not change my opinion," said K. "One cannot refer to these legends in court, can one?" The painter laughed. "No, one cannot," he said. "Then it is useless to discuss it," K. said; he wanted to temporarily accept all the painter's opinions, even if he found them unlikely and contradictory to other accounts. He did not have the time to verify or refute everything the painter said against the truth; it was already a great achievement if he could persuade the painter to help him in any way, even if it was not decisive. Therefore, he said: "Let us set aside the real acquittal; you mentioned two other possibilities." "The apparent acquittal and the delay. Those are the only ones that matter," said the painter. "But would you not, before we discuss them, remove your coat? You must be hot." "Yes," said K., who had been focused only on the painter's explanations, but now, reminded of the heat, felt strong sweat breaking out on his forehead. "It is almost unbearable." The painter nodded, as if he understood K.'s discomfort very well. "Could we not open the window?" K. asked. "No," said the painter. "It is just a fixed glass pane; it cannot be opened." Now K. realized that he had been hoping all along that either the painter or he would go to the window and throw it open. He was prepared to breathe in the fog with his mouth wide open. The feeling of being completely cut off from air made him dizzy. He lightly slapped the featherbed beside him and said in a weak voice: "This is uncomfortable and unhealthy." "Oh no," said the painter in defense of his window. "Because it cannot be opened, even though it is just a simple pane, the heat is better retained here than through a double window. But if I want to ventilate, which is not very necessary since air is coming in through the cracks in the beams, I can open one of my doors or even both." K., somewhat comforted by this explanation, looked around to find the second door. The painter noticed this and said: "It is behind you; I had to block it with the bed." Only then did

K. see the small door in the wall. "Everything here is far too small for a studio," said the painter, as if he wanted to preempt any criticism from K. "I had to set up as well as I could. The bed in front of the door is, of course, in a very poor position. The judge, for example, whom I am currently painting, always comes through the door by the bed, and I have also given him a key to this door so that he can wait for me here in the studio even when I am not home. However, he usually comes early in the morning while I am still asleep. It always tears me from the deepest sleep when the door opens beside the bed. You would lose all respect for the judges if you heard the curses with which I greet him when he climbs over my bed in the morning. I could take the key away from him, but that would only make it worse. Here, all doors can be easily broken off their hinges." Throughout this entire conversation, K. pondered whether he should take off his coat; he finally realized that if he did not, he would be unable to stay here any longer. He therefore removed his coat but laid it over his knees so he could put it back on if the discussion ended. Hardly had he taken off his coat when one of the girls called out: "He has already taken off his coat," and they could be heard pressing against the cracks to see the spectacle for themselves. "The girls believe," said the painter, "that I will paint you and that is why you are undressing." "Oh," said K., only slightly amused, for he did not feel much better than before, even though he was now sitting in his shirtsleeves. Almost grumpily, he asked: "What did you call the other two possibilities?" He had already forgotten the terms. "The apparent acquittal and the delay," said the painter. "It is up to you which one you choose. Both are attainable with my help, of course not without effort; the difference in this regard is that the apparent acquittal requires a concentrated temporary effort, while the delay requires a much lesser but more lasting effort. So first, the apparent acquittal. If you wish for this, I will write a confirmation of your innocence on a sheet of paper. The text for such a confirmation has been passed down to me from my father and is completely unassailable. With this confirmation, I will make the rounds with the judges I know. I will start, for example, by presenting the confirmation to the judge I am currently painting this evening when he comes to the session. I will present him the confirmation, explain to him that you are innocent, and vouch for your innocence. But that is not merely an external vouching; it is a real binding guarantee." In the painter's gaze lay a reproach that K. would impose the burden of such a guarantee on him. "That would be very kind," said K. "And the judge would believe you and still not really acquit me?" "As I said," replied the painter. "Furthermore, it is by no means certain that everyone would believe me; some judges, for example, will demand that I bring you to him myself. In that case, you would have to come along. However, in such a case, the matter is already half won, especially since I will, of course, inform you beforehand about how to behave with the respective judge. It is worse with the judges who will dismiss me outright—this will also happen. We will have to do without them, although I will certainly not fail to make multiple attempts; but we can afford this, as individual judges cannot decide the outcome here. Once I have a sufficient number of signatures from the judges on this confirmation, I will take it to the judge who is currently handling your case. I might also have his signature, in which case everything will progress a little faster than usual. In general, however, there are not many obstacles left at that point; it is then a time of utmost confidence for the accused. It is strange, but true, that people are more confident during this time than after an acquittal. No particular effort is required anymore. The judge has the guarantee of a number of judges in the confirmation, can acquit you without worry, and will undoubtedly do so after carrying out various formalities to please me and other acquaintances. You then leave the court and are free." "So I am free," K. said hesitantly. "Yes," said the painter, "but only apparently free, or better expressed, temporarily free. The lower judges, to whom my acquaintances belong, do not have the right to acquit definitively; only the highest court, completely unreachable for you, me, and all of us, has that right. We do not know what it is like there, and, by the way, we do not want to know either. The great right to free someone from the accusation is thus not possessed by our judges, but they do have the right to release from the charge. This means that if you are acquitted in this way, you are for the moment released from the accusation, but it continues to loom over you and can, as soon as the higher order comes, immediately take effect. Since I am in such good contact with the court, I can also tell you how the distinction between real and apparent acquittal is shown purely externally in the regulations for the court offices. In a real acquittal, the case files are to be completely laid aside; they vanish entirely from the proceedings—not only the charge, but also the trial and even the acquittal are destroyed; everything is destroyed. In contrast, with an apparent acquittal, no further changes have occurred to the record, other than that it has been enriched with the confirmation of innocence, the acquittal, and the reasoning for the acquittal. Otherwise, however, it remains in the proceedings; it will, as required by the uninterrupted traffic of the court offices, be forwarded to the higher courts, returned to the lower ones, and thus pendulate with larger and smaller swings, with greater and lesser stagnations. These paths are unpredictable. From the outside, it may sometimes appear that everything has long been forgotten, the record lost, and the acquittal a complete one. An insider would not believe that. No record is lost; there is no forgetting in court. One day—no one expects it—some judge takes the record in hand, realizes that in this case the accusation is still alive, and orders immediate arrest. I have assumed here that a long time passes between the apparent acquittal and the new arrest; this is possible, and I know of such cases, but it is equally possible that the acquitted person comes home from court and is already met by agents waiting to arrest him again. Then, of course, the free life is over." "And the trial starts anew?" K. asked, almost in disbelief. "Indeed," said the painter, "the trial starts anew, but there is again the possibility, just like before, to obtain an apparent acquittal. One must gather all one's strength again and not give up." The latter the painter perhaps said under the impression that K., who was somewhat slumped, made on him. "But," asked K., as if he wanted to preempt any revelations from the painter, "isn't obtaining a second acquittal more difficult than the first?" "One cannot," replied the painter, "say anything definite in this regard. You probably think that the judges would be biased against the accused due to the second arrest? That is not the case. The judges have already foreseen this arrest when they acquitted. This factor has hardly any effect. However, for countless other reasons, the mood of the judges as well as their legal assessment of the case may have changed, and the efforts for the second acquittal must therefore be adapted to the changed circumstances and must generally be as vigorous as those before the first acquittal." "But this second acquittal is again not final," K. said, turning his head dismissively. "Of course not," said the painter, "the second acquittal is followed by the third arrest, the third acquittal by the fourth arrest, and so on. That is inherent in the concept of apparent acquittal." K. fell silent. "The apparent acquittal does not seem advantageous to you," said the painter, "perhaps the delay suits you better. Shall I explain the nature of the delay to you?" K. nodded. The painter had leaned back comfortably in his chair, his nightshirt wide open, one hand slipped beneath it, stroking his chest and sides. "The delay," said the painter, looking ahead for a moment as if searching for a fully accurate explanation, "consists in keeping the trial permanently in the lowest stage of proceedings. To achieve this, it is necessary that the accused and the helper, but especially the helper, remain in constant personal contact with the court. I repeat, this requires no such exertion as obtaining an apparent acquittal, but much greater attention is needed. One must not lose sight of the trial; one must visit the respective judge at regular intervals and also on special occasions and seek to keep him friendly in every way. If one is not personally acquainted with the judge, one must have known judges influence him without giving up immediate discussions. If nothing is overlooked in this regard, one can reasonably assume that the trial will not progress beyond its initial stage. The trial does not stop, but the accused is almost as secure from a conviction as if he were free. Compared to the apparent acquittal, the delay has the advantage that the future of the accused is less uncertain; he is spared the terror of sudden arrests and does not have to fear that, just when his other circumstances are least favorable, he will have to undertake the efforts and excitements associated with obtaining an apparent acquittal. However, the delay also has certain disadvantages for the accused that should not be underestimated. I am not thinking here that the accused is never free; he is not in the true sense during the apparent acquittal either. There is another disadvantage. The trial cannot stand still without at least apparent reasons for doing so. Therefore, something must happen in the trial outwardly. Various orders must be made from time to time, the accused must be interrogated, investigations must take place, etc. The trial must always turn within the small circle to which it has been artificially confined. This naturally brings certain inconveniences for the accused, which you should not imagine to be too severe. Everything is merely superficial; the interrogations, for example, are quite short; if one has no time or inclination to go, one may excuse oneself; one can even, with certain judges, set the orders in advance for a long time together; it essentially only concerns the fact that one, being the accused, must report to the judge from time to time." Even during the last words, K. had placed his coat over his arm and stood up. "He is already getting up," it was immediately called from outside the door. "Are you going to leave already?" asked the painter, who had also gotten up. "It must be the air driving you away from here. I am very sorry. I had much more to say to you. I had to keep it very brief. But I hope I have been understandable." "Oh yes," said K., whose head ached from the effort of forcing himself to listen. Despite this confirmation, the painter summarized everything once more, as if he wanted to give K. some comfort for the way home: "Both methods have in common that they prevent a conviction of the accused." "But they also prevent a real acquittal," K. said softly, as if ashamed to have realized that. "You have grasped the essence of the matter," said the painter quickly. K. placed his hand on his winter coat but could not even decide to put it on. He would have preferred to pack everything up and run outside into the fresh air. The girls could not persuade him to put on his coat, even though they were already calling out to each other that he should dress. The painter was eager to interpret K.'s mood somehow and therefore said: "You have probably not yet decided regarding my suggestions. I approve of that. I would even have advised you against deciding immediately. The advantages and disadvantages are very finely balanced. One must weigh everything carefully. However, one must not lose too much time." "I will be back soon," said K., who in a sudden decision put on his coat, threw the mantle over his shoulder, and rushed to the door, behind which the girls had started to scream. K. thought he could see the screaming girls through the door. "But you must keep your word," said the painter, who had not followed him, "otherwise I will come to the office to inquire myself." "Please unlock the door," said K., pulling at the handle, which the girls were holding tightly outside, as he could feel from the counterpressure. "Do you want to be bothered by the girls?" asked the painter. "You should rather use this exit," and he pointed to the door behind the bed. K. agreed and jumped back to the bed. But instead of opening the door there, the painter crawled under the bed and asked from below: "Just a moment longer. Would you not like to see a painting that I could sell you?" K. did not want to be rude; the painter had indeed taken care of him and promised to help him further, and due to K.'s forgetfulness, they had not even discussed the payment for the help yet, so K. could not turn him down and allowed himself to see the painting, even though he was trembling with impatience to leave the studio. The painter pulled out a pile of unframed pictures from under the bed, which were so covered in dust that when the painter tried to blow the dust off the topmost picture, it swirled before K.'s eyes, choking him for quite a while. "A heath landscape," said the painter, handing K. the picture. It depicted two frail trees standing far apart in the dark grass. In the background was a colorful sunset. "Beautiful," said K., "I will buy it." K. had spoken so briefly without thinking, so he was relieved when the painter, instead of taking offense, picked up a second picture from the floor. "Here is a counterpart to this picture," said the painter. It might have been intended as a counterpart, but there was not the slightest difference from the first picture; here were the trees, here the grass, and there the sunset. But K. cared little about that. "They are beautiful landscapes," he said, "I will buy both and hang them in my office." "The motif seems to please you," said the painter, retrieving a third picture, "it is fortunate that I have another similar picture here." But it was not similar; it was rather the completely identical old heath landscape. The painter took advantage of this opportunity to sell old pictures. "I will take this one as well," said K. "How much do the three pictures cost?" "We will discuss that next time," said the painter. "You are in a hurry now, and we will stay in touch. Besides, I am glad that you like the pictures; I will give you all the pictures I have down here. They are all heath landscapes; I have painted many heath landscapes. Some people dismiss such pictures because they are too dark, but others, and you belong to them, love just the dark." But K. had no sense for the professional experiences of the begging painter now. "Pack all the pictures up," he called, interrupting the painter, "my servant will come tomorrow and pick them up." "It is not necessary," said the painter. "I hope to be able to provide you with a carrier who will go with you." And he finally leaned over the bed and unlocked the door. "Step onto the bed without hesitation," said the painter, "everyone does that when they come in here." K. would have taken no consideration even without this invitation; he had even already placed a foot on the feather bed when he looked through the open door and pulled his foot back. "What is that?" he asked the painter. "What are you astonished about?" asked the painter, astonished himself. "It is the court offices. Did you not know that there are court offices here? Court offices are almost on every attic; why should they be missing here? My studio actually belongs to the court offices; the court has made it available to me." K. was not so much shocked to find court offices here; he was mostly shocked about himself, about his ignorance regarding court matters. As a basic rule for the behavior of an accused person, it seemed to him essential to always be prepared, never to be surprised, not to look to the right innocently when the judge stood beside him on the left—and he repeatedly violated this fundamental rule. Before him stretched a long corridor, from which a breeze wafted, making the air in the studio feel refreshing by comparison. Benches were arranged on both sides of the corridor, just like in the waiting room of the office responsible for K. There seemed to be precise regulations for the arrangement of offices. At the moment, the traffic of parties there was not very large. A man sat there half-lying, burying his face in his arms on the bench and seeming to sleep; another stood in the half-dark at the end of the corridor. K. now climbed over the bed, and the painter followed him with the pictures. They soon encountered a court servant —K. could now recognize all court servants by the gold button they wore on their civil suit beneath the ordinary buttons—and the painter instructed him to accompany K. with the pictures. K. swayed more than he walked; he pressed his handkerchief against his mouth. They were already close to the exit when the girls stormed toward them, so K. could not escape them either. They had clearly seen that the second door of the studio had been opened and had taken the detour to enter from that side. "I can no longer accompany you," the painter laughed under the pressure of the girls. "Goodbye. And don't take too long to think!" K. did not even look back at him. On the street, he took the first cab that came his way. He wanted to get rid of the servant, whose gold button continuously stung his eyes, even though he likely did not stand out to anyone else. In his eagerness to serve, the servant wanted to take a seat on the driver's box, but K. chased him away. It was already well past noon when K. arrived at the office. He would have liked to leave the pictures in the cab but feared that on some occasion he would be compelled to present them to the painter. He therefore had them brought into the office and locked them in the bottom drawer of his desk to protect them from the gaze of the deputy director for at least the next few days.

## 8
# MERCHANT BLOCK · DISMISSAL OF THE LAWYER

Finally, K. had decided to withdraw his representation from the lawyer. Though doubts about whether this was the right course of action could not be entirely dispelled, the conviction of its necessity prevailed. This decision drained K. of much of his energy on the day he planned to visit the lawyer; he worked particularly slowly, had to stay at the office for a long time, and it was already past 10 o'clock by the time he finally stood before the lawyer's door. Even before he rang the bell, he considered whether it might be better to dismiss the lawyer by phone or in writing, as a personal conversation would certainly be very awkward. Nevertheless, K. ultimately did not want to forgo this meeting; any other form of dismissal would be accepted silently or with a few formal words, and K. would never learn how the lawyer received the dismissal or what consequences this dismissal might have for him according to the lawyer's not insignificant opinion, unless Leni could find out something. However, if K. sat across from the lawyer and caught him off guard with the dismissal, K. could easily glean everything he wanted from the lawyer's face and demeanor, even if the lawyer did not reveal much. It was even possible that he might be convinced that it would be better to leave the defense to the lawyer, and then he would withdraw his dismissal.

The first knock on the lawyer's door was, as usual, in vain. "Leni could be quicker," K. thought. But it was already an advantage that the other party was not interfering, as they usually did, whether it was the man in the dressing gown or someone else starting to bother him. As K. pressed the button for the second time, he glanced back at the other door, but this time it remained closed as well. Finally, two eyes appeared at the peephole of the lawyer's door, but they were not Leni's eyes. Someone unlocked the door but briefly pushed against it, calling back into the apartment, "It's him," and then opened it fully. K. had been pressing against the door because he could already hear the hurried turning of a key in the lock of the other apartment door behind him. Therefore, when the door finally opened before him, he stormed into the anteroom and saw Leni, who had been the subject of the door opener's warning call, running away in her shift through the corridor that led between the rooms. He watched her for a moment and then looked for the door opener. It was a small, thin man with a full beard, holding a candle in his hand. "Are you employed here?" K. asked. "No," the man replied, "I am a stranger here; the lawyer is only my representative. I am here regarding a legal matter." "Without a coat?" K. asked, gesturing with a hand at the man's inadequate clothing. "Oh, forgive me," the man said and illuminated himself with the candle as if he were seeing his own state for the first time. "Is Leni your mistress?" K. asked bluntly. He had slightly spread his legs and intertwined his hands behind his back, feeling superior to the thin man just by possessing a sturdy overcoat. "Oh God," the man exclaimed, raising one hand in frightened defense before his face, "no, no, what do you think?" "You look credible," K. said with a smile, "but still— come." He waved to him with his hat and let him go ahead. "What is your name?" K. asked on the way. "Block, merchant Block," the little man said, turning around at this introduction, but K. did not let him stop. "Is that your real name?" K. asked. "Of course," came the reply, "why would you doubt it?" "I thought you might have reason to conceal your name," K. said. He felt as free as one is when speaking to lowly people in a foreign place, keeping everything about himself to himself, only calmly discussing the interests of others, thus elevating them before himself but also able to disregard them at will. At the door of the lawyer's study, K. stopped, opened it, and called to the merchant, who had obediently continued on, "Not so fast, shine the light here." K. thought Leni might have hidden here; he had the merchant search all the corners, but the room was empty. In front of the picture of the judge, K. held the merchant back by the suspenders. "Do you know him?" he asked, pointing upward with his index finger. The merchant lifted the candle, squinting upward, and said, "It's a judge." "A high judge?" K. asked, positioning himself sideways in front of the merchant to observe the impression the picture made on him. The merchant looked up admiringly. "It's a high judge," he said. "You don't have much insight," K. said. "Among the low investigative judges, he is the lowest." "Now I remember," said the merchant, lowering the candle, "I've heard that too." "But of course," K. exclaimed, "I forgot, of course you must have heard it." "But why, why?" the merchant asked while he moved toward the door, urged by K. with his hands. Outside in the corridor, K. said, "You know where Leni is hiding?" "Hiding?" the merchant said, "no, but she should be in the kitchen making the lawyer some soup." "Why didn't you say that right away?" K. asked. "I wanted to lead you there, but you called me back," replied the merchant, looking confused by the contradictory orders. "You probably think you're very clever," K. said, "so lead me!" In the kitchen, K. had never been before; it was surprisingly large and well-equipped. The stove alone was three times the size of ordinary stoves; the rest was indistinguishable, as the kitchen was now only illuminated by a small lamp hanging at the entrance. Leni stood at the stove in a white apron as usual, pouring eggs into a pot on a spirit burner. "Good evening, Josef," she said with a sidelong glance. "Good evening," K. replied, gesturing with one hand to a chair standing aside for the merchant to sit on, which he did. K. then moved very close behind Leni, leaned over her shoulder, and asked, "Who is the man?" Leni wrapped one hand around K.'s waist, stirred the soup with the other, pulled him forward to her, and said, "He's a pitiable man, a poor merchant, a certain Block. Just look at him." They both looked back. The merchant sat on the chair K. had pointed to; he had blown out the candle, whose light was now unnecessary, and was pressing the wick with his fingers to prevent the smoke. "You were in your shift," K. said, turning her head back toward the stove with his hand. She remained silent. "Is he your lover?" K. asked. She reached for the soup pot, but K. took both her hands and said, "Now, answer!" She said, "Come to the study; I will explain everything to you." "No," K. said, "I want you to explain it here." She clung to him and wanted to kiss him, but K. pushed her away and said, "I don't want you to kiss me now." "Josef," Leni said, looking at K. pleadingly yet openly in the eyes, "you won't be jealous of Mr. Block, will you?" "Rudi," she then said, turning to the merchant, "help me, you see, I'm being suspected; let the candle be." One might have thought he was not paying attention, but he was fully aware. "I wouldn't know why you should be jealous," he said, rather unresponsive. "I actually don't know either," K. said, smiling at the merchant. Leni laughed aloud, seizing K.'s moment of inattention to loop her arm around him and whispered, "Leave him for now; you see what kind of person he is. I've taken care of him a little because he has a large clientele with the lawyer, for no other reason. And you? Do you still want to speak with the lawyer today? He is very ill today, but if you want, I will register you. But you will definitely stay with me overnight. You haven't been with us for so long; even the lawyer has asked about you. Don't neglect the trial! I also have various things to tell you that I have learned. But for now, take off your coat!" She helped him take it off, took his hat, rushed off with his things into the anteroom to hang them up, then ran back and looked after the soup. "Should I first register you or bring him the soup first?" "Register me first," K. said. He was irritated; he had initially intended to discuss his matters with Leni, particularly the questioned termination, but the presence of the merchant had taken away his desire to do so. Now, however, he considered his matter too important for this little merchant to possibly intervene decisively, so he called Leni, who was already in the hallway, back. "Bring him the soup first," he said, "he should strengthen himself for the conversation with me; he will need it." "You are also a client of the lawyer," the merchant said quietly from his corner, as if to confirm. However, this was not well received. "What does that concern you?" K. said, and Leni said, "Will you be quiet?" "Then I will bring him the soup first," Leni said to K. and poured the soup into a plate. "Then it's only to be feared that he will fall asleep soon; after eating, he falls asleep quickly." "What I will tell him will keep him awake," K. said, wanting to continually imply that he intended to discuss something important with the lawyer, hoping Leni would ask him what it was, and only then would he ask her for advice. But she dutifully fulfilled only the expressed orders. As she passed by him with the cup, she deliberately brushed against him gently and whispered, "While he eats the soup, I will register you right away, so I can have you back as soon as possible." "Just go," K. said, "just go." "Be a bit friendlier," she said, turning around in the doorway with the cup once more.

K. watched her; it was now finally decided that the lawyer would be dismissed. It was probably for the best that he couldn't discuss it with Leni beforehand; she hardly had a complete understanding of the situation and would surely have advised against it. She might have actually dissuaded K. from going through with the dismissal this time, leaving him in doubt and unrest. Eventually, he would have made his decision regardless, as it was too compelling. However, the sooner it was carried out, the less damage would be prevented. Perhaps the merchant knew something about it.

K. turned around; the merchant barely noticed as he immediately wanted to get up. "Stay seated," K. said, pulling a chair next to him. "Have you been a long-time client of the lawyer?" K. asked. "Yes," said the merchant, "a very long-time client." "How many years has he represented you?" K. asked. "I'm not sure how you mean that," said the merchant. "In business legal matters—I have a grain business—the lawyer has represented me since I took over the business, so about 20 years. In my own case, which you're probably alluding to, he has represented me since the beginning, which is now over 5 years. Yes, well over 5 years," he added, pulling out an old wallet. "I have everything written down; if you want, I can give you the exact dates. It's hard to keep track of everything. My case has probably been going on for much longer; it started shortly after my wife died, and that was over $5\frac{1}{2}$ years ago." K. moved closer to him. "So the lawyer also takes on regular legal matters?" he asked. This connection between business and law seemed incredibly reassuring to K. "Of course," said the merchant, then whispered to K., "People even say that he's more capable in these legal matters than in others." But then he seemed to regret what he had said, placing a hand on K.'s shoulder and saying, "I beg you, don't betray me." K. gently patted his thigh to calm him and said, "No, I'm not a traitor." "He is vengeful," said the merchant. "Against such a loyal client, he surely won't do anything," said K. "Oh yes," said the merchant, "when he is upset, he sees no differences; besides, I'm not really loyal to him." "Why not?" K. asked. "Should I confide that to you?" the merchant asked hesitantly. "I think you can," said K. "Well," said the merchant, "I will partially confide it to you, but you must also tell me a secret so we can hold each other accountable against the lawyer." "You are very cautious," said K. "But I will tell you a secret that will completely reassure you. What is the nature of your disloyalty to the lawyer?" "I have," said the merchant hesitantly and in a tone as if confessing something dishonorable, "I have other lawyers besides him." "That's not so terrible," K. said, a little disappointed. "Here it is," said the merchant, who was still breathing heavily from his confession but felt more trust due to K.'s remark. "It is not allowed. And it is least allowed to have other lawyers alongside a so-called lawyer. And that's exactly what I've done; I have five other lawyers in addition to him." "Five!" K. exclaimed, the number astonished him, "five lawyers besides this one?" The merchant nodded. "I'm currently negotiating with a sixth." "But why do you need so many lawyers?" K. asked. "I need all of them," said the merchant. "Would you not explain that to me?" K. asked. "Gladly," said the merchant. "Above all, I certainly don't want to lose my case; that's obvious. Therefore, I must not overlook anything that could benefit me; even if the hope for benefit in a certain case is very small, I cannot dismiss it. I have thus used everything I possess for the case. For example, I have withdrawn all my money from my business; previously, the offices of my business filled almost a whole floor, today a small room in the back house is enough where I work with an apprentice. This decline was of course not only due to the withdrawal of money but even more so due to the withdrawal of my labor. If one wants to do something for one's case, there's little time to deal with anything else." "So you still work at court yourself?" K. asked. "I'd like to know more about that." "I can only report little on that," said the merchant. "At first, I did try it, but soon I gave up. It's too exhausting and doesn't yield much success. Working and negotiating there has proven to be entirely impossible for me. Just sitting and waiting there is a great effort. You know the heavy air in the offices." "How do you know I was there?" K. asked. "I was just in the waiting room when you walked through." "What a coincidence!" K. exclaimed, completely taken in and forgetting the earlier ridiculousness of the merchant. "So you saw me! You were in the waiting room when I walked through. Yes, I did walk through there once." "It's not such a great coincidence," said the merchant. "I'm there almost every day." "I will probably have to go there more often now," said K., "only I doubt I will be received as honorably as I was then. Everyone stood up. They probably thought I was a judge." "No," said the merchant, "we greeted the court attendant then. We knew you were a defendant. Such news spreads very quickly." "So you already knew that," said K. "Then perhaps my behavior seemed arrogant to you. Was it not talked about?" "No," said the merchant, "on the contrary. But those are foolish notions." "What foolish notions?" K. asked. "Why do you ask about that?" said the merchant irritably. "You seem not to know the people there yet and may misinterpret it. You must consider that in this procedure many things come up repeatedly for which reason is insufficient; one is simply too tired and distracted for much, and in compensation, one resorts to superstition. I'm speaking of others, but I'm not any better myself. One such superstition is, for example, that many try to read the outcome of the trial from the defendant's face, especially from the shape of the lips. These people claimed that you would, judging by your lips, certainly and soon be convicted. I repeat, it's a ridiculous superstition and in most cases completely disproven by the facts, but when one lives in that society, it's hard to escape such opinions. Just think how powerful this superstition can be. You did address someone there, didn't you? He could hardly respond to you. There are indeed many reasons to be confused there, but one of them was also the sight of your lips. He later recounted that he believed he saw the sign of his own conviction on your lips." "My lips?" K. asked, pulling out a pocket mirror to look at himself. "I can't see anything special on my lips. And you?" "I can't either," said the merchant, "not at all." "How superstitious these people are," K. exclaimed. "Didn't I say so?" asked the merchant. "Do they socialize that much and exchange opinions?" K. said. "I have kept completely aside until now." "In general, they don't interact much," said the merchant. "That wouldn't be possible, there are too many. There are also few common interests. If sometimes a group appears to share a common interest, it soon proves to be an illusion. Nothing can be achieved collectively against the court. Each case is examined individually; it is indeed the most careful court. Therefore, nothing can be enforced together; only an individual sometimes achieves something in secret; only once it's achieved, do the others find out; no one knows how it happened. So there is no commonality; one does come together here and there in the waiting rooms, but little is discussed there. The superstitious beliefs have existed for ages and are almost self-replicating." "I saw the gentlemen there in the waiting room," said K. "Their waiting seemed so useless to me." "The waiting is not useless," said the merchant, "only the independent intervention is useless. I already mentioned that I now have five lawyers besides this one. One would think— I believed it myself at first— that I could fully leave the matter to them now. But that would be completely wrong. I can leave it to them less than if I only had one. You don't understand that, do you?" "No," said K., placing his hand reassuringly on the merchant's hand to calm him down, "I just want to ask you to speak a little slower; all of this is very important to me, and I can't quite follow." "Good that you reminded me," said the merchant. "You are a newcomer, a young one. Your case is half a year old, isn't it? Yes, I've heard about it. Such a young case! But I have thought through these matters countless times; they are the most obvious things in the world to me." "You must be glad that your case has progressed so far?" K. asked, not wanting to directly inquire about the merchant's situation. However, he didn't receive a clear answer. "Yes, I have been dragging my case on for five years," said the merchant, lowering his head, "it's no small accomplishment." Then he fell silent for a moment. K. listened to see if Leni would come. On one hand, he didn't want her to come because he still had many questions and didn't want to be interrupted in this confidential conversation with the merchant; on the other hand, he was annoyed that she was taking so long with the lawyer despite his presence, much longer than was necessary for serving the soup. "I still remember that time very well," the merchant began again, and K. immediately focused, "when my case was about as old as your case is now. I only had this lawyer then, but I wasn't very satisfied with him." Here, I'm learning everything, K. thought, nodding vigorously as if to encourage the merchant to share all the important details. "My case," the merchant continued, "did not progress; there were indeed investigations, and I attended every one, gathered evidence, presented all my business books to the court, which, as I later learned, wasn't even necessary. I kept running to the lawyer; he also submitted various requests—." "Various requests?" K. asked. "Yes, of course," said the merchant. "That's very important to me," said K. "In my case, he is still working on the first request. He hasn't done anything yet. I see now that he is neglecting me shamefully." "That the request isn't finished can have various legitimate reasons," said the merchant. "Moreover, it later turned out that my requests were completely worthless. I even read one myself through the kindness of a court official. It was learned, but essentially contentless. Above all, a lot of Latin that I don't understand, then pages of general appeals to the court, then flattery for certain specific officials who were not named but whom an insider would certainly have to guess, then self-praise of the lawyer, where he humbly prostrated himself before the court in a dog-like manner, and finally examinations of legal cases from ancient times that were supposed to resemble mine. These examinations were, as far as I could follow them, very carefully done. I don't want to pass judgment on the lawyer's work with all this; the request I read was only one of several, but in any case, and I want to speak about this now, I couldn't see any progress in my case then." "What kind of progress did you want to see?" K. asked. "You ask quite reasonably," said the merchant with a smile, "one can rarely see progress in this procedure. But back then, I didn't know that. I'm a merchant and was even more so at that time than I am today; I wanted tangible progress; the whole thing should move towards an end or at least take a proper upward trajectory. Instead, there were only agreements that mostly had the same content; I had the responses ready like a litany; several times a week, court messengers came to my business, to my home, or wherever they could find me, which was of course disruptive (at least today it's much better in this regard; a phone call disturbs me less), and among my business friends, particularly among my relatives, rumors about my case began to spread, so there were damages from all sides, but not the slightest sign indicated that even the first court hearing would take place in the near future. So, I went to the lawyer and complained. He gave me long explanations but firmly refused to do anything in my interest; no one has influence over the scheduling of the hearing, insisting on it in a request—as I demanded—was simply outrageous and would ruin both me and him. I thought: what this lawyer doesn't want or can't do, another will want and can do. I began looking for other lawyers. I'll say it right away: none demanded or enforced the scheduling of the main hearing; indeed, with a reservation I'll still speak about, it is really impossible regarding this point; thus, this lawyer didn't deceive me; but otherwise, I had no reason to regret turning to other lawyers. You may have heard a lot about the corner lawyers from Dr. Huld; he probably portrayed them as very contemptible, and they truly are. However, he always makes a small mistake when he speaks of them and compares himself and his colleagues to them, which I want to casually point out to you. He always refers to the lawyers in his circle as the "big lawyers" for distinction. That's incorrect; of course, anyone can call themselves "big" if they like, but in this case, only the court practice decides. According to this, besides the corner lawyers, there are also small and large lawyers. This lawyer and his colleagues are, however, only small lawyers, while the large lawyers, of whom I have only heard and never seen, stand in rank incomparably higher than the small lawyers, and these, in turn, stand higher than the despised corner lawyers." "The large lawyers?" K. asked. "Who are they? How does one get to them?" "So you've never heard of them," said the merchant. "There's hardly a defendant who, after hearing about them, wouldn't dream of them for a while. But don't let yourself be tempted. Who the large lawyers are, I don't know, and one probably can't get to them at all. I don't know of any case that could be definitively said they intervened. Some they defend, but you can't achieve that by your own will; they only defend those they want to defend. The matter they take on must have already gone beyond the lower court. Otherwise, it's better not to think about them, because otherwise, the discussions with the other lawyers, their advice, and their help seem so disgusting and useless; I've experienced it myself that one would prefer to throw everything away, lie in bed at home, and not hear about anything anymore. But that would of course be the dumbest thing to do, and one wouldn't have long peace in bed either." "So you didn't think about the large lawyers back then?" K. asked. "Not for long," said the merchant, smiling again, "unfortunately, one can't completely forget them; especially at night, such thoughts are favorable. But back then, I wanted immediate results, so I went to the corner lawyers."

"Look at you all sitting here together," Leni called out, returning with a cup and standing in the doorway. They were indeed packed closely together; with every slight movement, their heads bumped against each other. The merchant, who not only was small in stature but also hunched over, forced K. to bend down deeply if he wanted to hear everything. "Just a little longer," K. said to Leni, waving his hand impatiently, which was still resting on the merchant's hand. "He wanted me to tell him about my trial," the merchant said to Leni. "Go ahead, tell him," she replied. She spoke to the merchant affectionately, yet also condescendingly. K. didn't like that; he now realized that the man did have some value—firstly, he had experiences that he communicated well. Leni was probably judging him incorrectly. He watched with annoyance as Leni took the candle, which the merchant had been holding the whole time, away from him, wiped his hand with her apron, and then knelt beside him to scrape off some wax that had dripped onto his trousers. "You were going to tell me about the crooked lawyers," K. said, pushing Leni's hand away without further comment. "What do you want?" Leni asked, lightly swatting K. and continuing her work. "Yes, about the crooked lawyers," the merchant said, rubbing his forehead as if deep in thought. K. wanted to assist him and said, "They wanted immediate results, so they went to the crooked lawyers." "Exactly," the merchant replied but didn't continue. "Maybe he doesn't want to talk about it in front of Leni," K. thought, suppressing his impatience to hear more and choosing not to press him further.

"Did you sign me up?" he asked Leni. "Of course," she replied, "he's waiting for you. Let Block be; you can talk to him later, he's staying here anyway." K. hesitated. "He's staying here?" he asked the merchant, wanting his own answer; he didn't want Leni to speak of the merchant as if he were absent. Today, he felt an unspoken anger towards Leni. Once again, only Leni answered: "He often sleeps here." "Sleeps here?" K. exclaimed, thinking the merchant would only be waiting for him while he quickly dealt with the lawyer, and then they would leave together to discuss everything thoroughly and undisturbed. "Yes," Leni said, "not everyone gets to see the lawyer at any hour like you, Josef. You don't even seem surprised that the lawyer is still seeing clients at 11 PM, despite his illness. You take what your friends do for you far too much for granted. Well, your friends, or at least I, do it gladly. I don't want any other thanks, nor do I need any other, than that you love me." "Love you?" K. thought at first, and only then did it occur to him, "Well, yes, I love her." Still, he said, dismissing everything else, "He's seeing me because I am his client. If outside help were needed for that, one would have to beg and thank at every step." "He's terrible today, isn't he?" Leni asked the merchant. "Now I'm the absent one," K. thought, becoming almost angry with the merchant when he took up Leni's rudeness and said, "The lawyer sees him for other reasons as well. His case is actually more interesting than mine. Moreover, his trial is still in the early stages, so the lawyer is still happy to work on it. That will change later." "Yes, yes," Leni said, laughing at the merchant, "how he chatters! You can't believe a word he says," she turned to K. for this, "As nice as he is, he's just as talkative. Perhaps that's why the lawyer doesn't care for him much. In any case, he only sees him when he feels like it. I've tried very hard to change that, but it's impossible. Just think, sometimes I sign Block up, but he doesn't see him until the third day afterward. But if Block isn't there when he's called, everything is lost, and he has to be registered again. That's why I allowed Block to sleep here; it has happened before that he rang for him in the night. So now Block is also ready at night. However, it happens again that when the lawyer sees Block is there, he sometimes revokes his order to let him in." K. looked questioningly at the merchant. He nodded and said, as openly as he had spoken to K. before, perhaps distracted by embarrassment, "Yes, one becomes very dependent on one's lawyer." "He's only pretending to complain," Leni said. "He loves to sleep here, as he has often confessed to me." She went to a small door and pushed it open. "Do you want to see his bedroom?" she asked K., going over and looking from the threshold into the low, windowless room, which was completely filled by a narrow bed. To get into the bed, one had to climb over the bedpost. At the head of the bed, there was an indentation in the wall, where a candle, an inkpot, and a quill were neatly arranged, along with a bundle of papers, probably legal documents. "He sleeps in the maid's room?" K. asked, turning back to the merchant. "Leni arranged it for me," the merchant replied, "it's very advantageous." K. looked at him for a long time; perhaps the first impression he had of the merchant had indeed been correct; he had experience, as his trial had been going on for a long time, but he had paid dearly for that experience. Suddenly, K. could no longer bear the sight of the merchant. "Get him to bed," he called out to Leni, who seemed not to understand him at all. He himself wanted to go to the lawyer and, by resigning, free himself not only from the lawyer but also from Leni and the merchant. But just before he reached the door, the merchant spoke to him in a low voice: "Mr. Prosecutor," K. turned around with a scowl. "You've forgotten your promise," said the merchant, stretching out his hand towards K. from his seat, pleading. "You were going to tell me a secret too." "Indeed," K. said, also glancing at Leni, who was looking at him intently, "so listen: it's almost no secret anymore. I'm going to the lawyer now to dismiss him." "He's dismissing him," shouted the merchant, jumping up from his chair and running around the kitchen with his arms raised. He kept shouting, "He's dismissing the lawyer." Leni wanted to rush at K. immediately, but the merchant got in her way, for which she hit him with her fists. Still with her hands balled into fists, she ran after K., who had a significant lead. He was already in the lawyer's room when Leni caught up to him. He had firmly closed the door behind him, but Leni, holding the door open with her foot, grabbed him by the arm and tried to pull him back. But he gripped her wrist so tightly that she had to let him go with a sigh. She hesitated to enter the room, but K. blocked the door with the key.

"I have been waiting for you for a very long time," said the lawyer from his bed, placing a document he had been reading by candlelight on the nightstand and putting on a pair of glasses with which he scrutinized K. Instead of apologizing, K. said, "I'll be leaving soon." The lawyer ignored K.'s remark, as it was not an apology, and said, "I won't let you in at this late hour again." "That suits my purpose," K. replied. The lawyer looked at him questioningly. "Please, have a seat," he said. "Because you wish it," K. said, pulling a chair up to the nightstand and sitting down. "It seemed to me that you locked the door," the lawyer remarked. "Yes," K. replied, "it was for Leni's sake." He had no intention of sparing anyone's feelings. But the lawyer asked, "Was she being intrusive again?" "Intrusive?" K. asked. "Yes," the lawyer said, laughing, then fell into a coughing fit, and after it passed, began to laugh again. "Surely you must have noticed her intrusiveness," he asked, tapping K. on the hand, which K. had carelessly rested on the nightstand and quickly withdrew. "You don't seem to attribute much importance to it," said the lawyer, as K. remained silent, "the better. Otherwise, I might have had to apologize to you. It's one of Leni's peculiarities, which I have long since forgiven her, and I wouldn't mention it if you hadn't just locked the door. However, I probably need to explain this peculiarity to you the least, but you look so distressed that I will. This peculiarity consists in the fact that Leni finds most defendants attractive. She attaches herself to all of them, loves them all, and seems to be loved by all in return; to entertain me, she sometimes tells me about them when I allow it. I am not as surprised by the whole thing as you seem to be. If one knows what to look for, one often finds defendants quite beautiful. This, however, is a strange, in a sense, scientific phenomenon. The accusation does not cause any distinct, precisely measurable change in appearance. It is not like in other court cases; most of them continue their usual way of life and, if they have a good lawyer looking out for them, are not much hindered by the trial. Nevertheless, those with experience are able to recognize the defendants one by one from the largest group. You might ask, how? My answer won't satisfy you. The defendants are simply the most beautiful. It cannot be guilt that makes them beautiful, because—at least as a lawyer, I must say— not all of them are guilty, and it cannot be the right punishment that makes them beautiful now, since not all are punished; it must therefore lie in the proceedings against them that somehow clings to them. Of course, among the beautiful ones, there are particularly beautiful ones. But all are beautiful, even Block, that miserable worm."

K. remained completely composed as the lawyer finished speaking; he even nodded noticeably at the last words, thereby confirming his long-held view that the lawyer always attempted to distract him with irrelevant generalities, just as he had done this time, instead of addressing the main question of what actual work he had done for K.'s case. The lawyer noticed that K. was offering more resistance than usual, so he fell silent to give K. the opportunity to speak. When K. remained silent, he asked, "Did you come to see me today with a specific intention?" "Yes," K. replied, shielding the candlelight slightly with his hand to see the lawyer better, "I wanted to inform you that I am withdrawing my representation from you as of today." "Do I understand you correctly?" the lawyer asked, half rising in bed and propping himself up on one elbow. "I take it that way," K. said, sitting upright and alert. "Well, we can discuss this plan," the lawyer said after a moment. "It's no longer a plan," K. replied. "Perhaps not," said the lawyer, "but still, let's not rush into anything." He used the word "we," as if he had no intention of releasing K. and wanted to remain at least as an advisor, even if he could no longer be his representative. "It's not rushed," K. said, slowly getting up and stepping behind his chair, "it's well thought out and perhaps even too much so. The decision is final."

"Then allow me just a few more words," said the lawyer, lifting the comforter and sitting on the edge of the bed. His bare, white-haired legs trembled from the cold. He asked K. to hand him a blanket from the couch. K. fetched the blanket and said, "You are exposing yourself to a chill unnecessarily." "The situation is important enough," the lawyer replied, wrapping the comforter around his upper body and then tucking the blanket around his legs. "Your uncle is my friend, and you have also become dear to me over time. I openly admit that, and I have no reason to be ashamed of it." These sentimental words from the old man were very unwelcome to K., as they forced him into a more detailed explanation that he would have preferred to avoid. They also unsettled him, as he openly acknowledged, although they could never reverse his decision. "I appreciate your kind sentiments," he said, "and I acknowledge that you have taken my case as much to heart as you can and as you believe is beneficial for me. However, I have recently come to the conviction that this is not enough. Of course, I will never attempt to convince you, a much older and more experienced man, of my opinion; if I have sometimes unwittingly tried to do so, I ask for your forgiveness. But the matter, as you yourself expressed it, is important enough, and I believe it is necessary to intervene much more vigorously in the process than has been done so far."

"I understand you," said the lawyer, "you are impatient." "I am not impatient," K. replied somewhat irritably, no longer paying much attention to his words. "You may have noticed during my first visit when I came with my uncle that I did not care much for the process; if I were not forcibly reminded of it, I completely forgot about it. But my uncle insisted that I hand over my representation to you, and I did it to please him. Now one could have expected that the process would be even easier for me than before, since one hands over representation to a lawyer to relieve oneself of the burden of the process a little. However, the opposite has happened. Never before have I worried so much about the process as I have since you began to represent me. When I was alone, I did nothing in my case, but I hardly felt it; now, however, I had a representative, everything was set up for something to happen, I awaited your intervention incessantly and increasingly anxiously, but it never came. I did receive various updates from you about the court, which I might not have gotten from anyone else. But that is not enough for me if the process is now formally approaching me in secret." K. had pushed the chair away and stood upright with his hands in his coat pockets. "From a certain point in practice," the lawyer said quietly and calmly, "nothing fundamentally new happens anymore. How many parties in similar stages of their processes have stood before me and spoken similarly to you?" "Then," K. said, "all these similar parties were just as right as I am. That does not refute me at all."

"I didn't mean to refute you," the lawyer said, "but I wanted to add that I expected more judgment from you than from others, especially since I have given you more insight into the court system and my work than I usually do with parties. And now I must see that despite everything, you do not have enough trust in me. You are not making this easy for me." How the lawyer humbled himself before K.! Without any regard for the dignity that is undoubtedly most sensitive in this regard. And why did he do that? He was apparently a busy lawyer and a wealthy man; he should not have cared much about losing a client or the loss of earnings. Besides, he was in poor health and should have been mindful of having work taken off his plate. Yet he held on to K. so tightly! Why? Was it personal concern for the uncle, or did he genuinely view K.'s case as extraordinary and hope to distinguish himself in it, either for K. or—this possibility could never be ruled out—for his friends at the court? Nothing about him was apparent, no matter how scrutinizingly K. looked at him. One might almost assume he was waiting, with an intentionally closed demeanor, to see the effect of his words. But he seemed to interpret K.'s silence too favorably for himself, as he continued: "You will have noticed that while I have a large firm, I do not employ any assistants. It used to be different; there was a time when some young lawyers worked for me, but today I work alone. This is partly due to a change in my practice, as I have increasingly limited myself to legal matters of the kind you have, and partly due to the deeper understanding I have gained of these legal matters. I found that I could not leave this work to anyone else without committing a sin against my clients and the task I had taken on. However, the decision to do all the work myself had the natural consequences: I had to decline almost all requests for representation and could only accede to those who were particularly close to me—well, there are plenty of creatures, even quite nearby, who pounce on any scrap I throw away. And besides, I became ill from overexertion. But I do not regret my decision; it is possible that I should have declined more representations than I have, but that I have dedicated myself entirely to the processes I have taken on has proven to be absolutely necessary and has been rewarded by success. I once found a very nice description in a piece about the difference between representation in ordinary legal matters and representation in these legal matters. It said: one lawyer leads his client along a thread to the verdict, while the other lifts his client onto his shoulders and carries him, without setting him down, to the verdict and even beyond. That's how it is. But it wasn't entirely accurate when I said that I never regret this great work. When it is, as in your case, so completely unrecognized, then, well, then I almost do regret it."

K. became more impatient than convinced by these words. He somehow believed he could hear in the lawyer's tone what awaited him if he yielded again—the delays would start once more, references to the progress of the submissions, to the improved mood of the court officials, but also to the great difficulties that lay ahead in the work—in short, everything known to weariness would be brought up again to deceive K. with vague hopes and torment him with vague threats. This had to be definitively prevented, so he said: "What will you undertake in my case if you retain the representation?" The lawyer even acquiesced to this insulting question and replied, "I will continue with what I have already undertaken for you." "I knew it," K. said, "so now every further word is unnecessary." "I will make one more attempt," said the lawyer, as if what excited K. did not affect K. but him instead. "I suspect that you are not only led to the wrong assessment of my legal assistance but also to your other behavior because you are treated too well, or rather, seemingly carelessly, despite being the accused. This latter also has its reason; it is often better to be in chains than to be free. But I would like to show you how other defendants are treated; perhaps you can learn something from it. I will now call Block; please unlock the door and sit next to the bedside." "Gladly," K. said, doing as the lawyer requested; he was always willing to learn. However, to cover himself just in case, he asked, "But you have acknowledged that I am withdrawing my representation?" "Yes," said the lawyer, "but you can still reverse it today." He lay back down in bed, pulled the comforter up to his knees, and turned toward the wall. Then he rang the bell.

At the same time as the bell rang, Leni appeared, quickly glancing around to see what had happened; K. sitting quietly by the lawyer's bed seemed reassuring to her. She smiled and nodded at K., who was staring at her. "Get Block," said the lawyer. Instead of fetching him, she stepped just outside the door, called, "Block! To the lawyer!" and then slipped behind K.'s chair, probably because the lawyer turned away from the wall and seemed unconcerned. From then on, she distracted him by leaning over the back of the chair or gently and carefully running her hands through his hair and stroking his cheeks. Finally, K. tried to stop her by grabbing one of her hands, which she reluctantly allowed him to take.

Block arrived immediately upon the call but stood hesitantly at the door, seemingly debating whether to enter. He raised his eyebrows and tilted his head as if listening for the order to come to the lawyer to be repeated. K. could have encouraged him to enter, but he had resolved to break definitively not only with the lawyer but with everything in the apartment, and thus remained motionless. Leni was silent as well. Block realized that at least no one was driving him away and tiptoed in, his face tense, hands clenched behind his back. He had left the door ajar for a possible retreat. K. did not look at him at all but instead stared at the high feather bed, under which the lawyer was positioned, having pushed himself close to the wall so that he was not even visible. Then his voice was heard: "Block here?" he asked. This question struck Block, who had already moved quite a bit further in, like a blow to the chest and then to the back; he staggered, remained bent over, and said, "At your service." "What do you want?" asked the lawyer, "you come at an inconvenient time." "Was I not called?" Block asked more to himself than to the lawyer, holding his hands out defensively and ready to flee. "You were called," said the lawyer, "but still you come at an inconvenient time." And after a pause, he added, "You always come at an inconvenient time." Since the lawyer spoke, Block no longer looked at the bed; instead, he stared into a corner, listening as if the speaker's sidelong glance were too bright for him to bear. Listening was difficult as well since the lawyer spoke against the wall, quietly and quickly. "Do you want me to leave?" Block asked. "Well, now that you are here," said the lawyer. "Stay!" One might have thought the lawyer had not fulfilled Block's wish but rather threatened him with a beating, for now Block truly began to tremble. "I was with the third judge yesterday, my friend," said the lawyer, "and gradually directed the conversation towards you. Do you want to know what he said?" "Oh please," said Block. Since the lawyer did not respond immediately, Block repeated the request and leaned forward as if he were about to kneel. But K. snapped at him: "What are you doing?" he exclaimed. Since Leni had tried to stop him from making that exclamation, he also grabbed her second hand. It was not the pressure of love with which he held her; she sighed often and tried to free her hands from him. For K.'s exclamation, however, Block was punished, for the lawyer asked him: "Who is your lawyer?" "You are," said Block. "And besides me?" asked the lawyer. "No one but you," said Block. "Then follow no one else," said the lawyer. Block fully acknowledged this, glaring at K. with angry looks and shaking his head violently at him. If one had translated this behavior into words, it would have been coarse insults. With this man, K. had wanted to speak friendly about his own case! "I will not disturb you any longer," K. said, leaning back in the chair. "Kneel or crawl on all fours, do what you want; I will not concern myself with it." But Block still had a sense of dignity, at least towards K., for he advanced towards him, waving his fists and shouted as loudly as he dared in the lawyer's presence: "You must not speak to me like that; it is not allowed. Why do you insult me? And furthermore, here before the esteemed lawyer, where we both, you and I, are only tolerated out of mercy? You are no better a person than I am, for you too are accused and have a trial. But if you still consider yourself a gentleman, then I am just as much a gentleman, if not even greater. And I also want to be addressed as such, especially by you. If you think you are favored because you sit here and may listen quietly while I, as you put it, crawl on all fours, then I remind you of the old legal maxim: for the accused, movement is better than stillness, for he who is still may always, unbeknownst to him, be on a scale and weighed against his sins." K. said nothing; he could only stare at this confused man with unblinking eyes.

What changes had taken place in him in just the last hour! Was it the trial that threw him back and forth, making him unable to recognize who was a friend and who was a foe? Did he not see that the lawyer was intentionally humiliating him and had no other aim this time than to flaunt his power before K. and perhaps even to subdue K. in the process? But if Block was incapable of recognizing this or if he feared the lawyer so much that that recognition was of no help to him, how could it be that he was still clever or bold enough to deceive the lawyer and hide from him that he had other lawyers working for him as well? And how did he dare to confront K., since K. could easily reveal his secret? But he dared even more; he approached the lawyer's bed and began to complain about K. as well: "Mr. Lawyer," he said, "did you hear how this man spoke to me? One can still count the hours of his trial, and already he wants to lecture me, a man who has been in trial for five years. He even insults me. He knows nothing and insults me, who, as far as my weak abilities allow, have studied precisely what decorum, duty, and court customs require." "Do not concern yourself with anyone," said the lawyer, "and do what seems right to you." "Certainly," said Block, as if encouraging himself, and knelt down closely by the bed with a brief sidelong glance. "I am kneeling already, my lawyer," he said. But the lawyer remained silent. Block cautiously stroked the feather bed with one hand. In the silence that now prevailed, Leni, freeing herself from K.'s hands, said, "You are hurting me. Let me go. I am going to Block." She walked over and sat on the edge of the bed. Block was very pleased with her arrival; he immediately made lively yet silent gestures asking her to intercede with the lawyer for him. He evidently needed the lawyer's communications very urgently, but perhaps only for the purpose of utilizing them through his other lawyers. Leni probably knew exactly how to approach the lawyer; she pointed to the lawyer's hand and pursed her lips as if for a kiss. Immediately, Block executed the kiss on the hand and repeated it two more times at Leni's prompting. But the lawyer remained silent still. Then Leni leaned over the lawyer, her beautiful figure becoming visible as she stretched out, and brushed her hand over his long white hair, leaning deeply toward his face. This finally forced a response from him. "I hesitate to tell him," said the lawyer, and one could see him shake his head slightly, perhaps to become more aware of the pressure from Leni's hand. Block listened with his head lowered, as if he were transgressing a command by doing so. "Why do you hesitate?" asked Leni. K. had the feeling that he was hearing a rehearsed conversation that had been repeated many times and would be repeated many more, which would retain its novelty only for Block. "How did he behave today?" asked the lawyer instead of answering. Before Leni commented on this, she looked down at Block and observed for a moment how he raised his hands toward her and rubbed them together pleadingly. Finally, she nodded seriously, turned to the lawyer, and said, "He was calm and diligent." An old merchant, a man with a long beard, implored a young girl for a favorable testimony. Even if he had ulterior motives, nothing could justify him in the eyes of a fellow human being. He nearly degraded the observer. Thus, the lawyer's method worked; K. had fortunately not been subjected to it long enough that the client ultimately forgot the whole world and hoped to drag himself to the end of the trial along this misguided path. This was no longer a client; this was the lawyer's dog. If the lawyer had ordered him to crawl under the bed like a dog and bark from there, he would have gladly done so. As if K. were instructed to absorb everything being spoken here, to report it at a higher place, and to draft a report, he listened attentively and reflectively. "What did he do all day?" asked the lawyer. "I locked him in the maid's room," said Leni, "so he wouldn't disturb me while I worked, where he usually stays. Through the gap, I could occasionally check what he was doing. He was always kneeling on the bed, had the writings you lent him open on the windowsill, and was reading them. That left a good impression on me; after all, the window only leads into an air shaft and lets in almost no light. That Block was still reading showed me how obedient he is." "I am glad to hear that," said the lawyer. "But did he read with understanding?" During this conversation, Block incessantly moved his lips, evidently formulating the responses he hoped to hear from Leni. "Of course, I cannot answer that with certainty," said Leni. "In any case, I saw that he was reading thoroughly. He read the same page all day and followed the lines with his finger while reading. Whenever I looked in on him, he sighed as if reading were very laborious for him. The writings you lent him are probably difficult to understand." "Yes," said the lawyer, "they certainly are. I also do not believe that he understands anything from them. They are only meant to give him a sense of how tough the struggle is that I am fighting for his defense. And for whom am I fighting this tough battle? For—it's almost ridiculous to say it—for Block. He should also learn what that means. Has he studied continuously?" "Almost continuously," Leni replied, "only once did he ask me for water to drink. I handed him a glass through the gap. At 8 o'clock, I let him out and gave him something to eat." Block glanced at K. with a sidelong look as if something praiseworthy were being said about him and must also impress K. He now seemed to have good hopes, moved more freely, and shifted around on his knees. The more clearly he froze under the following words of the lawyer. "You praise him," said the lawyer. "But that makes it difficult for me to speak. The judge did not express himself favorably, neither about Block himself nor about his case." "Not favorably?" asked Leni. "How is that possible?" Block looked at her with such a tense expression as if he trusted her ability to turn the judge's already spoken words in his favor. "Not favorably," said the lawyer. "He was even unpleasantly disturbed when I started to talk about Block. 'Do not speak of Block,' he said. 'He is my client,' I said. 'You are being misused,' he said. 'I do not consider his case lost,' I said. 'You are being misused,' he repeated. 'I do not believe it,' I said. 'Block is diligent in the trial and always on top of his case. He almost lives with me to stay informed. Such zeal is not always found. Certainly, he is not personally pleasant, has ugly manners, and is dirty, but in procedural terms, he is irreproachable. I said 'irreproachable,' I exaggerated intentionally. To that, he said: 'Block is merely clever. He has accumulated a lot of experience and knows how to delay the trial. But his ignorance is far greater than his cleverness. What would he say if he learned that his trial has not even begun yet, if one were to tell him that not even the bell for the start of the trial has been rung?' 'Calm down, Block,' said the lawyer, for Block had begun to rise on shaky knees and clearly wanted to ask for clarification. This was now the first time the lawyer directly addressed Block with more detailed words. With tired eyes, he looked half-aimlessly, half at Block, who slowly sank back down to his knees under that gaze. "This statement from the judge has no significance for you," said the lawyer. "Do not be startled at every word. If this repeats itself, I will not tell you anything more. One cannot begin a sentence without you looking at one as if your final judgment were coming now. Shame on you before my client! You also undermine the trust he places in me. What do you want? You are still alive, you are still under my protection. Senseless fear! You read somewhere that the final judgment may unexpectedly come from anyone at any time. While that is true with many reservations, it is also true that your fear disgusts me and that I see it as a lack of the necessary trust. What did I say? I repeated the statement of a judge. You know, the different views accumulate about the procedure until it becomes impenetrable. This judge, for example, considers the start of the proceedings to begin at a different time than I do. A difference of opinion, nothing more. At a certain stage of the trial, according to old custom, a bell is rung. According to this judge, that begins the trial. I cannot tell you everything that speaks against this; you would not understand it either. It suffices for you to know that much speaks against it." Embarrassed, Block ran his fingers through the fur of the bedspread below; the fear due to the judge's statement occasionally made him forget his own subservience to the lawyer; he then only thought of himself and turned the judge's words over in his mind. "Block," said Leni in a warning tone, pulling him a little up by the collar of his coat. "Leave the fur now and listen to the lawyer." K. could not understand how the lawyer could have thought of winning him over through this performance. If he had not already driven him away before, he would have achieved it through this scene.

## 9

# IN THE CATHEDRAL

K. received the assignment to show some monuments to an Italian business associate of the bank, who was very important to them and was visiting the city for the first time. It was a task that he would have certainly considered an honor at another time, but now, as he struggled to maintain his reputation at the bank, he took it on reluctantly. Every hour he spent away from the office troubled him; although he could no longer make the most of his office time as he used to, he managed to fill many hours with only a flimsy pretense of actual work. His worries grew larger when he was not in the office. He believed he could see the deputy director, who had always been on the lookout, coming into his office from time to time, sitting at his desk, rummaging through his documents, meeting with parties that K. had been almost friendly with for years, and possibly even uncovering mistakes that K. felt threatened by from all directions during his work, mistakes he could no longer avoid. Thus, whenever he was assigned a business trip or even a small journey—such assignments had coincidentally increased lately— the suspicion arose that they wanted to temporarily remove him from the office to review his work, or at the very least, that they considered him somewhat dispensable in the office. Most of these assignments he could have easily declined, but he didn't dare, for if his fears were even slightly justified, refusing the assignment would mean admitting to his anxiety. For this reason, he accepted such assignments with apparent equanimity and even concealed a serious cold when he was supposed to go on a demanding two-day business trip, just to avoid the risk of being excused from the journey due to the currently rainy autumn weather. When he returned from this trip with a terrible headache, he learned that he was to accompany the Italian business associate the following day. The temptation to refuse this one request was very strong; above all, what they had planned for him was not directly related to business. However, fulfilling this social obligation to the business associate was undoubtedly important, just not for K., who well knew that he could only maintain his position through work successes, and that if he failed to achieve that, it would be completely worthless even if he unexpectedly charmed the Italian; he did not want to be pushed out of the work sphere for even a day, as the fear of not being allowed to return was too great—a fear he recognized as exaggerated, yet it still constrained him. In this case, however, it was almost impossible to come up with a reasonable objection; K.'s knowledge of Italian was not very extensive, but sufficient. The decisive factor, however, was that K. had some artistic knowledge from the past, which had become exaggeratedly known in the bank because he had once been a member of the association for the preservation of the city's monuments, albeit only for business reasons. Now, the Italian, as had been rumored, was an art lover, making K.'s selection as his companion entirely understandable.

It was a very rainy and stormy morning when K., filled with anger about the day ahead of him, arrived at the office at 7 a.m. to at least finish some work before the visit would take everything from him. He was very tired, having spent half the night studying an Italian grammar book to prepare a bit; the window, at which he had lately spent far too much time sitting, tempted him more than his desk, but he resisted and sat down to work. Unfortunately, just then the servant entered and announced that the director had sent him to check if the assistant director was already there; if he was, he should kindly come to the reception room, as the gentleman from Italy was already there. "I'm coming," said K., putting a small dictionary in his pocket, taking an album of the city's sights that he had prepared for the foreigner under his arm, and walking through the assistant director's office into the director's room. He was pleased to have arrived at the office so early and to be available right away, which no one had seriously expected.

The assistant director's office was, of course, still empty as in the dead of night; presumably, the servant was also supposed to summon him to the reception room, but it had been unsuccessful. When K. entered the reception room, the two gentlemen rose from their deep armchairs. The director smiled warmly, clearly very pleased with K.'s arrival, and immediately made the introductions. The Italian shook K.'s hand vigorously and laughingly called someone an early riser. K. didn't quite understand who he meant, and it was a strange word whose meaning he only guessed after a while. He replied with a few smooth sentences, which the Italian took with laughter, nervously stroking his gray-blue bushy mustache several times. This mustache was evidently perfumed, and one was almost tempted to lean in and smell it.

As everyone took their seats and a small introductory conversation began, K. noticed with great discomfort that he only understood the Italian in fragments. When he spoke calmly, K. understood him almost completely, but these were rare exceptions; most of the time, the speech spilled from his mouth, and he shook his head as if amused by it. However, in such speeches, he regularly fell into some dialect that had nothing Italian about it anymore, but which the director not only understood but also spoke, which K. could have anticipated, as the Italian was from Southern Italy, where the director had also spent several years. In any case, K. realized that the possibility of communicating with the Italian had largely been taken from him, as the Italian's French was also difficult to understand, and the mustache obscured the lip movements, which might have helped with understanding.

. . .

K. began to foresee many inconveniences; for the moment, he gave up trying to understand the Italian—in the presence of the director, who understood him so easily, it would have been unnecessary effort—and he limited himself to observing him irritably, how he rested deeply yet lightly in the armchair, how he often tugged at his short, sharply tailored jacket, and how he once raised his arms and moved his hands loosely in the joints, trying to convey something that K. could not grasp, despite leaning forward and keeping his eyes on his hands. Eventually, K., who otherwise was unoccupied and only mechanically followed the back and forth of the conversation, felt his earlier fatigue reasserting itself, and to his alarm, he caught himself just in time, having been about to stand up, turn around, and leave.

Finally, the Italian looked at his watch and jumped up. After bidding farewell to the director, he squeezed past K. so closely that K. had to push his armchair back to be able to move. The director, who surely recognized in K.'s eyes the distress he was in with regard to this Italian, intervened in the conversation so cleverly and delicately that it seemed he was only adding small suggestions, while in reality, he made everything the Italian brought up, as he relentlessly interrupted, understandable to K. in a nutshell. K. learned from him that the Italian still had a few business matters to attend to for the time being, that unfortunately he would have very little time overall, that he had no intention of rushing to see all the sights, but that he had instead decided—though only if K. agreed, the decision lying solely with him—to thoroughly visit only the cathedral. He was very much looking forward to making this visit in the company of such a learned and charming man—referring to K., who was occupied only with ignoring the Italian and quickly grasping the director's words—and he asked him, if it suited him, to meet him at the cathedral in two hours, around 10 o'clock. He himself hoped to be there by that time.

K. responded with something appropriate, the Italian first shook hands with the director, then K., and then again with the director, and

THE TRIAL

left, still talking but only half turned toward them, with both following him to the door. K. then stayed for a while with the director, who looked particularly unwell today. He felt the need to somehow apologize to K. and said—they stood close together in a confidential manner —that at first, he had intended to go with the Italian himself, but then —he gave no further reason—he had decided it better to send K. instead. If he didn't understand the Italian right away, he shouldn't be surprised, understanding would come very quickly, and even if he didn't understand much at all, it wouldn't matter much, as it was not so important for the Italian to be understood. Furthermore, K.'s Italian was surprisingly good, and he would surely manage excellently with the situation. With that, K. was dismissed.

He spent the remaining free time writing down rare vocabulary he needed for the cathedral from the dictionary. It was a highly tedious task; servants brought the mail, officials came with various inquiries and stood at the door because they saw K. busy, but did not move away until K. had listened to them. The assistant director couldn't resist interrupting K., coming in often, taking the dictionary from his hand, and leafing through it apparently without purpose. Even groups appeared in the dimness of the hallway when the door opened and hesitated to bow, wanting to attract attention but unsure if they were seen—all of this revolved around K. as if he were the center, while he assembled the words he needed, then searched in the dictionary, wrote them out, practiced their pronunciation, and finally attempted to memorize them. His previously good memory seemed to have completely abandoned him; sometimes he became so angry with the Italian, who was causing him this effort, that he buried the dictionary under papers with the firm intention of not preparing any longer. But then he realized that he could not walk silently with the Italian in front of the artworks in the cathedral, and he pulled the dictionary out again with even greater fury.

Just at 9:30, when he was about to leave, a phone call came in. Leni wished him a good morning and asked how he was doing. K. hurriedly thanked her and mentioned that he couldn't possibly engage in a conversation right now because he had to go to the cathedral. "To the cathedral?" Leni asked. "Well, yes, to the cathedral." "Why to the cathedral?" Leni said. K. tried to explain briefly, but scarcely had he begun when Leni suddenly said, "They're rushing you." K. could not tolerate the pity he hadn't provoked and didn't expect; he bid farewell with two words but added, as he hung up the receiver, partly to himself and partly to the distant girl who could no longer hear him, "Yes, they are rushing me."

Now it was already late, and there was a real danger that he wouldn't arrive on time. He drove there in the car, and at the last moment, he remembered the album that he hadn't had a chance to deliver in the morning, so he took it with him now. He held it on his lap and drummed anxiously on it the whole way. The rain had lessened, but it was damp, cool, and dark; one would see little in the cathedral, but K.'s cold would certainly worsen due to standing on the cold tiles for a long time.

The cathedral square was completely empty. K. remembered that even as a small child, he had noticed that in the houses surrounding this narrow square, almost all the window curtains were always drawn. Given the weather today, this was more understandable than usual. The cathedral also seemed deserted; of course, no one would think of coming here now. K. walked through both side aisles and encountered only an old woman, wrapped in a warm cloth, kneeling in front of a Marian image and gazing at it. From a distance, he then saw a limping servant disappear through a wall door. K. had arrived on time; just as he entered, it struck ten, but the Italian was not there yet. K. returned to the main entrance, stood there for a while, uncertain, and then took a stroll around the cathedral in the rain to see if the Italian might be waiting at some side entrance. He was nowhere to be found. Could the director have misunderstood the time? How could one ever understand these people correctly? However it was, K. had to wait for him for at least half an hour. Since he was tired, he wanted to sit down. He went back into the cathedral, found a small carpet-like piece on a step, pulled it with his foot in front of a nearby bench, wrapped himself tighter in his coat, flipped up his collar, and sat down. To distract

## THE TRIAL

himself, he opened the album, flipped through it a little, but soon had to stop, as it became so dark that when he looked up, he could hardly distinguish any details in the nearby side aisle.

In the distance, a large triangle of candlelight sparkled on the main altar. K. couldn't say for certain whether he had seen them before. Perhaps they had just been lit. The church attendants were professional sneaks; you hardly noticed them. When K. turned around by chance, he saw not far behind him a tall, strong candle affixed to a pillar also burning. As beautiful as it was for illuminating the altar images, which mostly hung in the darkness of the side altars, it was completely inadequate; rather, it increased the darkness. It was both reasonable and rude of the Italian not to have come; there would have been nothing to see, and one would have had to settle for searching a few images with K.'s flashlight. To see what he could expect, K. went to a nearby small side chapel, climbed a few steps up to a low marble railing, and leaned over it to illuminate the altar image with his lamp. The eternal light hovered disturbingly in front of it. The first thing K. saw and partially guessed was a large armored knight depicted at the very edge of the image. He leaned on his sword, which he had thrust into the bare ground in front of him—only a few blades of grass sprouted here and there. He seemed to be attentively observing an event that was unfolding before him. It was remarkable that he remained standing there and did not approach. Perhaps he was meant to stand guard. K., who hadn't seen images for a long time, looked at the knight for a while, even though he had to keep blinking his eyes as he couldn't tolerate the green light from the lamp. When he then swept the light over the rest of the image, he found a burial of Christ in a conventional depiction; it was, by the way, a newer painting. He put the lamp away and returned to his place.

It was probably unnecessary to wait for the Italian, but outside there was certainly pouring rain, and since it was not as cold here as K. had expected, he decided to stay for the time being. Nearby was the large pulpit, with two empty golden crosses lazily reclining on its small round roof, their tips crossing each other. The outer wall of the balustrade and the transition to the supporting column were formed by green foliage, into which small angels reached, sometimes lively, sometimes at rest. K. stepped in front of the pulpit and examined it from all sides; the stonework was extraordinarily meticulous, and the deep darkness between the foliage and behind him seemed captured and held in place. K. placed his hand in one of the gaps and then carefully felt the stone, of which he had previously been unaware of the existence of this pulpit. Then he noticed a church attendant standing behind the next row of benches, dressed in a hanging, wrinkled black coat, holding a snuffbox in his left hand and observing him. "What does this man want?" thought K. "Am I suspicious to him? Does he want a tip?" However, when the church attendant realized that K. had noticed him, he pointed with his right hand, still holding a pinch of tobacco between two fingers, in some vague direction. His behavior was almost incomprehensible; K. waited for a little while, but the church attendant did not stop pointing and even emphasized it with nods of his head. "What does he want?" K. quietly asked himself, not daring to call out here; then he pulled out his wallet and squeezed through the next bench to reach the man. But the attendant immediately made a defensive gesture with his hand, shrugged his shoulders, and limped away. With a similar gait to this hurried limping, K. had tried to imitate riding horses as a child. "A childish old man," thought K. "His mind is only good enough for church service now. He stops when I stop and lurks to see if I want to keep going." Smiling, K. followed the old man through the entire side aisle almost to the height of the main altar; the old man continued to point at something, but K. deliberately did not turn around, knowing that the pointing served no other purpose than to distract him from the old man's path. Finally, he truly let him go; he did not want to frighten him too much, and he also did not want to completely scare off the apparition in case the Italian should still come.

As he entered the nave to look for his seat, where he had left the album, he noticed a small side pulpit almost adjacent to the altar choir benches, quite simple, made of bare, pale stone. It was so small that from a distance it appeared to be an empty niche intended for a statue. The preacher could hardly take a full step back from the railing. Moreover, the stone arch of the pulpit began unusually low and rose, though completely unadorned, in such a way that a man of average height could not stand upright there but had to constantly lean over the railing. The whole setup seemed designed to torment the preacher; it was incomprehensible why this pulpit was needed when there was already the other large and intricately decorated one available.

K. would not have noticed this small pulpit if there hadn't been a lamp attached to it, like the ones usually prepared just before a sermon. Was a sermon about to take place? In the empty church? K. looked down the narrow staircase that led to the pulpit, which seemed so slender that it was meant not for people, but merely to adorn the column. But at the bottom of the pulpit, K. smiled in amazement; the clergyman was indeed there, holding onto the railing, ready to ascend, and looking at K. Then he nodded slightly, prompting K. to make the sign of the cross and bow, which he should have done earlier. The clergyman gave himself a little push and ascended the pulpit with quick, short steps. Was a sermon really about to begin? Perhaps the verger was not entirely out of his mind and had meant to summon the preacher, which was certainly quite necessary in the empty church. Besides, there was still an old woman somewhere in front of a statue of Mary who also should have come. And if it was already to be a sermon, why wasn't it announced by the organ? But it remained silent, only faintly glimmering from the darkness of its great height.

K. considered whether he should leave in a hurry; if he didn't do it now, there was no chance he could during the sermon, and he would have to stay for its duration. He was losing so much time in the office, and he was no longer obliged to wait for the Italian. He looked at his watch; it was 11 o'clock. But could there really be a sermon? Could K. represent the congregation all by himself? What if he had been a stranger who just wanted to visit the church? Fundamentally, he was nothing else. It was absurd to think that a sermon would take place now at 11 o'clock on a weekday in the most dreadful weather. The clergyman — it was undoubtedly a clergyman, a young man with a smooth, dark face — seemed to be going up only to turn off the lamp that had been mistakenly lit.

But that was not the case; the clergyman rather adjusted the light, turning it up a bit more, then slowly turned toward the railing, which he grasped with both hands at the angular edge. He stood there for a while, looking around without moving his head. K. had stepped back quite a bit and leaned with his elbows on the front church bench. With uncertain eyes, he looked somewhere, without pinpointing the exact location, at the church servant, who was hunched over, peacefully curling up as if he had completed his task. What a silence reigned now in the cathedral! But K. had to break it; he had no intention of staying here. If it was the clergyman's duty to preach at a certain hour, regardless of the circumstances, he could do so; it would succeed without K.'s presence, just as K.'s presence would certainly not enhance its effect. Slowly, K. began to move, tiptoeing along the bench, then made his way into the wide main aisle and walked there undisturbed, except for the fact that the stone floor echoed softly with the faintest step, and the arches subtly, but continuously, resonated in various, methodical progressions. K. felt a bit abandoned as he walked alone through the empty benches, perhaps observed by the clergyman. It also seemed to him that the size of the cathedral was right at the edge of what was still bearable for humans. When he reached his previous spot, he almost hastily grabbed the album he had left behind there. He had nearly crossed the area of the benches and was approaching the open space between them and the exit when he heard the clergyman's voice for the first time. A powerful, practiced voice. How it filled the cathedral, ready to receive it! But it was not the congregation that the clergyman called; it was unmistakably clear, with no room for excuses—he called: Josef K.!

K. paused and looked down at the floor. For now, he was still free; he could still walk away and escape through one of the three small, dark wooden doors not far in front of him. This would mean that he did not understand, or that he did understand but did not want to care. However, if he turned around, he would be trapped, for then he would have confessed that he understood well, that he truly was the one being called, and that he wanted to follow. If the cleric had called him again, K. would surely have left, but since everything remained silent while K. waited, he turned his head slightly to see what the cleric was doing now. The cleric stood calmly at the pulpit as before, but it was clear that he had noticed K.'s head movement. It would have been a childish game of hide-and-seek if K. had not fully turned around. He did so and was beckoned closer by the cleric with a wave of his finger. Now that everything could happen openly, K. — partly out of curiosity and to shorten the matter — walked towards the pulpit with long, sweeping strides. He paused at the first pews, but the cleric seemed to think the distance was still too great; he extended his hand and pointed with a sharply lowered index finger to a spot just in front of the pulpit. K. complied, having to tilt his head back significantly to still see the cleric. "You are Josef K.," the cleric said, raising a hand on the railing in an indeterminate gesture. "Yes," said K., thinking about how openly he had always stated his name before; it had become a burden for him over time, and now people he was meeting for the first time also knew his name; how nice it was to introduce oneself first and then be known. "You are accused," the cleric said particularly softly. "Yes," K. replied, "I have been informed of that." "Then you are the one I am looking for," said the cleric. "I am the prison chaplain." "Oh, I see," said K. "I called you here," the cleric continued, "to talk with you." "I didn't know that," K. said. "I came here to show a tourist the cathedral." "Leave the trivialities," said the cleric. "What do you have in your hand? Is it a prayer book?" "No," K. replied, "it's a booklet of city sights." "Put it down," said the cleric. K. threw it away so forcefully that it opened and dragged a crumpled page a bit across the floor. "Do you know that your case is not looking good?" the cleric asked. "It seems that way to me too," K. said. "I have made every effort, but so far without success. However, I have not yet completed my submission." "How do you envision the outcome?" the cleric asked. "I used to think it had to end well," K. said, "but now I sometimes doubt even that. I don't know how it will end. Do you?" "No," said the cleric, "but I fear it will end badly. They consider you guilty. Your case may not even get beyond a lower court. For now, at least, your guilt is presumed." "But I am not guilty," K. said. "It is a mistake. How can a person be guilty at all? We are all humans here, one like the other." "That is true," said the cleric, "but that is how the guilty tend to speak." "Do you also have a prejudice against me?" K. asked. "I have no prejudice against you," said the cleric. "Thank you," K. said. "But all the others involved in the proceedings have a prejudice against me. They instill it in the uninvolved as well. My position is becoming increasingly difficult." "You misunderstand the facts," said the cleric. "The judgment does not come all at once; the proceedings gradually lead to a judgment." "So that's how it is," K. said, lowering his head. "What do you plan to do next in your case?" the cleric asked. "I want to seek help," K. said, raising his head to see how the cleric would judge this. "There are still certain possibilities that I have not exploited." "You seek too much external help," the cleric said disapprovingly, "especially from women. Don't you realize that this is not true help?" "Sometimes, and even often, I could agree with you," K. said, "but not always. Women have great power. If I could get some women I know to work together for me, I would have to succeed. Especially with this court, which consists almost entirely of womanizers. Show a woman to the examining magistrate from afar and he rushes to get to the courtroom and the defendant just in time." The cleric tilted his head towards the railing; it seemed as if the canopy of the pulpit was pressing down on him. What kind of storm might be outside? It was no longer a gloomy day; it was already deep night. No stained glass from the large windows could break the dark wall even with a shimmer. And just now, the sacristan began to extinguish the candles on the main altar one by one. "Are you angry with me?" K. asked the cleric. "You may not know what kind of court you serve." He received no answer. "These are just my experiences," K. said. It remained silent above. "I did not mean to offend you," K. said. Then the cleric shouted down to K., "Don't you see even two steps ahead?" It was shouted in anger, but at the same time like someone who sees another about to fall and, startled, shouts out carelessly and involuntarily.

Both remained silent for a long time. Surely, the clergy member could not see K. clearly in the darkness below, while K. could see the clergy member distinctly in the light of the small lamp. Why didn't the clergy member come down? He hadn't given a sermon; K. had only shared some information that, if he were to pay close attention, would likely do him more harm than good. However, it seemed that K. could undoubtedly sense the clergy member's good intentions. It was not impossible that he might find common ground with him if he came down; it was not impossible that he might receive decisive and acceptable advice from him, advice that would, for example, show him not how to influence the trial, but how to break free from it, how to avoid it, how to live outside of it. This possibility had to exist; K. had often thought about it recently. But did the clergy member know of such a possibility? Perhaps he would reveal it if asked, despite belonging to the court himself, and despite having suppressed his gentle nature and even shouted at K. when K. had attacked the court.

"Will you not come down?" K. said. "It's not like you have to give a sermon. Come down to me." "I can come down now," said the clergy member, perhaps regretting his shouting. As he took the lamp off its hook, he said, "I had to speak to you from a distance first. I am easily influenced otherwise and forget my duties."

K. was waiting for him at the bottom of the stairs. The clergyman extended his hand to him from a higher step as he descended. "Do you have a moment for me?" K. asked. "As much time as you need," said the clergyman, handing K. the small lamp to carry. Even nearby, a certain solemnity did not leave his demeanor. "You are very kind to me," K. said. They walked side by side in the dark side aisle. "You are an exception among all those who belong to the court. I trust you more than anyone else I know among them. I can speak openly with you." "Don't deceive yourself," said the clergyman. "What should I be deceived about?" K. asked. "You are deceiving yourself about the court," said the clergyman. "In the introductory writings of the law, it says of this deception: before the law stands a gatekeeper. To this gatekeeper comes a man from the countryside and asks for admission to the law. But the gatekeeper says that he cannot grant him entry at the moment. The man thinks it over and then asks if he will be allowed to enter later. 'It is possible,' says the gatekeeper, 'but not now.' Since the door to the law stands open as always and the gatekeeper steps aside, the man bends down to look through the door into the interior. When the gatekeeper notices this, he laughs and says: 'If it tempts you so much, try to enter despite my prohibition. But keep in mind: I am powerful. And I am only the lowest gatekeeper. There are gatekeepers from hall to hall, one more powerful than the other. Even I cannot bear the sight of the third.' Such difficulties the man from the countryside did not expect; the law should be accessible to everyone at all times, he thinks. But when he now looks closely at the gatekeeper in his fur coat, his large pointed nose, and his long, thin, black, Tartar beard, he decides to wait until he receives permission to enter. The gatekeeper gives him a stool and lets him sit down sideways at the door. There he sits for days and years. He makes many attempts to be admitted and tires the gatekeeper with his pleas. The gatekeeper often conducts small interrogations with him, asking him about his homeland and many other things; however, these are indifferent questions, like those asked by great lords, and in the end, he always tells him that he still cannot admit him. The man, who has equipped himself with many provisions for his journey, uses everything he has, no matter how valuable, to bribe the gatekeeper. The latter accepts everything but says: 'I only accept it so that you don't think you have missed out on anything.' During the many years, the man observes the gatekeeper almost without interruption. He forgets the other gatekeepers, and this first one seems to him the only obstacle to entering the law. He curses the unfortunate circumstance loudly in the early years; later, as he grows old, he only mutters to himself. He becomes childish, and since in his years of studying the gatekeeper he has also recognized the fleas in his fur collar, he even asks the fleas to help him and persuade the gatekeeper. Eventually, his eyesight weakens, and he does not know whether it is truly getting darker around him or if his eyes are just deceiving him. However, he now recognizes in the darkness a light that shines unquenchably from the door of the law. Now he does not have much longer to live. Before his death, all his experiences over the years coalesce into a question he has not yet asked the gatekeeper. He gestures to him, as he can no longer lift his stiffening body. The gatekeeper must bend down deeply to him, for the size differences have turned greatly against the man. "What do you still want to know?" asks the gatekeeper. "You are insatiable." "Everyone strives for the law," says the man, "how is it that in all these years no one but me has requested entry?" The gatekeeper realizes that the man is already at the end of his life, and to reach his fading hearing, he shouts at him: "No one else could gain entry here, for this entrance was meant only for you. I am now going and closing it."

"The gatekeeper deceived the man," K. said immediately, drawn strongly to the story. "Don't be hasty," the cleric replied, "don't adopt another's opinion without scrutiny. I have told you the story in the exact wording of the text. There is nothing in it about deception." "But it is clear," K. said, "and your first interpretation was entirely correct. The gatekeeper only conveyed the redeeming message when it could no longer help the man." "He was not asked earlier," the cleric said, "and remember that he was only a gatekeeper, and as such, he fulfilled his duty." "Why do you believe he fulfilled his duty?" K. asked. "He did not fulfill it. His duty was perhaps to deny entry to all strangers, but he should have let in this man, for whom the entrance was intended." "You do not have enough respect for the text and distort the story," said the cleric. "The story contains two important statements from the gatekeeper regarding entry, one at the beginning and one at the end. One statement reads: that he cannot grant him entry now, and the other: this entrance was meant only for you. If there were a contradiction between these two statements, you would be right, and the gatekeeper would have deceived the man. However, there is no contradiction. On the contrary, the first statement even points to the second. One could almost say that the gatekeeper went beyond his duty by offering the man a future possibility of entry. At that time, it seems his only duty was to deny the man entry, and in fact, many commentators on the text are surprised that the gatekeeper made that insinuation at all, as he appears to love precision and watches over his office strictly. For many years, he does not leave his post and only closes the gate at the very end; he is very aware of the importance of his service, for he says: 'I am powerful,' he has reverence for his superiors, for he says: 'I am just the lowest gatekeeper,' he is not talkative, for during those many years, he only asks what are called 'dispassionate questions,' he is not bribable, for he says about a gift: 'I accept it only so you do not believe you have missed something,' he is neither to be moved nor offended when it comes to fulfilling his duty, for it is said of the man, 'he tires the gatekeeper with his pleas.' Finally, his appearance also suggests a pedantic character, with his large, pointed nose and long, thin, black, Tartar-like beard. Can there be a more dutiful gatekeeper? However, other traits blend into the gatekeeper's character, which are very favorable for the one requesting entry, and which make it understandable that he could go a little beyond his duty in that insinuation of a future possibility. It cannot be denied that he is a bit simple-minded and, in connection with that, somewhat conceited. Even if his statements about his power and the power of the other gatekeepers and their even unbearable appearance for him— I say, even if all these statements may be correct in themselves, the way he presents these statements shows that his understanding is clouded by simplicity and arrogance. The commentators say about this: 'A correct understanding of a matter and misunderstanding of the same matter do not completely exclude each other.' In any case, one must assume that this simplicity and arrogance, however minor they may seem, weaken the guarding of the entrance; they are gaps in the character of the gatekeeper. Additionally, the gatekeeper seems to be naturally friendly; he is not always just an official. Right from the first moments, he makes a joke that he invites the man to enter despite the explicitly stated prohibition, then he does not send him away but gives him, as it is said, a stool and allows him to sit beside the door. The patience with which he endures the man's pleas over all those years, the small interrogations, the grace with which he allows the man to loudly curse the unfortunate fate that has placed the gatekeeper here— all this suggests feelings of compassion. Not every gatekeeper would have acted that way. And finally, he bends down deeply at a gesture to give the man the opportunity for one last question. Only a slight impatience— the gatekeeper knows that everything is coming to an end— is expressed in the words: 'You are insatiable.' Some even go further in this interpretation and believe that the words 'You are insatiable' express a kind of friendly admiration that is certainly not free from condescension. In any case, the figure of the gatekeeper concludes differently than you believe." "You know the story better than I do and for a longer time," K. said. They were silent for a moment. Then K. said, "So you believe the man was not deceived?" "Don't misunderstand me," the cleric said, "I am only showing you the opinions that exist about it. You should not pay too much attention to opinions. The text is unchangeable, and opinions are often just an expression of despair about it. In this case, there is even an opinion that it is precisely the gatekeeper who is deceived." "That is a far-reaching opinion," K. said. "How is it justified?" "The justification," the cleric replied, "is based on the simplicity of the gatekeeper. It is said that he does not know the inner workings of the law but only the path he must walk before the entrance again and again. The ideas he has about the inner workings are considered childish, and it is assumed that he himself fears what he wants to instill fear about in the man. Yes, he fears it more than the man does, for the man wants nothing more than to enter, even after he has heard about the terrible gatekeepers of the inner sanctum, while the gatekeeper, on the other hand, does not want to enter; at least nothing is known about that. Others say that he must have already been inside, for he was once taken into the service of the law, and that could only have happened inside. To this, one can reply that he could also have been appointed gatekeeper by a call from inside and that he at least should not have been deep inside, since he can no longer bear the sight of the third gatekeeper. Furthermore, it is not reported that during all those years he has said anything about the inner workings except for remarks about the gatekeepers. He may have been forbidden to do so, but he has not spoken about the prohibition either. From all this, one concludes that he knows nothing about the appearance and significance of the inner workings and is under a delusion about it. But he is also supposed to be under a delusion about the man from the countryside, for he is subordinate to this man and does not know it. That he treats the man as a subordinate can be recognized from much that you may still remember. That he is indeed subordinate to him is supposed to be equally evident according to this opinion. Above all, the free man is superior to the bound man. Now the man is indeed free; he can go wherever he wants, only entry into the law is forbidden to him, and moreover, only by one person, the gatekeeper. If he sits down on the stool beside the gate and stays there for his whole life, this is done voluntarily; the story does not mention any coercion. The gatekeeper, on the other hand, is bound to his post by his office; he is not allowed to leave, and apparently, he also cannot go inside, even if he wanted to.

Moreover, although he is in the service of the law, he serves only for this entrance, thus also only for this man, for whom this entrance is meant alone. For this reason, he is subordinate to him. It is to be assumed that for many years, for an entire man's lifetime, as it were, he has only performed an empty service, for it is said that a man comes, thus someone of manhood, meaning that the gatekeeper had to wait a long time before his purpose was fulfilled, and he had to wait as long as it pleased the man, who came voluntarily. But even the end of the service is determined by the man's end of life, thus he remains subordinate to him until the end. And it is repeatedly emphasized that the gatekeeper seems to know nothing about all this. However, nothing remarkable is seen in this, for according to this opinion, the gatekeeper is in an even deeper delusion regarding his service. Ultimately, he speaks of the entrance and says: 'I am going now to close it,' but at the beginning, it is stated that the gate to the law stands open as always; if it is always open, always meaning regardless of the lifespan of the man for whom it is intended, then the gatekeeper will not be able to close it. Opinions vary on whether the gatekeeper, with his announcement that he will close the gate, is merely responding or emphasizing his duty or wants to set the man in remorse and sorrow at the last moment. However, many agree on the point that he will not be able to close the gate. They even believe that at least in the end, he is also subordinate to the man in his knowledge, for the man sees the brilliance that breaks forth from the entrance of the law, while the gatekeeper, as such, is presumably standing with his back to the entrance and does not show by any expression that he has noticed a change." "That is well justified," K. said, having repeated certain parts of the cleric's explanation quietly to himself. "It is well justified, and I now believe that the gatekeeper is deceived. However, I have not departed from my earlier opinion, for both overlap partially. It is inconclusive whether the gatekeeper sees clearly or is deceived. I said the man is deceived. If the gatekeeper sees clearly, one might doubt that; if the gatekeeper is deceived, then his deception must necessarily transfer to the man. The gatekeeper is then not a deceiver, but so simple-minded that he should be immediately dismissed from his service. You must consider that the deception in which the gatekeeper finds himself harms him not at all, but harms the man a thousandfold." "Here you encounter a counter-opinion," the cleric said. "Some say that the story gives no one the right to judge the gatekeeper. No matter how he may appear to us, he is nonetheless a servant of the law, thus belonging to the law, thus removed from human judgment. One should not believe that the gatekeeper is subordinate to the man. To be bound by his service only to the entrance of the law is incomparably more than to live freely in the world. The man comes to the law; the gatekeeper is already there. He has been appointed to service by the law; to doubt his worthiness is to doubt the law." "I do not agree with this opinion," K. said, shaking his head, "for if one adheres to it, one must accept everything the gatekeeper says as true. But that is not possible, as you have explained in detail yourself." "No," the cleric said, "one does not have to accept everything as true; one only has to regard it as necessary." "A gloomy opinion," K. said. "Lies are made part of the world order."

K. said this in conclusion, but it was not his final judgment. He was too tired to grasp all the implications of the story; it led him into unfamiliar lines of thought, into unreal matters more suited for discussion among court officials than for him. The simple narrative had become distorted, and he wanted to shake it off. The clergyman, who was now showing great sensitivity, tolerated this and silently accepted K.'s remark, even though it surely did not align with his own opinion.

They walked on in silence for a while, K. kept close to the clergyman, not knowing in the darkness where he was. The lamp in his hand had long since gone out. Once, a silver statue of a saint flickered right in front of him, glimmering only with the sheen of silver before disappearing back into the darkness. To avoid being completely dependent on the clergyman, K. asked him, "Aren't we near the main entrance now?" "No," said the clergyman, "we are far from it. Do you want to leave already?" Although K. had not thought about it at that moment, he immediately replied, "Of course, I must leave. I am the assistant manager of a bank; they are waiting for me. I only came here to show a foreign business associate the cathedral." "Well," said the clergyman, extending his hand to K., "then go." "But I can't find my way in the dark by myself," K. said. "Go left to the wall," said the clergyman, "then keep going along the wall without leaving it, and you will find an exit." The clergyman had taken just a few steps away, but K. already called out loudly, "Please, wait a moment." "I will wait," said the clergyman. "Don't you want anything from me?" K. asked. "No," said the clergyman. "You were so kind to me before," K. said, "and explained everything to me; now you are sending me off as if you don't care about me." "You must leave," said the clergyman. "Well," K. said, "you should see that." "You should first realize who I am," said the clergyman. "You are the prison chaplain," K. said, stepping closer to the clergyman; his immediate return to the bank was not as urgent as he had claimed, and he could very well stay here a little longer. "So I belong to the court," said the clergyman. "Why would I want anything from you? The court wants nothing from you. It accepts you when you come and releases you when you go."

## 10
# END

On the eve of his 31st birthday — it was around 9 PM, a time of silence on the streets — two gentlemen arrived at K.'s apartment. Dressed in overcoats, pale and stout, with seemingly immovable top hats. After a brief formality at the entrance regarding their initial entry, the same formality was repeated on a larger scale at K.'s door. Although he had not been informed of their visit, K. was also dressed in black, sitting in an armchair near the door, slowly putting on new, tightly fitting gloves, as one does when expecting guests. He immediately stood up and looked at the gentlemen with curiosity. "So you are here for me," he asked. The gentlemen nodded, one pointed with his top hat in hand at the other. K. admitted to himself that he was expecting another visitor. He walked to the window and glanced again at the dark street. Almost all the windows on the opposite side were also dark, with many curtains drawn. In one illuminated window on the upper floor, small children were playing behind a grate, reaching for each other with their little hands, still unable to move from their spots. "Old subordinate actors are sent to me," K. thought to himself, looking around to convince himself once more. "They are trying to dispose of me in a cheap way." K. suddenly turned to them and asked, "Which theater do you play in?" "Theater?" one gentleman asked, with twitching corners of his mouth, looking to the other for advice. The other behaved like a mute, struggling with a stubborn organism. "You are not prepared to be asked," K. told himself and went to fetch his hat.

Even on the stairs, the gentlemen wanted to link arms with K., but he said, "Not until we're in the street; I'm not sick." However, right at the gate, they intertwined with him in a way that K. had never experienced with anyone before. They held their shoulders tightly behind his, didn't bend their arms, but used them to envelop K.'s arms fully; below, they grasped K.'s hands with a practiced, irresistible grip. K. walked stiffly between them, and the three of them formed such a unit that if one had been struck, all would have been affected. It was a unity that could almost only be formed by the lifeless.

Under the streetlights, K. tried several times, as difficult as it was in their close arrangement, to see his companions more clearly than he had been able to in the twilight of his room. Perhaps they are tenors, he thought, noticing their heavy double chins. He felt disgusted by the cleanliness of their faces. One could almost still see the cleansing hand that had gone into the corners of their eyes, that had rubbed their upper lips, that had scraped the creases at their chins.

When K. noticed this, he stopped, and as a result, the others stopped as well; they were at the edge of an open, deserted square adorned with features. "Why were you sent specifically?" he exclaimed more than he asked. The gentlemen seemed to have no answer; they waited with their free arm hanging down, like caregivers when a patient wants to rest. "I'm not going any further," K. said experimentally. The gentlemen did not need to respond to this; it was enough that they did not loosen their grip and attempted to lift K. away from the spot, but K. resisted. "I won't need much more strength; I will use all I have now," he thought. He remembered the flies that struggle to escape from a sticky trap with their torn legs. "The gentlemen will have a hard time."

From a lower street, Miss Bürstner climbed up a small staircase to the square before them. It wasn't entirely certain if it was really her, although the resemblance was indeed striking. However, K. didn't care whether it was definitely Miss Bürstner; he simply became aware of the futility of his resistance. There was nothing heroic about his opposition, about the difficulties he now posed for the gentlemen, or about his attempts to savor the last semblance of life in defense. He set off, and the joy he brought to the gentlemen also reflected back on him. They now tolerated him determining the direction of their path, which he chose to follow the route that Miss Bürstner was taking—not because he wanted to catch up to her or because he wanted to see her for as long as possible, but simply to ensure he wouldn't forget the reminder she represented for him. "The only thing I can do now," he told himself, and the rhythm of his steps matched that of the two others, confirming his thoughts, "the only thing I am doing now is to maintain a calm and balanced mind until the end. I always wanted to dive into the world with twenty hands, and for a purpose that cannot be condoned. Was that wrong? Should I now show that not even a year-long process could teach me? Should I leave as a dim-witted person? Should people be able to say that at the beginning of the process I wanted to end it, and now, at its conclusion, I want to start it all over again? I don't want that to be said. I am grateful that on this path, I have been given these half-silent, uncomprehending gentlemen, and that it has been left to me to tell myself what is necessary."

The young lady had meanwhile turned into a side street, but K. was already able to part with her and gave himself over to his companions. All three now walked in complete agreement across a bridge in the moonlight, eagerly mirroring every small movement K. made; when he turned slightly towards the railing, they also turned to face that way. The water, shimmering and glistening in the moonlight, split around a small island where clumps of leaves from trees and shrubs were piled together. Beneath them, now invisible, gravel paths led to comfortable benches where K. had stretched and relaxed on many a summer. "I didn't even want to stop," he said to his companions, embarrassed by their eagerness. One seemed to give the other a gentle reproach behind K.'s back regarding the misunderstood stopping, and then they continued on.

They passed through several ascending streets, where police officers stood or walked here and there; sometimes in the distance, sometimes quite close. One officer, with a bushy mustache and his hand on the hilt of his saber, stepped purposefully close to the rather suspicious group. The gentlemen hesitated, and the police officer seemed about to say something when K. forcefully urged them forward. He often turned around cautiously to see if the officer was following; but once they had a corner between themselves and the officer, K. started to run, and despite their heavy breathing, the gentlemen had to run along as well.

They quickly left the city, which seamlessly transitioned into fields in this direction. A small, abandoned, and desolate quarry was located near a still urban house. Here, the gentlemen stopped, whether this place had been their destination from the very beginning, or they were simply too exhausted to continue walking. They released K., who waited in silence, removed their top hats, and wiped the sweat from their foreheads with handkerchiefs as they looked around the quarry. The moonlight lay everywhere with a naturalness and calmness that no other light possesses.

After exchanging some pleasantries about who was to carry out the next tasks — the gentlemen seemed to have received their orders in full — one of them approached K. and began to remove his coat, vest, and finally his shirt. K. involuntarily shivered, prompting the gentleman to give him a light, reassuring pat on the back. He then carefully folded the clothes, treating them as items that would still be useful, even if not in the immediate future. To avoid leaving K. without movement in the somewhat cool night air, he took him under the arm and walked him back and forth a bit while the other gentleman searched the quarry for a suitable spot. Once he found it, he signaled, and the other gentleman guided K. over. It was near the quarry wall, where a loose stone lay. The gentlemen seated K. on the ground, leaned him against the stone, and rested his head on top. Despite all their efforts and K.'s cooperation, his position remained very forced and unconvincing. One gentleman then asked the other to leave him alone for a moment to lay K. down, but this too did not improve the situation. Eventually, they left K. in a position that wasn't even the best among those they had already achieved. Then one gentleman opened his coat and took out a long, thin, double-edged butcher's knife from a sheath attached to a belt worn over his vest. He held it up and tested the sharpness in the light. Again, the disgusting pleasantries began, one handed the knife over K. to the other, who then passed it back over K. K. now knew exactly that it would have been his duty to grasp the knife himself as it hovered from hand to hand above him and to plunge it in. But he did not do it; instead, he turned his still-free neck and looked around. He could not fully assert himself, could not take all the work away from the authorities; the responsibility for this final mistake lay with the one who had denied him the remaining strength needed for it. His gaze fell on the top floor of the building adjacent to the quarry. Like a flash of light, the window shutters of a window there swung open, and a person, weak and thin in the distance and height, leaned far forward with a sudden motion and stretched out their arms even further. Who was it? A friend? A good person? Someone who cared? Someone who wanted to help? Was it an individual? Was it everyone? Was there still help? Were there objections that had been overlooked? Surely there were. Logic may be unshakeable, but it does not resist a person who wants to live. Where was the judge he had never seen? Where was the high court to which he had never come? He raised his hands and spread all his fingers.

But at K.'s throat, the hands of one man were laid, while the other plunged a knife into his heart and twisted it twice. With breaking eyes, K. still saw how the gentlemen, close to his face, leaned against each other, cheek to cheek, watching the decision unfold. "Like a dog!" he said; it was as if shame was meant to outlive him.

# AFTERWORD

Strange and profound, like all expressions of life, was Franz Kafka's attitude toward his own work and any publication. The issues he faced in dealing with this matter, which must therefore also guide every publication from his estate, cannot be overestimated in their seriousness. The following serves at least as a preliminary assessment:

Almost everything Kafka published was taken from him through my cunning and persuasion. This does not contradict the fact that he often experienced great happiness during long periods of his life due to his writing (though he always referred to it merely as "scribbling"). Anyone who was fortunate enough to hear him read his own prose in a small circle, with captivating passion and a rhythm that no actor could ever achieve, felt immediately the genuine, untamed creative urge and passion behind his work. The reason he ultimately rejected it lay first in certain sad experiences that led him to self-sabotage and, consequently, to a form of nihilism towards his own work; in addition, it was also due to the fact that he held this work to the highest religious standards, which it could not meet, given its many complexities. The possibility that his work could have been a strong help to many who strive for faith, nature, and perfect mental health likely meant nothing to

# AFTERWORD

him, as he was relentlessly serious in his own search for the right path and had to give counsel to himself first, not to others.

Thus, I interpret Kafka's negative stance toward his own work. He often spoke of the "wrong hands reaching out to him while he was writing" — also mentioning how the written and even published work could distract him in his further endeavors. He faced many obstacles before a volume of his work was released. Nevertheless, he found genuine joy in the finished beautiful books and occasionally in their effects, and there were times when he regarded both himself and his work with a similarly benevolent gaze, never completely without irony, but with a friendly irony that concealed the immense pathos of his relentless striving for the highest.

In Franz Kafka's estate, no will was found. In his desk, among many other papers, there was a folded note written in ink with my address. The note reads as follows:

Dearest Max, my last request: Everything in my estate (that is, in the bookcase, linen cupboard, desk, at home and in the office, or wherever else anything might have been placed that catches your attention) in the form of diaries, manuscripts, letters, both foreign and my own, drawings, and so on, should be completely and unread burned, as well as everything written or drawn that you or others whom you ask on my behalf might possess. Letters that are not to be handed over to you should at least be committed to be burned by those who hold them. Your Franz Kafka.

Upon closer inspection, an older, yellowed sheet written in pencil was also found. It states:

Dear Max,

Perhaps this time I will not get up anymore; the onset of pneumonia is quite likely after a month of lung fever, and even the fact that I am writing this will not fend it off, despite having a certain power. In this case, here is my final wish regarding

# AFTERWORD

everything I have written: Of all that I have written, only the following books are to be considered: *Judgment, The Stoker, Metamorphosis, In the Penal Colony, The Country Doctor*, and the story *A Hunger Artist*. (The few copies of *Meditation* may remain; I do not want to burden anyone with the task of destroying them, but nothing from it should be reprinted.)

When I say that those five books and the story are valid, I do not mean that I wish for them to be reprinted and preserved for future generations; on the contrary, should they be completely lost, that would correspond to my true desire. However, since they already exist, I do not want to prevent anyone from keeping them if they wish to do so.

In contrast, everything else I have written (published in magazines, in manuscript form, or in letters) is, without exception, to be destroyed as soon as possible. This includes anything that can be obtained or requested from the recipients (you know most of the recipients; it mainly concerns ........., especially do not forget the few notebooks that .... has) — all of this is to be burned, and I kindly ask you to do this as soon as possible.

Franz

---

If I categorically refuse to carry out the herostratic act that my friend demands of me, I have the most compelling reasons for this.

Some of these reasons are not suitable for public discussion. However, even those that I can share are, in my opinion, entirely sufficient to understand my decision.

The main reason: when I changed my profession in 1921, I told my friend that I had made my will, in which I asked him to destroy this and that, to review other things, and so on. In response, Kafka showed me the note written in ink that was later found in his desk, which said: "My will will be very simple — the request to you to burn everything."

## AFTERWORD

I also remember very clearly the answer I gave at that time: "If you seriously expect me to do something like that, I am telling you now that I will not fulfill your request." The entire conversation was conducted in that joking tone that was common between us, yet with the underlying seriousness that we always assumed was there for each other. Convinced of the seriousness of my refusal, Franz would have had to appoint another executor if his own provision had been of absolute and final seriousness.

I am not grateful to him for plunging me into this difficult moral dilemma, which he must have foreseen, as he knew the fanatical admiration I had for every word he spoke. This admiration led me, over the 22 years of our untroubled friendship, among other things, to never throw away even the smallest note or postcard that came from him. — By the way, the phrase "I am not grateful" should not be misunderstood! What does even the heaviest moral conflict weigh against the endless blessing I owe to my friend, who has been the very backbone of my entire intellectual existence?

Further reasons: the order of the pencil sheet was not followed by Franz himself, as he later explicitly granted permission for parts of the 'Meditation' to be reprinted in a newspaper and for three more novellas to be published, which he himself combined with the "Hunger Artist" and handed over to the publisher Die Schmiede. Both decisions also stem from a time when my friend's self-critical tendencies had reached their peak. However, in his final years, his entire existence took an unforeseen, new, happy, and positive turn that mitigated this self-hatred and nihilism. — My decision to publish the estate is further facilitated by the memory of all the bitter struggles I endured to force each individual publication of Kafka's works, often begging for them. Yet he ultimately reconciled with these publications and was relatively satisfied. — Finally, with a posthumous publication, a number of motives fall away, such as the concern that publication could hinder further work or call to mind the shadows of personally painful periods in life. How much Kafka's non-publication was intertwined with the issue of his way of life (a problem that now, to our immense sorrow, no longer troubles us) is evident from many conversations, including the

# AFTERWORD

following letter he wrote to me: "... I won't include the novels. Why stir up the old efforts? Just because I haven't burned them so far? ... I hope to do so next time I come. What is the point of keeping such 'even' artistically unsuccessful works? Is it the hope that these pieces will somehow come together into a whole, some instance of appeal to which I can turn when I am in need? I know that this is not possible, that no help will come from there. So what should I do with these things? Should those who cannot help me also harm me, as must be the case, given this knowledge?"

I feel very strongly that there remains a part of me that would want to prohibit publication for particularly sensitive individuals. However, I consider it my duty to resist this very enticing temptation of sensitivity. What is crucial, of course, is not any of the arguments presented so far, but solely the fact that Kafka's estate contains the most wonderful treasures, including some of the very best he has ever written. Honestly, I must admit that this single fact of literary and ethical value would have been sufficient (even if I had no objection against the strength of Kafka's last will) to determine my decision with a precision to which I would have nothing to oppose.

Unfortunately, Franz Kafka has become his own executor in part of his legacy. I found ten large quarto notebooks in his apartment—only their covers remain, the contents completely destroyed. Furthermore, he has reportedly burned several writing pads. In the apartment, there was only a collection (about a hundred aphorisms on religious topics), an autobiographical attempt that remains unpublished for now, and a pile of disordered papers that I am currently reviewing. I hope that among these papers there will be some completed or nearly completed stories. Additionally, I was handed an (unfinished) animal novella and a sketchbook.

The most precious part of the legacy consists of the works that were removed from the author's grim reality in time and secured. These are three novels. 'The Fireman,' the already published story, forms the first chapter of one novel set in America, for which the concluding chapter also exists, so it should not exhibit any significant gaps. This novel is with a friend of the deceased; the other two—"The Castle" and "The

## AFTERWORD

Trial"—I brought to myself in 1920 and 1923, which is a true comfort to me today. Only these works will show that the true significance of Franz Kafka, who until now could justifiably be considered a specialist, a master of the minor arts, lies in the grand epic form.

However, with these works, which may fill about four volumes of a posthumous edition, the radiance of Kafka's enchanting personality is by no means exhausted. Although a publication of the letters cannot be thought of for the time being, each of which possesses the same naturalness and intensity as Kafka's literary work, a small group will soon set about collecting everything that remains as an expression of this unique individual. To give just one example: how many of the works that, to my bitter disappointment, were no longer found in Kafka's apartment, did my friend read to me or at least read parts of, or tell me about their plans! What unforgettable, entirely original, and deeply profound thoughts he shared with me! As far as my memory and strength allow, nothing shall be lost.

I took possession of the manuscript of the novel "The Trial" in June 1920 and organized it right away. The manuscript has no title, but Kafka always referred to the novel as "The Trial" in conversation. The division into chapters as well as the chapter titles are from Kafka himself. Regarding the arrangement of the chapters, I relied on my intuition. However, since my friend had read a large part of the novel to me, my intuition for organizing the papers could rely on those memories. — Franz Kafka considered the novel to be unfinished. Before the existing final chapter, several stages of the mysterious trial were meant to be depicted. However, according to the poet's verbally expressed view, the trial should never progress to the highest court, making the novel, in a sense, unfinishable, i.e., capable of being continued infinitely. The completed chapters, along with the concluding final chapter, clearly illuminate both the meaning and form of the work, and anyone who is not informed that the poet intended to continue working on the piece (he refrained from doing so because he turned to a different atmosphere of life) will hardly feel its gap. — My work on the large bundle of papers that this novel represented at the time was limited to separating the completed chapters from the unfinished ones. I will leave the unfinished ones for the concluding volume of the posthumous edition; they contain nothing essential for the progression of the plot. One of these fragments was included by the poet himself under the title "A Dream" in the collection "A Country Doctor." The completed chapters are gathered and arranged here. Of the unfinished chapters, I have only included one, which is clearly nearly complete, with a slight rearrangement of four lines as Chapter 8. — In the text, I naturally made no changes. I only transcribed the numerous abbreviations (e.g., instead of F. B., I wrote out "Fräulein Bürstner" — instead of T., I wrote out "Titorelli") and corrected a few minor oversights that clearly remained in the manuscript only because the poet did not subject it to a definitive review.

Max Brod.